CON MAN

CHAPTER ONE

The gorgeous redhead leaned forward across my favorite table at my favorite restaurant, and from the look in her eyes, I already knew what was coming next.

"So, what do you think?" she asked. "Should we take this conversation back to my hotel room?"

The two of us were seated at a prime patio table at *Ocean*, a fairly classy restaurant bordering the south end of Central Park. We'd been having a pleasant conversation from our outdoor post, enjoying the mid-summer breeze which was made blessedly cooler from the shade of our umbrella. We'd been planning to indulge in a leisurely meal as we talked, but Charise's question ensured that this little luncheon was going to be cut rather short.

I eased back in my chair and assessed the fiery-haired bombshell seated across from me. Her invitation was unmistakable, and I found myself letting out with an exasperated breath. "I think there's been a misunderstanding."

"Well, maybe I should have been a little clearer," she purred, sliding a finger to trace along the swell of her ample breast. "I'm hoping you'll be able to, ah, *teach* me a thing or two about what a man really wants."

"That's not what I do." I'd encountered this scenario a time or two, and I'd learned it was best to just confront the situation head-on, without mincing words. "Look, Charise, I think you've been misinformed about what kind of service I provide. I'm not a sex therapist; I'm an image consultant."

I'm the founder and CEO of *Swan, Inc.,* New York City's preeminent makeover service. People who felt stuck in the "ugly duckling" stage of their lives came to me for transformation. My services provided much more than a simple makeover, though. Aside from helping these ladies out with a new hairdo and some clothes, I also offered some intensive remodeling of their self-esteem. Reputedly, these methods helped to unleash a woman's inner sexpot.

It kinda went with the territory. The sex appeal was simply a happily unexpected side effect of the confidence training I provided.

Charise blinked a few times in my direction, clearly confused. "I was told that you teach women to be absolute maneaters. And after I saw the change in Darla Haagen... I mean, she was positively *glowing* by the time you got through with her. She said you were a godsend. She said she never experienced a better eight weeks in her entire life. I'm sorry. I guess I just assumed..."

"Sometimes people do. I'm not offended."

Most of the time, a new client and I will have engaged in a series of emails prior to our first meeting. Even if we haven't, it was easy enough for them to do their homework on their own; my website clearly lays out what it is that I do. But sometimes, like in the case with Charise, here, people jumped to their own conclusions and thought they were merely hiring a high-priced escort. Hell, even if I *was* in the sex therapy business, actual sex isn't a part of the therapy provided.

I gave Charise a smile, trying to put her at ease regarding the mixup. Essentially, the woman had just offered herself up on a silver platter only for me to turn her down. Rather than dwell on her undoubtedly bruised ego, I decided to point her in the right direction. "In fact, if you're looking for a sex therapist, I can recommend someone for you. I know a guy out in Arizona—his name is Justice Drake and he's the best at what he does. But he and I don't work in the same field, understand?"

Charise tipped her head to the side and eyed me curiously. "No. I guess I *don't* understand. I thought I was hiring you to teach me how to please a man."

"Yes, to a point. Essentially what I do is teach you how to please *yourself.*" Charise's lip curled, confirming that her mind was spinning all over again. Before she could jump to another conclusion, I added, "I teach *confidence.* That's it. When you think about it, that's the sexiest trait of all, wouldn't you agree?"

I could see the shift in her posture as my words finally sunk in. "But I already have confidence."

"Yes, you certainly do. Rightfully so."

She gave me a flattered smile for that. "So, I guess this isn't going to be a good fit, is it?"

"I'm sorry, no, it's not."

There was an awkward pause between us as the situation sank in, until finally, she let out with a resigned sigh. "Well," she said agreeably as she rose from her chair. "It looks like my little sex-school adventure is going to turn into a shopping marathon instead." She gave me a smile and held out her hand. "It was a pleasure to meet you, Luke."

I came around to her side of the table to give her a hug. "You too, Charise."

When we pulled away from each other, there was a devilish twinkle in her eye as she purred, "You know, Luke... Just because I'm not hiring you for sex, that doesn't mean we can't have a little fun off the clock. Armed with nothing but false information and your photograph, I flew all the way out here from Houston, and I have to say, you're even more delicious than your picture. I'd hate to think the sexy vacation I was planning is actually going to be a complete letdown. I could use some company over the next couple of months while I'm here."

I couldn't contain my smirk as I answered, "That is one tempting offer, Charise. Truly. But I'm going to have to respectfully decline your generous proposition. Something tells me you're going to have one hell of a vacation without me. Here," I added, pulling out my wallet and digging around for my associate's business card. "Maybe after you've torn up New York for a few days, you'll decide to reroute to Sedona. Give Drake a call. He really knows his stuff."

She took the card from my hand, flicking it around her fingers as she said, "I will. I promise."

One of my brows raised as I added, "Although you strike me as someone who's already well-schooled in this area."

Charise grinned as she gave me a last peck on the cheek before jaunting across the patio and into the park.

My morning appointment was a bust, and my afternoon appointment wasn't scheduled to be here for another two hours. Since now I had some time to kill, I decided to take a walk to clear my head. I asked Fernando to hold my table, then slipped out of the gated patio and into the courtyard.

There were a few high-end boutiques that bordered this end of the park, so I did a little window shopping. Eyed up a new suit in the display at Brooks Brothers; checked out a kickass watch in the front case of Tiffany's. When my stomach started growling, I became aware of my abandoned lunch, and stopped off at a corner pushcart to get a dirty-water dog with the works.

I loved the city. The noise, the crowds... hell, I even loved the traffic. New York never lets you forget it's alive. It was the best place in the world to strike out on one's own, to test a person's mettle. You could live out your every dream or disappear into a sea of faces. Do whatever you wanted to do; be whoever you wanted to be.

I headed back to Ocean and hit the men's room to clean up before my next appointment, throwing a couple bucks in the attendant's tray and giving a quick glance in the mirror as I ran a hand through my hair.

I wasn't always this good-looking.

Before you can accuse me of being an arrogant, conceited jerk, I'll tell you that the personal assessment of my handsomeness is mentioned without spectacle or vanity of any kind.

Well, maybe a *little* pride, but that's it. And I'm only proud because it took a ton of hard work to get myself looking this way.

So, I'm not going to apologize for being hot. I earned it.

Countless hours at the gym, consultations with fashion gurus, and a whole helluva lot of mental reprogramming all combined to create the man you see standing before you today.

Fact is, before I was one of the "beautiful people," I used to view an attractive person with the same sort of indifference as I would a hot air balloon.

Pretty to look at, but there's no substance to it.

Strange that I should've made my living as an image consultant, right? If I had such disregard for external beauty, then why did I make it my mission to help women achieve the height of theirs?

And no. Before you can ask, I'll tell you emphatically that I did *not* start this whole venture as some elaborate scheme to pick up chicks. I'm not looking to hit on them. I'm looking to *help* them.

Unfortunately, the sad fact is this: I've been where these women are now. I know from firsthand experience what it's like to be ignored or downright snubbed for not looking like those people you see on your television screens. Society as a whole has always been impressed with such superficial qualities in a person. Looking good is the easiest way to catch a guy's eye, and if a woman is coming to me to help her land a man, she's going to have to understand that men appreciate external beauty above all else.

At least they think they do.

That's why the second part of my service is even more important than the first. Yes, I'll whip your body into shape. Yes, I'll hook you up with hair and makeup professionals. But while all that is happening, I'll be working on your *in*ternal assets. Pointing out your positive attributes, trying to teach you how to use them to your advantage. Building your confidence in little baby steps until you're ready to do it on your own.

At the end of it all, you'll have reached a point where you don't even need that spa-day makeover, but you'll get it just the same. Although by then, it'll merely be icing on an already delicious cake.

CHAPTER TWO

I was a few minutes early getting back to the restaurant, but as I made my way onto the patio, a woman who was obviously *not* my client was occupying my table. I guess I couldn't have expected Fernando to just leave his station empty for two entire hours, but this woman didn't look like she was ready to wrap up anytime soon.

She was preoccupied with perusing the menu, allowing me an extra minute to peruse *her*. It didn't take more than a glance to assess that she was gorgeous, and I allowed myself to appreciate the view. Blonde hair pulled back in an artless ponytail, the entire mass shining in the midday sun, model-high cheekbones above a full, luscious mouth, a bottom lip pinched between her teeth as she scanned the specials.

It was almost intimidating.

Now. I know I just got through telling you that I held no stock in a pretty face. And for the most part, I meant it. But that was then and this is now and the fact of the matter is that I happened to be a red-blooded American male. I couldn't *not* notice a beautiful woman. The difference between me and most of my gender, however, was that looks alone didn't sell me. I needed more than that.

I was curious to see if a killer personality went along with the killer looks, and figured there was no better time than the present to find out. I normally found that a pairing like that was a rarity, but what the hell. It was worth the shot. I had a few minutes to kill before one, so why not spend my wait with a little company? Realizing I had the perfect opening, I figured I could use the seating mixup to my advantage. I formulated an effective line as I closed the few paces that separated us, confident that I could win her over with my *witty repartee*.

But then she looked up.

I stopped dead in my tracks as I was met with the most incredible blue eyes I'd ever seen in my life. They were peeking through a fringe of heavy lashes, putting the sky to shame and tripping me up something fierce.

The look on her face was apprehensive, though, and seeing that slip in her armor caused the most terrifying thought to seep into my brain: *Wait. Is this my one o'clock?*

No. Wasn't possible. There was simply no way.

Please don't let this be my new client. Please don't let this—

"Lucas Taggart?" she asked. Her voice was a soft melody wrapped in an alluring timidity that reverberated all the way down my spine.

Not good.

"Yes," I replied through sandpaper before clearing my throat. "You must be Ainsley Carrington."

I was sure that the second misunderstanding of my day was about to take place. The girl I was looking at could hardly be considered an ugly duckling. She didn't need an image consultant; her image was already perfectly fine just the way it was.

Fresh. Natural. Beautiful.

Totally. Fucking. Hot.

She rose from her chair to shake my hand. "It's nice to finally meet you, Lucas."

Her yellow sundress hugged a trim figure, subtle curves in all the right places. Her perfume assaulted me, and I inhaled the sweet floral scent against my will.

This was bad. This was very, very bad.

8

"Nice to meet you, too, Miss Carrington. But please don't call me Lucas."

Her face immediately flushed as her eyes found her shoes. "Oh, I'm sorry! Should I have called you Mr. Taggart? I didn't mean to—"

"No, of course not," I offered, dipping my head to bring her eyes back to mine. What I saw there tipped me off to the reason she was here. As physically beautiful as she was, the poor girl was a nervous rabbit. I should have known better than to start out with a criticism, for godsakes. Why did I have to fluster her right off the bat? "I just meant that nobody calls me 'Lucas.' If we're going to be on a first name basis, you can call me Luke."

She smiled politely as she removed her hand from my grasp. I hadn't even realized I was still holding onto it. "I'd like that. Thank you."

The first sight of her smile made my heart stutter in my chest before I was able to collect myself and shake out of the schoolboy stupor.

Jesus. There was no way I could take this job. How could I? My entire career was based on instilling confidence, and yet I felt mine had disappeared within two minutes of meeting this woman. She was... *stunning*. I didn't think I'd be able to stop staring at her long enough to do my job properly.

I was thinking of the most delicate way to foist her off on another consultant, someone who'd be able to maintain his professionalism for godsakes, when I found myself offering, "Why don't we have a seat? I'll order us a couple drinks and we can get down to it."

Ainsley smoothed her skirt behind her knees and sat down, saying, "I was so nervous about meeting with you today. Thank you so much for agreeing to see me." I watched her tuck a stray lock of that blonde hair behind her ear, her fingers shaking as she stared down at her place setting. I didn't know what had happened to turn this beautiful girl into such an insecure wallflower, but I *did* know that I was intrigued. There was some serious untapped potential sitting across that table.

Within seconds, I was suddenly reversing my earlier decision. Regardless of my personal doubts, I decided passing this particular client along to someone else was not a viable option. Ainsley didn't need *someone*. She needed *me*. She needed a confidence boost from a guy who was experienced enough to give it to her and I was the best con man there was, so to speak. I wouldn't be doing her any favors by turning her away. Fact was, I could help her. I knew her story from my own past experience. How hard it must have been for her to take that first step and seek out my services. Harder still for her to actually send me that initial email. Practically a miracle that she followed through with our meeting today.

I can do this. Ainsley Carrington was no different than any other client. The thought strengthened my resolve.

I waved a waiter over and ordered a bottle of Pellegrino. "Is that alright with you, Ainsley?"

She placed a napkin across her lap as she answered, "That sounds perfect, thank you." As the waiter left us, Ainsley's blank gaze met mine in expectation. "So, should I... Do you need to know why I'm here?"

"I already know why you're here."

It always helped me to better understand my potential clients if I was granted a minute to assess their situation, and I was pretty sure I already had Ainsley Carrington figured out. Being an introvert allowed for a lifetime of observing people, and I'd learned how to pick up on their signals. Most of the time, they weren't even aware they were giving them off. People are easy to read if you take the time to pay attention.

"Is it that obvious?" she lamented, organizing the silverware at her place setting.

I shrugged in an attempt to ease her mind. "So, you're shy. Big deal. The only 'obvious' thing to me is that you're finally doing something about it."

Ainsley shook her head and sighed. "Gosh, I must be even more of a dud than I thought. I grew up so sheltered, and now here I am, twenty-five years old, and I have no life!"

"I'll help you change that."

"I'm *really* insecure."

"But what do you have to be insecure about? You're hot."

I wasn't big on blowing smoke up people's asses, but part of my program was to offer constant assurance. I always discovered at least one positive attribute that I could reinforce repeatedly, getting them used to the idea of believing it about themselves. It normally took me a little while to come up with an honest compliment, however, because I wasn't in the habit of lying to my clients. But I hadn't put any forethought into that "hot" comment; it just sort of slipped out.

And it was one hell of an understatement.

But Ainsley avoided the commentary about her looks, and instead, a smile eked through as she tried to answer casually, "Luke, it's okay. I know I'm not... you know... *fun*."

What does fun have to do with being hot?

I eased back into my chair, absently tapping a fingertip against the linen tablecloth as I took in her words. I knew all too well what it felt like to be socially inhibited. "Well, I can definitely help you there. But Ainsley," I added cautiously, "I feel it's only right to be honest with you. My course encompasses a lot more than learning how to be the life of the party. We've got some hard work ahead of us, but I'm already thinking you're gonna be tough enough to handle it." As skittish as she seemed, I had already picked up an underlying resolve. Determination went a long way, and hers would serve her well.

She extended a genuine smile at me, and I felt my heart lurch. She had a gorgeous smile; lovely, full lips and delicate, straight teeth that would *not* be needing a bleaching. I mentally crossed the customary Laser-White visit off my Week Four checklist, and attempted to get this meeting back on track.

This was the part where I'd normally launch into my schpiel, but I didn't want to overwhelm her more than I already had. Sure, all my clients were lacking confidence, but this one was downright petrified. I felt that one wrong move would send her scurrying for the hills.

"So," I said, attempting to ease into some talking points. "Maybe we should start with a Q and A? That's always an easy way to break the ice."

Ainsley rearranged the napkin across her lap and directed her next words toward it. "Well, good, because I'm not really sure how this works. I know you change women's lives, but I guess I'm still unclear as to how."

"Well," I started in. "It's more like I help women change their *own* lives." When she seemed receptive to hearing more, I gave her the standard rundown, explained the role I'd be playing through it. Told her about the schedule we'd be keeping, the exercises I had planned, the homework she'd be expected to do. Mind you, I barely scratched the surface, but I was trying to keep from overwhelming her while still answering her question.

It was hard not to notice the charming way she listened intently while simultaneously avoiding any sort of prolonged eye contact. It was kind of adorable.

I was pretty distracted by Ainsley's fidgeting—and, you know, by her hotness—but I managed to get through my presentation without embarrassing myself.

Shocker.

I wrapped up the diatribe with my standard footnote. "I'll be asking a lot of you over these next weeks. Some things will seem entirely effortless, while others will be well out of your comfort range. I only ask that you trust me. In return, I will grant you complete and utter honesty. If there's ever any question about what we're doing or why, I'd like you to ask me straight out. I'll always tell you the truth. This program works best when that honesty is a two-way street, however, so I'm hoping I can expect the same from you."

Ainsley nodded her head in acceptance just as the waiter delivered our drinks. The interruption was a good enough excuse to cease my monologue and propose a toast. "To new beginnings," I offered, holding my stem glass out to Ainsley. "And happily ever afters."

She seemed to like the idea of that, smiling as she clinked her glass to mine. "You make it sound like life is a fairytale."

I shot her my most effective smirk, looking right into those incredible blue eyes of hers as I answered, "It's high time you started living like it was."

CHAPTER THREE

Rain. Dark. Faint music in the background.

Where am I?

Wait. WHO am I?

The panic floods in and consumes every fiber of my being. My eyes crack open but my body is unable to move. My face is against the blacktop, my cheek scraping against wet gravel. The moisture from the road below joins forces with the deluge from above and soaks me to the bone.

Cold.

I open my eyes a bit more. Smoke? Fog?

Someone's running toward me. Just a silhouette at first. His face comes into focus, worried but kind. It calms me. He kneels down beside me, places a hand on my back. I flinch.

Pain.

"The ambulance will be here any minute. You just hang tight, son. You're going to be alright."

His voice is distressed, horrified. But it soothes me anyway.

Shards of metal near my hand. Glass. Something sticky on my head.

Bright lights. Loud voices.

Everything goes black.

I woke up in a cold sweat yet again, my heart racing. The same nightmare had plagued my sleep before, but it had been a few months since the last time. The details sometimes changed, but the outcome was always the same: A twelve-year-old me, lying on that wet street, bloody and bruised, my father in a panic at my side.

The vague pictures disappeared into non-descript images with every second I was distanced from my sleep. But even while dreaming, the details always eluded me. I tried to grasp onto them, but the further I was separated from the nightmare, the quicker it vanished into the ether. It was like trying to grab a handful of cloud.

I lay in my bed, confused and frustrated yet again as I attempted to put the jumbled puzzle pieces of my dream into some sort of cohesive timeline:

It's always raining. I know that much.

What I can't remember is how the accident happens. I can see the car in a heap of twisted metal, a semi truck turned on its side, Lenny Kravitz playing on the radio. I can practically feel the gravel under my cheek, the damp blacktop seeping through my clothes, the sticky blood dripping down my face. My father, so worried, running from the wreckage toward me, checking for injuries along my body, afraid to scoop me off the ground. The terror in his voice as he tries to make small talk, keep the conversation light.

Thing was, the vision wasn't just a bad dream. It was also a memory.

The very first memory I have of my life, to be specific.

Oh, yeah. While I was so busy filling you in on what a swell-looking guy I am, I forgot to mention the most important thing about me: My brain is a mess. I have a condition known as *Profound Retrograde Amnesia*. Basically, I have no memory of my life before the accident; no memory of the child I once was.

From all accounts, it would seem better that I forgot.

I pulled back the covers and hopped in the shower. My domain was the junior suite in the house, seeing as my father occupied the master.

Yeah, yeah. I still lived in my father's house, but I don't think you can blame me. Not only did he like the idea of keeping me close, but the "house" in question was actually a humongous mansion. I had a separate entrance that led to a separate wing, so it was almost like living on my own anyway. The two of us had plenty of room to lead separate lives.

It's just that most of the time, we chose not to.

My father is Frederick Taggart, CEO of Worldwide Consulting.

Don't let the high-brow title fool you. The man was no whiz kid in the business world. He simply got lucky when he took a risk on a few tech stocks at the right time, and has been living the high life ever since.

He moved us to the affluent neighborhood of Greenhaven in Rye, an obscenely opulent suburb of Westchester County on the outskirts of New York City. Even then, we were clearly "new money," and a status like that didn't warrant much respect from the bluebloods that lived here. *Nuevo riche* was one step above hillbilly as far as they were concerned. Prestige and respect were saved for Old Wealth in most moneyed communities, and this New Yorkian utopia was no different.

Greenhaven was the microcosmic equivalent to a larger Manhattan mentality, only with bigger houses and even bigger egos. The town enabled its residents to show off all that scratch they'd swindled from nine to five while still allowing for a quick commute into the city. Most of our neighbors were CEOs themselves, reigning supreme over the bevy of working stiffs who helped to line their pockets.

Dad didn't quite fit the mold.

His name wasn't ever tossed about with any of the other movers and shakers in town. Even though he'd changed his lifestyle to reflect his new bank account, he couldn't change the fact that he'd only recently amassed his fortune. And that he did it without relying on the broken backs of a common-man workforce was practically reprehensible.

Even before he had the audacity to strike it rich on his own, he was a bit of a wild man. Back in the day, he was a real lost soul, or so I've been told. His parents had died within a year of each other while he was still a teenager, and he had no other relatives to speak of. He sold the family home and moved into a one-bedroom, cockroach-infested tenement in the crappy NYC neighborhood known as Alphabet City. *To find himself*, he said. At that point in his life, he'd been "rudderless. Didn't have a single ambition outside of where to eat the next meal." Apparently though, he was quite the ladies' man, and I will express my gratitude for the good genes here when I say that the guy was one helluva handsome bastard back in the day. He had enough cash socked away to fund his bar tab and skirt-chasing, and spent the better part of his twenties doing little else with his life.

Then in 1984, he met my mother.

The framed picture on his nightstand shows her as a feather-haired blonde, but even with the outdated hairstyle and blue eyeliner, you could tell she was a knockout. Dad sure as hell must have thought so. He's always said that from the first minute he met her, he was "immediately smitten."

Almost overnight, the late nights and carousing came to an end. She lived in Jersey, so Dad moved out to Shermer Heights to be closer to her. They dated on and off for three years until she got pregnant with me, but even still, they chose not to get married. They never did, at least not officially, but that never stopped Dad from referring to her as his "wife."

17

According to my father, my birth was "the greatest thing that ever happened" to them. He's never hidden his love for me, but I think he likes to exaggerate the extent of my mother's affections. Piecing together the years between their courtship and my adolescence is only slightly less frustrating than trying to figure out my dream, and barely more informative. Dad doesn't like to talk too much about it, so those years have only been offered to me in snippets. Tiny, anecdotal bits of their life and mine that I'm expected to add into a whole. The edges are fuzzy and the picture never works out quite right, so I can only give you the nutshell version of what I know for sure:

Mom wanted Dad to be more serious... He bought some stocks... He got lucky a couple years later when they paid off... He built this house...

She never moved in.

Supposedly, my mother took issue with his flightiness over the years, and finally up and left the both of us the day after my twelfth birthday. Dad hired a team of private detectives to find her, and when they did, she still refused to come home.

And then... the accident happened.

It was one hell of a rough year for him to get through. It wasn't exactly a cakewalk for me either, seeing as I spent most of it in a hospital bed. But the heartbreak of my mother leaving was his and his alone. I didn't even remember her, so I didn't have anything to miss. I was almost grateful for the messed-up brain, because unlike him, I never had to deal with the pain of her absence.

One of the few perks of being an amnesiac.

Can you imagine being my father during that time? His wife leaves him, and then just one short month later, his son almost dies. It was always easier for me to put my troubles in perspective when compared to that.

Even though Dad wrote my mother off years ago, he never truly got over her. He still kept a few framed pictures of her around the house but I'm not with her in a single one. Then again, there are hardly any baby pictures of me at all. She took them all with her when she left, so I guess that shows *some* sort of affection, right? Of course I have no recollection of it which is just as well. I've had to rely on my father's memory to fill me in on the missing twelve years of my life.

I'm not bitter or regretful about any of this, if you can believe it. My reality is the only one I've ever known, and I wouldn't trade the life I lead now for anything. It is what it is and I've learned to adapt.

My father, however, insists that my brain can be fixed. A few times a year, I'll humor him and meet with any new neurologist he's found, embark on whatever cockamamie new treatment plan he's researched. It's a small price to pay to keep him optimistic about my situation. The guy has never given up, I'll give him that.

I adjusted the lapels of my light gray suit before heading down the hall where I met up with Dad in the kitchen. Before I could even pour myself a cup of coffee, he launched in. "Good morning, Lucas!"

"Morning, Pop."

"Heading into the city?"

"Yes. Signing a new client."

"Wow, that's great!" He got up to join me at the espresso bar and offer a pat on the back. "You know, when you started this venture, I wasn't sure how far you'd be able to go with it."

"Gee, thanks," I shot back through a laugh.

Dad laughed along with me. "I had faith in *you*, numbskull. I just wasn't sure if all those pretty-pretty-princesses-in-training would fork over all that scratch. I can't believe what you charge."

My father never quite lost that chip on his shoulder when it came to rich people. Even though he was one of them.

"It's a drop in the bucket for most of them," I said.

"Oh, don't I know it." He checked his watch, and I readied myself for what was coming next. "By the way, did you get a chance to call Dr. Mandelbaum?"

He'd found yet another doctor for me to see, and I was supposed to get in touch with him yesterday. I guess I got distracted by Ainsley, because I didn't think about anything else but her for the rest of the night.

"Sorry, Pop. I completely forgot." His pursed lips showed his disappointment, so I quickly added, "But I'll do it today. Promise."

CHAPTER FOUR

I parked around the corner from my favorite diner on 44th Street. It was a non-descript dive right in the heart of Times Square that served the best egg-white omelets in the world. I had just enough time before my appointment with Ainsley to grab a quick breakfast, and my mouth was already watering. But before I could get in the door, my phone buzzed. I pulled it from my breast pocket and looked at the screen. Unknown number.

"Hello?"

"Mr. Taggart. This is Dr. Mandelbaum. Your father asked me to call."

"Oh, yes." Shit. I guess the old man made the decision that *he* was going to be the one to put the wheels in motion. "Thank you. Sorry if you've been waiting for me to reach out first. To be honest, I don't know what he thinks you can do for me."

"Well, it's PRA, yes?"

"Yes."

"Duration?"

"Sixteen years."

There was a sigh from the doctor's end, and I readied myself to hear The Speech.

"Well, as you know, the longer the synapses take to reconnect, the less chance you'll have that they'll ever do so."

"Yes, Doctor. So I've been told."

"Any hallucinations? Schizophrenic episodes?"

"No. Never. Vivid dreams, that's about it."

"Hmm. Maybe you should come in to discuss your options. I'd like to meet with you. There may still be a path we can take."

I was only half-listening. Many, many other doctors had had their hopes dashed in the past. I, however, had stopped hoping years ago. I'd accepted that my condition was permanent, and didn't really feel like wasting any more time chasing down a pipe dream.

But then I had the vision of how excited my father looked this morning, and reluctantly realized that I didn't want to let him down. "Sure, Doc. It can't hurt to hear you out."

"No guarantees, you understand."

"Of course."

"Are you free later this month? Let's say Monday the twenty-second, around two o'clock?"

"I believe I am."

"Wonderful. I'll have my receptionist text you the address."

"Sure thing, thanks. See you then."

I'd been absently pacing the sidewalk as I spoke with Dr. Mandelbaum. By the time I hung up, I was completely distracted. I must have turned a little too abruptly to head into the diner... because I managed to slam into a woman coming out the door.

The collision almost knocked me off my feet, and sent her coffee cup hurtling to the ground.

"Puñeta!" she said, staring at the spilled drink.

My eyes followed hers toward the sidewalk at our feet where I took notice of the brown splatter that was seeping into her beige, high-heeled shoes. "Oh man. I'm so sorry."

Great. This was exactly what I needed to start my day. And I was pretty sure the brick wall I'd just collided with didn't appreciate the start to *her* day, either.

Her head was down so I couldn't see her face, but her body already told me she was a big girl—only a few inches shorter than me and almost as broad—draped in a long, beige blazer.

She swiped a hand over her forehead and pulled her shiny, black hair back in a fist as her head rose. I was met with an incredible pair of dark brown eyes that were smiling as they met mine. "I was really looking forward to that coffee."

Relief washed away my guilt as I saw her handling my attack with grace and humor. "Well, lucky for you, I just happen to know where you can get another one."

I offered to replace her drink and she accepted, so I held out the door for the both of us to go back inside. I put in the order for our coffees, then handed over a stack of napkins I'd grabbed from the dispenser.

She immediately bent over to blot at her shoes, but gave up almost as quickly, sighing as she straightened. "These are suede. I might be screwed, here."

"I'm really sorry. I've got a shoe guy if you'll let me get them cleaned for you."

She raised an eyebrow at me. "You have a *shoe guy?* Who has a shoe guy?"

"I do, I guess," I said through a snicker.

"Is he nearby? I've really got to get to the office."

"Westchester."

The look on her face went from impressed to discouraged as we grabbed our coffees and headed back outside. "Fancy. But that doesn't do us much good from midtown." She hitched her bag over her shoulder and held her cup out toward me in a toast. "Thanks for the coffee, though."

She turned to walk away as I stood there, feeling really bad about ruining her shoes... But then, inspiration struck. I checked my watch, realizing I'd be pushing the limits of my time constraints, but found myself calling out anyway. "Hey, listen. There's a shoe store around the corner. Let me buy you a new pair and then I'll take these to my guy. I'll get them back to you, good as new."

She turned toward me slowly, raising the same skeptical brow at me as she'd done before. "A man I just met wants to buy me a new pair of shoes so he can take my used ones. Hmmm. You don't have any kind of weird foot thing, do you? Is this your scam? Randomly spilling coffee on women's shoes so you can do weird stuff with them at home?"

She was feisty. I had to give her that much. I kept my smile at bay as I explained, "A man you just met feels extraordinarily guilty for *ruining* said shoes and would like to make things right."

Her wary smile turned into a full grin. "Well, hell, I'd be an idiot to turn down a new pair of shoes. Lead the way!"

We walked around the corner to Broadway, and I directed her into *Kate Spade*. We were greeted by an overly enthusiastic sales clerk who said his name was Colin as my new friend wandered around the showroom. She wasted no time before pointing to a pair of gold, high-heeled sandals, and Colin scurried off to retrieve the selection in her size.

"Are you sure you want to do this?" she asked.

"Of course. Why would you ask?"

"I'm just not sure you're fully aware of where you brought me. This isn't exactly Payless."

The comment had me snickering as I found a place to sit. I figured this might take a while.

She pulled off her beige blazer to reveal a matching short-sleeved blouse and tailored skirt. Both pieces of clothing hugged her curves and showed off her shape.

Huh.

My first impression out on the sidewalk had been that she was fat, but I soon realized that my first impression hadn't been quite right. While she definitely had some extra meat on her bones, the better description would actually be... *voluptuous*. A larger version of a typical hourglass figure—huge tits and rounded hips; a sizeable, luscious ass.

The chick was a bombshell.

I wished I'd met her as one of my clients. Shave sixty or seventy pounds off this woman and she could be a knockout. Healthy, shiny, black hair that fell in thick waves over her shoulders. Smooth, caramel-brown skin. Mischievous, deep, dark-chocolate eyes. Full lips. Decent teeth.

Colin came back with the box of her chosen shoes, and my new friend pulled out the pair of sandals. She bent over to strap them around her ankles, and I couldn't help but to catch a glimpse of cleavage. I'd barely snuck a peek when she raised her head and caught me.

"I know my tits are mesmerizing, but try to control yourself."

I chuckled and held my hands up.

She smirked as she straightened, checking out her feet in the wall mirror. Women are seriously entertaining as all hell whenever they try on new stuff. The pose is always the same: Hands on hips, three-quarter turn from the mirror, head cocked to the side. This woman was no exception.

I watched her twirl her ankle as she assessed her feet with a satisfied pout. "I think these will do." She picked her stained heels off the floor and packed them into the box before handing the whole shebang over to me. "And lucky you, they're on sale," she said, tapping at the price sticker. "You got off easy."

I couldn't control the snicker that escaped my throat. This chick was a piece of work. "The entertainment value alone was worth twice as much," I said, shooting her a playful smirk. Babes always loved the smirk, and I figured why not give this girl a thrill?

She took one look at my *smoldering mug* and let out with a disappointed, "Man, do you really know how to spin a line of bullshit."

The fact that she saw right through me immediately had me busting out in a laughing fit. *Crash and burn!* So much for my foolproof move.

Once I regained my composure, I checked my watch and realized I was officially running late. "Okay. Bullshit aside, we both have places to be this morning." I held the box up between us. "My guy will need a few days with these. I'll be in touch when I hear from him. Sound like a plan?"

"Sure does. Here. Give me your phone." She held her hand out toward me, so I dug my phone from my breast pocket and forked it over. I settled up at the register as she punched her number in, shaking her head and saying, "Don't make me regret this, Shoe Freak. If I don't hear from you, I'm going to assume the worst."

She handed it back to me and I checked her name. "Mia Cruz," I said, quickly shooting her a text. "My name's Luke Taggart. Pleasure doing business with you."

WEEK ONE: ASSESSMENT

Come up with a plan of action
Set a workout schedule
Meet with nutritionist to lay out a diet plan

CHAPTER FIVE

Ainsley's and my first meeting yesterday was more of an interview, a free consultation. Today, our second appointment was about nailing down a schedule and hammering out the details.

We chose the lobby of the *TRU Times Square* to chat about the game plan. The TRU was a modern, impressive hotel right in the heart of the city, and one of the few places where I suggested my clients check in for the duration of our time together—whether they lived near here or not. It was always easier to access my clients when I knew where to find them, plus the seclusion from their friends and family allowed for complete immersion in my program. Since Ainsley lived all the way out in Westport anyway, the temporary move was a necessity.

There were a few seating areas set up, small clusters of white couches at right angles to one another with low, marble tables anchoring each conversational space.

I had just made myself comfortable on one of the sofas when Ainsley glided in. Even from across the room, she was easy to spot. A girl like that couldn't go unnoticed if she tried.

And hell if she didn't try her damnedest.

Ramrod straight posture, save for her head, which was pointed toward her clasped hands. Somehow, she navigated across the expansive lobby, walking toward me as if she were anticipating a communion wafer before nodding in my direction and lowering herself primly... to a completely separate couch from mine.

We can share a couch, sweetheart. I don't bite.

I couldn't help but smile, knowing that this beautiful little wallflower was only weeks away from full bloom. I'd make sure of that. It wouldn't be a problem so long as I concentrated solely on my work over the next two months. It wasn't like I could act on my attraction to her before then anyway.

The thing was, I didn't date my clients. Ever. It was the second most important rule I had for myself. Not only would it be a breach of trust, but it would be pretty sleazy as well. These women paid me a lot of money for professional help. Taking advantage of that situation would be wrong on a lot of different levels.

Once our eight weeks were up, however...

"Good morning, Ainsley. Have you settled into your room okay?" I asked.

"Yes, thank you. I've never been here before. It's lovely."

You're lovely, I thought. But instead of voicing my compliment aloud—which would have had her bolting from the sofa quicker than had it burned her—I switched gears in an attempt to open her up. "I'm glad you like it." I checked the impulse to cover her hands with one of my own, and instead resorted to teasing. "Have you been to the restaurants yet? The pool? The bars?"

My questions caused a slight grin to slip through. "No, can't say as I have."

"Lemme guess," I said through a smirk. "Room service alone in your suite last night?"

That caused her to smile even wider as she finally met my eyes. "You must be psychic."

I was struck all over again by those gorgeous blue eyes staring into mine. Was it just me or was she finding it just as hard to look away? The girl was positively beautiful, no two ways about it. I couldn't wait for the day that I would have those eyes looking at me with more than just curiosity.

Until then, we had some details to discuss.

I pulled some papers from my briefcase and slid them across the table toward her. "This is just a preliminary contract to get us started," I explained. "It's a general list of the services I'll be providing and a rundown of what's expected of you as a client. I'll draw up a more comprehensive agreement next week once we have a customized schedule in place."

She scanned through the pages as I tried to ignore the charming way she chewed her bottom lip. I was wondering what it would be like to chew that lip for her until her question jogged me out of the vision. "Umm... What's this at Number Four?" she asked. *"Client will actively participate in all agreed-upon assignments regardless of his or her personal opinions, doubts, or misgivings about said assignment.* Sounds rather... *authoritarian* of you."

I chuckled and explained, "That's just a fancy way of asking you to trust me. Remember when we talked about stepping outside your comfort zone? We won't get anywhere if we're constantly butting heads over your assignments. I'll need you to be open to new experiences."

Ainsley mulled that over before answering, "You want me to be a willing participant in this huge change to my life, is that right?"

"Pretty much."

I was a bit blown away by her enthusiastic surrender, so I was unprepared for her mischievous blue eyes as she looked up and asked, "Okay... So what would you change about me?"

"Nothing."

My reply was returned automatically. Unthinkingly. Dangerously.

Dammit.

Ainsley's vacant gaze sliced through me as I cleared my throat and added, "What I meant is that you're very beautiful already. I don't claim to be able to improve on what God has already graced you with."

Smooth, Taggart.

Her cheeks actually flushed as she looked down at her lap. "Thank you." She let out with a little giggle and added, "That's very effective."

"What is?"

"The way you just dive in like that." When my eyebrows drew together in confusion, she clarified, "Instilling confidence right from the very beginning. Saying things to make your clients feel good."

"I don't… It wasn't a line. I didn't say it just to make you feel good." When I was met with her crestfallen face, I realized I must have sounded like a world class jerk. "But I'm glad it did," I amended truthfully.

Jackass.

"So," I started in, trying to bring the conversation back around to business. Exclusively business. "This is normally the part where we discuss what you're hoping to get out of working with me."

"Well, I'm not sure exactly. As I've already mentioned, I'm too introverted, so maybe I thought you'd help me come out of my shell?"

"Absolutely."

"Because, right now, I mean… *I have the hardest time talking to men,*" she admitted in a near-whisper, as if she were mortified to say such a thing aloud.

"You seem to be doing okay in that department."

"If I had to pay this much to every man I wanted to have a conversation with, I'd go broke!"

31

Her response was so unexpected that I found myself sputtering out a laugh. "It's easier to talk to me because you're paying me?"

She shrugged and answered, "It's easier to talk to you because I'm not trying. You asked me to be honest, and honest is easier than charming."

Her honesty *was* charming. It was interesting as all hell to see her relaxing into our conversation, saying what was really on her mind. I got the impression that she was finally allowing herself to speak freely for the first time this morning, maybe the first time ever in her life. As proud as I was about it, I didn't want to scare her off by calling her out for it just yet. "We'll work on upping your conversation skills with the opposite sex. Anything else?"

"Yes." She lowered her head and spoke the next part toward her clasped hands. "I want to be... I want to be *sexy*. I never learned how to do that."

I knew it was hard for her to voice such an admission, and I was humbled that she already trusted me enough to say what she was really thinking. The good thing was, my program didn't work if a client wasn't willing to put themselves completely out there, and the fact that Ainsley was already diving in headfirst was encouraging.

The problem was, she was already *incredibly* sexy.

I could have told her as much, but that would have started me down a slippery slope. I barely had a hold over my attraction to her as it was. "I think you'll learn a *lot* of new things by the end of this," I said, dodging the bullet. "So," I added, getting us back on track. "I never did find out what brought you to me."

I didn't realize until long after our first meeting yesterday that I had interrupted her when she tried to tell me about her reasons for coming to see me. I was so stunned by how gorgeous she was that I overcompensated by trying to come off as a know-it-all.

But one of the most important lessons I could impart was teaching a woman how to find her own voice. It wasn't too late to start over.

"I saw your website. I read the testimonials. You seemed like the guy to go to."

"Thank you, but I meant what prompted your search in the first place?"

She hesitated for a brief pause, placing the contract across her lap and scrunching her brows, trying to find the right words. Finally, she just gave a shrug and went for it. "*Well*... I guess you could say I'm... *husband hunting*."

Husband hunting? Shit!

I don't know why I was so surprised; most of my clients came to me for that very reason. But dammit, I guess I was blinded by my own lust for this *particular* client.

Didn't mean the revelation wasn't a blow to my ego, however. I thought she was into me. I mean, it seemed like a foregone conclusion. When you think about it, we actually owed it to the greater good to hook up. It was defying the natural order of things for two beautiful people to deny themselves the pleasure of each other's bodies.

But Jesus. I couldn't imagine she was gearing up to fuck *me* if her sights were set on *husband hunting*. I hadn't yet sorted out the part of my brain that was screaming to "get this woman into bed immediately." My thoughts hadn't danced anywhere *near* "lifelong commitment."

But that's obviously what she was looking for.

We were clearly not on the same page.

I kept my displeasure in check as I responded, "I can't imagine it will be a very difficult hunt. Guys must be lining up for a chance to be with you."

Her lips turned up slightly as she shook her head. "You sure are smooth about it, I'll grant you that."

Her comment caught me off guard, and my brows furrowed in confusion. "Smooth about what?"

"Luke, it's okay. Stop trying to *sell* me on this little adventure. I'm already in!"

Despite my frustration with the situation, I was pleased to see Ainsley's enthusiasm. I handed her a pen and she happily signed her name in a swirly, feminine script. But then, in a zealous burst of joy, she raised the contract to her face and planted a kiss on the corner.

And that was it. That's what did it. I lost my shit when I saw that goddamned lipstick stain on the paper. That little pink kiss pushed me right over the fucking edge.

I'd never had such an instant chemical reaction to a woman before. I'd been attracted to plenty of girls over the years, but with Ainsley? It was primal. I almost couldn't control myself.

I wanted to comb my fingers through her hair, pull her in for a kiss, slip my tongue between those gorgeous pink lips. I wanted to slide my hand up her skirt, lay the both of us down on the sofa, sink myself into her. I wanted to take her back to her room and spend the next twelve hours exploring every inch of her perfect body, maybe let her wrap those pink lips around me, maybe return some lip service of my own...

Jesus. I had to get out of there before I did something stupid.

I shook my head to rid myself of the vision and shifted in my seat, trying to focus on the task at hand. Ainsley didn't sign on for this. She didn't ask to be the target of my bizarre infatuation. She came to me for help, and I've done nothing but drool over her since the first minute I met her. She deserved better than that.

For chrissakes, Taggart, you've got a job to do.

I snapped back into professional mode and wrapped up our meeting by presenting Ainsley with the customary questionnaire booklet—an intensive, twenty-two page personality assessment that I could use as a reference guide throughout the program. "Take it back to your room and look through it. I expect it to be filled out in full by our next appointment tomorrow morning. In the meantime, you'll be working on your first field assignment."

"Field assignment?"

"Yes. While I'll be right with you during most of your tasks, I can't be with you every minute of the day. A lot of your work will be done on your own."

She seemed apprehensive, but she was willing to hear me out. She closed her eyes and took a deep breath before asking, "Okay, shoot."

"I want you to start thinking positively. No getting down on yourself. Focus only on your good qualities." When she opened her mouth to protest, I spoke before she could argue that she didn't have any. "*If you're not sure*, the questionnaire should help you discover what they are."

Ainsley turned it over in her hands, asking, "Anything else, *sir?*"

I ignored her taunt and answered, "Yes." I pulled a small journal from my briefcase and handed it over. It was a nondescript 5x7 notebook with a blue cover that matched her eyes. "I want you to jot down any thoughts you have over the next eight weeks. Spend a few minutes every night to assess the day's events and your feelings about them. This notebook isn't for me. It's for you. I promise you I'll never so much as crack the cover. Your thoughts and feelings will remain your own. Guard it with your life. I suggest you store it in the room safe."

"Aye aye, captain."

I had to smile at that one. We stood up to part ways, but not before I could summarize our meeting. "So. Focus on the positive. No negativity. Get cracking on that journal. Complete the questionnaire. I'll see you tomorrow."

And then I got the hell out of there.

CHAPTER SIX

"Two more, Jared."

Jared and I were winding down his workout but I wanted him to finish with a bang. I'd just upped the weight on the benchpress machine and he was definitely struggling with the difference. His arms were shaking and sweat was pouring from his brow as he groaned in protest. "Seriously, dude? You said 'two more' ten reps ago."

"Just these last two, I promise. C'mon. You can do it."

Jared grumbled as he readied himself for another lift.

That's right. I have male clients. Surprised? Shame on you if you were. I told you this wasn't just some elaborate scheme to pick up women. My male clients aren't as numerous as my women, but they *are* just as desperate to change.

Jared cursed through the last two reps until finally, he lowered the bar and collapsed against the bench. "I can't do this!"

"What are you talking about? You just *did* it. Great job."

He sat up and wrapped a towel around his neck. "No, I can't do *this* anymore. Why should I even bother? Nothing's going to change. It's not going to make any difference."

Ah. The Week Two Doldrums. It wasn't so out of the ordinary for a client's frustration to peak at this point. When they first meet me, they're skeptical, but optimistic. Even after the contracts are signed, they start off wary. But soon enough, the promise of a new life gives them a burst of adrenaline which carries them through the early stages of my program. After a few days of buying into the hope, however, their pre-programmed insecurities take over and bring us back to Square One.

I looked down at my exhausted client, feeling his pain. "I have a special surprise for whenever this moment hits. Want to see it?"

Jared wiped his face down with the towel and offered a resigned, "Yeah, sure. What?"

I pulled my wallet from my nearby gym bag and rifled through the stack of business cards until I found what I was looking for, then handed over a timeworn photograph.

Jared eyed the picture of a teenaged me, all one-hundred-and-ten pounds of scrawny body, metal mouth, and stupid hair. "Is this you?" he asked incredulously.

"Yep. The thing I remember most about this picture is that it was taken about thirty seconds before Jimmy McKinley shoved me into a dumpster."

"No fucking way."

I snickered while reclaiming the photo. "Yes way. The thing is, I wanted to show you that I understand. I get why you're feeling so down right now. I was you once. Worse, actually."

That made him smile.

"My point is," I went on, holding the picture next to my head, "if I can turn this skinny dork into the man you see standing before you today, think of what I can do with *you*."

I may have exaggerated when I said I was born with good genes. I guess I was, but man, did they take their sweet old time manifesting on my body. That may be the case now, but growing up, I was your typical scrawny geek. I'm not just saying that to be modest, like those gorgeous supermodels who try to convince us they had buck teeth and bad skin before emerging into the classic beauties they are today. I truly was a full-on nerd. Reformed now, thankfully, but back in the day, I was pretty hopeless.

During my teen years, I was as awkward as they come. Braces, army-issue crewcut, emaciated body. I didn't even have some stellar personality to make up for it, so I tended to shy away from people. Finding a group of guys to hang with seemed unlikely and getting a girlfriend was completely out of the question. I spent my hours at school with my nose in a book, and my free time in front of the TV. Not exactly the most popularity-inducing traits for a socially inept teen.

But now? Well, hell. Now I'm Batman.

I'm a downright, modern-day, vigilante hero… and my superpower is de-geekifying.

"Okay, let's wrap it up; you've worked hard enough for one afternoon. I want you to stretch for the next ten minutes and then we can call it a day."

CHAPTER SEVEN

I'd dropped off Mia Cruz's shoes at the cobbler a few days before, so they were ready when I swung by this evening. I'd sent her a text to meet me at the diner of our demise, but she said she wouldn't be available until after eight o'clock. Then she said she'd much rather meet at *The Blue Bar*, because she'd "had a damn day and needed a damn drink."

So now I was walking around New York City with her shoes in a shopping bag, really regretting my lack of planning. But why would I have thought she'd be busy doing anything else? It's not like guys were banging down her door or anything. What else would a girl like that be doing with her free time?

In any case, it looked like my plans were going to have to change. I called Ainsley to see if she wouldn't mind bumping our appointment back to nine, then walked the length of 44th to cross into the Theater District.

I used my walk to think about the schedule I'd be presenting her with tonight. I had grappled all day over the best course of action to take, and was confident that I had come up with a personalized agenda that would guarantee her success. Every client was different, and I always made sure that my program was custom-tailored to suit their individual needs.

For some of them, it was best to just rip off the Band-Aid. I'd have them on stage singing karaoke during Week One.

For Ainsley, confidence-building would require a more delicate touch.

I made my way through the lobby of The Algonquin Hotel and headed for The Blue Bar. The place was practically a historic institution in this city. Back in the day, it was the most popular hangout for Broadway actors and acclaimed writers to come and throw back a few. Dorothy Parker and her entourage used to hold court right there in the lobby. Hirschfeld's art could be seen hanging on practically every wall. Hell, James Dean used to live at The Iroquois, located right next door.

The building housed a couple of bars and restaurants, but they've all changed over from their original forms since the old days. My father had brought me to The Oak Room on my twenty-first birthday so we could share a few drinks. He bought us a bottle of Macallan Rare Cask, and we put a good-sized dent in it before he checked us into a room where I could pass out. The Oak Room had since been redesigned as The Blue Bar, and I took a moment to appreciate the new look. It used to be a classy, wood-paneled, trip-back-in-time. Now, it was a modernized, neon, smooth-jazz venue. Still classy, though.

There was a real winner stationed in the corner who was way too excited to be playing the piano. Most of the people in the room weren't paying him any mind, but I couldn't take my eyes off the guy. Dude was lost in his own baby-grand world. I chuckled to myself as I took a seat at the bar, watching his hands floating over the keys as if he thought he were a magician, not a musician. Talented, so I could see why The Blue Bar hired him, but Jesus. Take it easy, maestro.

* * *

At 8:05, Mia whirled through the door in a frenzied blur of monochromatic gray. I waved her over to the bar, and she let out with a relieved sigh, greeting me with a breathy, "Glenlivet. Neat. Lots of it."

I chuckled and put in her order as she removed her raincoat and settled herself down on the stool next to mine. She ran her fingers through a damp mass of black hair, fluffing the waves over her shoulders.

"How long has it been raining?" I asked.

She lowered her eyebrows and curled her lip. "How long have you been in here?"

"About two hours."

"Hmmm." She motioned a finger toward my glass. "Drunk yet?"

I couldn't help but smile. "Not yet. But I'm working on it."

The bartender placed Mia's scotch in front of her, and she wasted no time clinking her glass to mine. "Well, I guess I've got some catching up to do. *Salud*."

With that, she tipped her head back and downed her drink in a single sip. "Mmmm," she groaned in satisfaction before placing her glass on the bar. She caught the bartender's eye and gestured for another round before turning to me and smiling. "Did you bring the goods?"

I grabbed the bag at my feet and handed it over. Mia opened the box inside and pulled out her newly cleaned shoes for inspection before grinning ear to ear and hugging them to her chest. "Oh my babies! Welcome home!" She tossed them back in the box and deposited the bag at her feet. "Thanks so much for taking care of this. You really went above and beyond."

"Nah," I said, waving her off. "It was the least I could do."

"No. The least you could do would be nothing. What you *did* was essentially hook me up with two brand new pairs of shoes! The least *I* could do is cover tonight's bar tab."

I didn't want to have to explain that I wasn't going to be there for very long; I had that appointment with Ainsley in about an hour. But the TRU *was* right down the street... I figured I had enough time for a couple more drinks.

"Look at this guy," Mia said, nodding her head toward the piano player. "Does he think he's the shit or what?"

I snickered, but didn't bother telling her I'd been thinking the same thing.

"*Huele bicho*," she added with a roll of her eyes.

I didn't speak a lick of Spanish, and asked, "Welly beacho?"

"Dick sniffer."

I almost spit out my drink. Damn, she was funny. And likable. And I gotta say, it was a relief to just sit and *talk* with somebody.

I didn't have a lot of friends, and I didn't have the social wherewithal to seek them out. With all my transformation from shy nerd to confident stud, I still hadn't learned how to form lasting friendships. Not surprising when you consider my job basically entailed only bonding with people for pre-designated chunks of time. I didn't meet new people very easily, so the best prospects for friendship were my clients. Most of them were women, however, and most of *them* didn't live anywhere near here. But such was the transient nature of my business.

My therapist liked to say that I've purposely set my life up this way to avoid any long-term relationships. That my mother's abandonment is at the root of my controlling nature and fear of commitment. As if I were specifically keeping any potential friends at arms' length, and the only women I allowed into my life were the ones who'd be contractually bound to split once our

43

eight weeks were through. That I preferred to bang a hundred different broads rather than build anything of value with a single one of them. That I *wanted* women to use me and throw me away.

For the record... she was wrong.

Before Ainsley, it simply never occurred to me to try and convert any of my clients into girlfriends. I mean, how unprofessional would *that* be? There were a few that I liked over the years, but I always made a point to tone down the flirting. With Ainsley, the suppression was tenfold.

I was feeling a bit suppressed all around.

It had been a while since I'd struck up a conversation with a woman outside of my client base. Mia wasn't somebody I wanted to have sex with, but she was *here*. It was probably a good idea to test out the old mojo every now and again. Make sure I could still deliver the goods.

I was gearing up to throw out a suggestive line, but Mia beat me to the punch. "*I* have had quite the day."

"Oh you have, have you?"

She snickered as she answered, "Oh, yes." She cupped a hand to her mouth and leaned in conspiratorially to whisper, "I went through an entire case of condoms today!"

Whoa. What? I wasn't sure I heard her right, and my eyes tightened in confusion.

Mia laughed and clapped her hands before explaining, "The Trojan account. They just gave it to me. I spent all day with my team, brainstorming the best way to sell them. Trojan wants to highlight their *variety* in the new set of ads. Who knew there were so many different types of sausage casings? You should see the box of debauchery sitting in my office right now." She took a

44

sip from her drink and added, "Very. Interesting. Day. To say the least."

I'd started coughing at her use of the words "sausage casings," but Mia didn't join in with my choked laughter until the last of her rant.

I arched a brow in her direction. "I suppose it would have helped to know that you were in *advertising*."

"Oh yeah. Sorry. I'm a marketing analyst at *Manhattan Media*."

"Was that so hard?"

The frustration in her voice was obvious as she answered, "It will be."

"How so?" I asked.

She gave a shrug and attempted to deliver casually, "Well, come this January, I'll be vying for Vice President."

"No shit?"

"A *lotta* shit."

"Huh?"

Mia sighed. "The current VP is looking to retire next year. He likes me, so he's been grooming me to take over the position, but the board wants to install the owner's pisant little nephew instead."

"Still. That's pretty impressive."

"I'm glad you think so. Because I'm freaking the hell out."

"Why's that?"

I flinched as she dropped her head on the bar with a *thunk*, her voice muffled as she responded, "Because I have no idea how I'm going to do this." She raised her head and looked at me to add, "I don't stand a chance, right? I've never been a boss!"

"Hey, you seem pretty bossy to me."

She gave me a *durr hurr* face and said, "I am completely lacking the confidence necessary to win this job."

The word confidence was like a lightbulb going off, and my brain immediately kicked into overdrive. Who better to help Mia gain confidence than a confidence *expert*?

I couldn't help the sly grin that spread across my face, prompting her to ask, "Why is this amusing you?"

I sat back in my chair and crossed my hands over my stomach. "Because I haven't told you yet what it is that *I* do."

WEEK TWO: OBSERVATION

Evaluate strengths
Watch confident people in action

CHAPTER EIGHT

"*Ten* things?"

It was the second time Ainsley had repeated those words back to me, and I couldn't help but chuckle at her dismay. "Yes, Ainsley. Ten things you like about yourself. C'mon. This shouldn't be too hard. Don't think too much about it. Just write down the first things to pop into your brain. That's normally the best way to handle it."

She chewed on her bottom lip, her pencil frozen in place above the paper. "That thing was more extensive than the SATs," she said, pointing an accusing finger at the questionnaire booklet I was perusing. Completing it was the first solo assignment I had given her for the week, and it shouldn't have been so difficult to take care of during all that free time she had between our daily workouts.

It had been five days since we first met. Five days since I was knocked out by her killer looks, four days since I started fantasizing about taking her to bed, three days since she showed up for our first workout session wearing a hot pink sports bra and booty shorts, and one day since I finally caved and jerked off because of it.

Not my proudest moment.

I was planning to use her cardio time today to assess her answers, but instead, I was forced to play exam moderator in order to keep her on task. The last page of the booklet had been suspiciously left blank, so I had ripped it out and handed it over for her to fill out. Instead of getting our workout underway, she was sitting at a table outside of the gym gnawing on a pencil as she stared at the lone sheet of paper in front of her, finishing what should have been taken care of days ago. I knew it wasn't easy for her to flay herself open like this, which is why I was able to keep my patience about it.

Ainsley, however, wasn't feeling quite as serene. She jabbed her pencil toward me and asked, "I've already told you my life story in those pages and now you want me to tell you what I *like* about myself?" She shook her head at the table as I stood there trying not to laugh at the entire tableau playing out before me.

I mean, the outburst itself was pretty amusing. But the fact that she seemed to be wholly invested in provoking me this morning was just too entertaining for words. It was a completely unexpected new side to her. She showed up for today's session wearing a pair of black stretch pants and a tiny white T-shirt that said EVERYTHING HURTS AND I'M DYING across the front, which made me think she was also developing a bit of humor along with her defiance.

Good signs.

I couldn't hide my grin as I answered, "Well, I figure there won't be much of you I don't know by the end of our two months together, but it's better to learn as much as I can as early as I can."

Two months. Two entire months of what I was sure was going to be unmitigated torture, trying to keep things on a professional level.

My grin disappeared as Ainsley grumbled and went back to work. After an eternity, she handed the paper over, and I set her up on the stepper while I looked it over. I'd already glanced through the rest of the booklet, but now I had the time to really assess her answers. I was mostly curious about what she'd written today, however, so I started there.

PLEASE LIST TEN THINGS YOU ALREADY LIKE ABOUT YOURSELF:

1. I'm nice

Agreed.

2. I try to be a good person

Good for her. That's important.

3. My hair
4. My eyes

Glad she appreciates some of those killer looks.

5. I have decent fashion sense

That she does. A little conservative for my tastes, but we could work on it.

6. Excellent fingernails

I stopped scanning her list at that one. I looked up and asked, "Excellent fingernails?"

Ainsley never broke stride on the stepper and simply wiggled her fingers in my direction. "They never break. I know girls who spend hundreds at the nail salon every month, but I hardly go at all. It's my best physical feature."

I was pretty sure that I could name about twenty better ones, but if Ainsley found pride in her fingernails, I wasn't going to tear her down.

7. My dog

That one threw me. "Whoa, hold on. Number seven? *Your dog? This hardly counts as something you like about *yourself*."

"Of course it does."

"How so?"

"Because I trained him." I shook my head, chuckling at her logic. "Hey, don't knock my awesome dog," she said through her panting. "Fluffernutter was the best."

That was about all I could take. *"Fluffernutter?"*

She gave a shrug and explained, "I was ten. I named him after my favorite thing."

That shocked me. Who knew a pristine Connecticut rich girl like Ainsley was even aware of what a Fluffernutter was, much less that it was her favorite thing?

God, I was practically in love with her already. Good thing she impressed me early because I wasn't exactly blown away by the rest of her list. Check it out:

8. I have a green thumb

Yawn.

9. I can identify all 151 of the most common flower types in the U.S.

Bigger yawn.

I mean, really? I don't think I'm being too out of line by finding both of those things incredibly boring. But I guess when you've spent your life sheltered within the walls of your family home, you don't get too many chances to learn how to be dazzling.

That's where I came in.

10. *I can roll my tongue*

Alright. Now we were talking.

Before I could stop myself, I barked out a request. "Lemme see."

"See what?" Ainsley asked.

I couldn't hide my smirk as I answered, "Number ten."

She almost lost a step as she giggled up a storm, but she finally calmed down and stuck her tongue out at me. Sure enough, it was formed in a perfect curly-Q.

"I'm impressed," I busted. "Hey, I'm gonna grab a water. You want?"

She answered with a breathy, "Yes! Thank you."

I beat a quick exit out the gym doors and practically ran into the hallway, adjusting myself in my shorts the second I was out of her line of sight. I couldn't get the vision of Ainsley's tongue out of my mind. I wanted to wrap my arms around her waist, lower her down from the stepper, and suck that tongue right into my mouth.

I threw a few bucks in the vending machine and retrieved two bottles of water, one of which I used to roll across my forehead in an attempt to cool off. I leaned against the wall and pressed the sweating bottle to my heated skin, trying like all hell to get my brain straight. I was going to have to do a better job of keeping my attraction to this woman in check from now on.

After all, I was supposed to be grooming her for *husband hunting*.

I grumbled to myself at the thought.

CHAPTER NINE

Mia and I had spent the rest of our time at The Blue Bar the other night talking shop. She told me more about her career issues, and I told her more about *Swan, Inc.* She was intrigued with the premise of my business, and fascinated by the tales of my clients' successes.

I was at a point in my career where I didn't need to seek out clients anymore; the word-of-mouth had spread and I rarely bothered with advertising. So, it was an odd position I found myself in, trying to convince Mia to sign on. Surprisingly, it didn't take much prompting on my part. After a few drinks and a quick sales pitch, she was on board.

The thing was, I knew I could help her. My program was all about confidence-building. It didn't matter whether it was to land a man or a job.

She had a bubbly personality, so the social aspects of moving up the corporate ladder weren't going to be a problem. No. Her issues lay squarely with speech-giving and team-building. She didn't like to be the center of attention, all eyes trained on her. I assumed it was because of her weight. Not a problem. I'd whip that overgrown bod into shape and she'd be strutting her stuff soon enough.

And that's why our very next follow-up appointment was taking place at the gym.

Mia showed up for our first workout session wearing a gray scoop-neck T-shirt that accentuated her full bust, and a pair of black stretch pants that hugged her curvy ass. I couldn't wait to see what I could turn her into. Her shape was right; there was just too much of it. Eight entire weeks of high-intensity cardio should kickstart her into better form.

"You ready to get this party started?" I asked.

Mia threw her towel on a nearby chair as she answered, "As I'll ever be."

"Good," I said. "Come have a seat so we can get the paperwork out of the way first."

I had her meet me at *Crunch* on 38th not only because it was a great gym, but because it was close to midtown. Since she had a full-time job, we had to schedule her workouts during the evening hours, and I had to imagine that rallying for a gym session after a full day of nine-to-five wasn't the easiest thing to do. I gave her a ton of credit for going along with it.

We took a seat on the black leather bench in the lobby area. I pulled the sizeable stack of pages out of my duffle bag and dropped them down on the white Formica table with a *thunk*.

"What the hell is that?" she asked, wide-eyed. "Do I need to sign away my firstborn? My *soul?*"

I chuckled as I answered, "I know it seems intimidating, and yeah, maybe I went a little overboard on the personality assessment here, but we don't need to go over everything tonight. This," I said, placing my hand over the pile of papers, "is homework." When she shot an *oh really?* look at me, I assured her, "I promise, you'll breeze right through it. This, however," I added, pulling off the top four pages, "has to be taken care of now."

I started to explain some of the details as Mia scanned the contract, but she was already waving for a pen before I could finish. She took a few minutes to scrawl something on the bottom of the final page as I craned my neck to see what she'd written, but I couldn't get a clear enough view until she handed the paper back to me:

CLIENT has no patience to haggle over the terms of this anal-retentive contract at the present moment. She is simply signing the ridiculous thing in order to get her workout underway. Owner/Proprietor of Swan, Inc. agrees that he will discuss the terms at a later date, and be open to adjustments at that time. Because there's no way in hell that CLIENT is doing half this stuff.

She'd signed her name underneath, and added X_____ for me to do the same.

I'd started chuckling at her amendment, but it was the sight of that X that pushed me over the edge. I was cracking up as I motioned for Mia to hand me the pen, and enthusiastically signed my name on the line. I stuffed the papers back into my bag and rose from my seat before holding out Mia's towel toward her.

"Anal-retentive?" I asked as she stood up. "I like to think of myself as detail-oriented."

Mia gave a huff, threw the towel around her neck, and said, "Taggart, you're so tight that if you stuck a lump of coal up your ass, in two weeks it would turn into a diamond."

I did a double-take at her comment, less annoyed at the fact that it was insulting and more impressed that she was quoting one of my favorite movies. "Ferris Bueller?" I asked.

"You know it."

"That I do."

Seeing as she was a girl after my own heart, and seeing as she wasn't going to sign the official contract, I figured we could seal the deal in a more unconventional way. I was smirking as I held out my palm for a handshake. "Here's to newfound confidence and old eighties movies."

"And shoes," she added, meeting my grasp.

"Of course. We can't forget the shoes."

We were both chuckling as I led her into the gym. "Always an adventure doing business with you, Cruz."

I had her start on the treadmill, a full thirty minutes of moderately-paced power-walking. I didn't know if I was pushing her too much for her very first workout, but I did know I wouldn't be doing her any favors by going too easy. I had her follow up on the stepper, and then a condensed session of weight training.

She carried out her first day without complaint, but she was definitely wiped out.

After a quick shower and costume change, we headed over to Hoboken for the second part of tonight's assignment, which is why we were currently settled in at a dilapidated wood table at *The Duplex West* to see a band.

"Band" might be overstating things, however.

Def Bowler Jam was a fairly terrible rock ensemble. These guys were bad. Like really, really bad. Their instrumentals were barely recognizable and their lead singer was tone deaf.

I couldn't get enough of them.

Mia pulled her wide-eyed gaze from the stage to shoot an accusing glare at me. "Wasn't there a worse band we could go see tonight?

"What do you mean?" I asked with mock confusion. "This is the hottest ticket in town."

"Then I feel bad for the town."

I laughed my ass off. I couldn't help it. The jig was up. "Don't. This neighborhood loves these guys. Zero talent and all."

"Okay, so I'm not crazy. They're not exactly... good, right?"

"No, not at all. But that's the idea."

"What is? Taking me to see a crappy band?"

"Yes," I laughed out. "It's Observation Week. Have you ever seen a more confident lead singer than *that* guy?" I pointed to the stage just as Harvey dropped to his knees and screeched out an ear-splitting final note. "And you can make fun of them all you want; it won't stop them. They know they suck. They just love to play, and they get to do it here every Thursday night."

She rolled her eyes and took a sip of her club soda. "So," she said. "Do you like all old movies or just ones from the eighties?"

The abrupt change of subject caught me off guard, until I realized she was just continuing our conversation from earlier. "I think my father would probably pass out if he heard you calling eighties movies 'old.'"

"You know what I mean."

I did. I gave a shrug and answered, "Probably all old movies. You?"

"I like all movies, period. But eighties are my favorite."

"Which one tops your list?"

She didn't even hesitate as she answered, "Well, aside from the fact that Eric Stoltz is the hottest redhead ever in Some Kind of Wonderful—"

"Never saw it."

"Blasphemy!" she declared. "Sweet and romantic. Totally underrated."

I arched an eyebrow at her. "Please don't tell me it's your favorite movie just because you think the actor is hot."

"No. *Even though* I think he's hot, The Princess Bride gets the win."

"Never saw that one either. Isn't that a kids' movie?"

"No way," she said, shaking her head with conviction. "Try and find a grown woman who *doesn't* swoon anytime Wesley says 'as you wish.' Be still my beating heart," she said, fluttering her eyelashes dramatically.

Def Bowler Jam launched into "I Want You to Want Me" (I think), and the noise level rose to unparalleled heights. It caused Mia and me to cease with our conversation, at least for the time being. It was a good enough excuse to use the time to sit back and observe her. Every moment spent with her up until now had been on fast forward.

She was high-energy. Thought fast, talked fast, moved fast. The latter was pretty surprising when you take her larger bod into account. Walking around looking like that showed she had more confidence than I had given her credit for, at least.

Wait. You know what? I'm an asshole.

I stabbed at the lime in the bottom of my glass, thinking that it was shitty of me to make assumptions about her life based on her looks. It was wrong of me to treat her as a "safe" target for flirting practice that night at The Blue Bar, and I'm glad I didn't get much of a chance to do so. She was way cool and a lot of fun.

She deserved better than that.

CHAPTER TEN

Once a year, the best students from the School of Visual Arts were given the opportunity to paint a mural on the outside of the building. People came from miles around to watch its creation.

Ainsley and I were two of them.

There was a large courtyard adjacent to the school, and it was there that we set up shop. We were able to find a piece of real estate amidst all the people throwing Frisbees, playing music, talking, laughing. I laid our blanket out on the lawn and unpacked the lunch that I'd put together earlier this morning. Nothing too crazy; just some fruit, some crackers, and a couple bottles of water. And oh yeah. Two Fluffernutter sandwiches.

Yeah, fine, you caught me. I was trying to impress her. So what.

Ainsley smoothed her skirt behind her knees and lowered herself to the blanket as modestly as possible. She was wearing a short pink sundress covered in little white flowers, and it knocked me right the fuck out. She was so completely unaware of how naturally seductive she was.

The artists had already begun their painting. They had a scaffolding set up against the wall that allowed two people to splash large swaths of color on the upper part of the mural. We couldn't tell what the finished product was going to be yet, but at the very least, it was pretty interesting to watch.

Ainsley seemed to be enjoying it, anyhow. Her face just lit up as she watched the artists go to town on their project, excitedly commenting on their pigment choices and brushstrokes.

I, on the other hand, was simply enjoying my present company. With the relaxed setting, I could almost pretend that Ainsley and I were on a date, not an assignment.

"This is so amazing," Ainsley gushed. "One of my favorite things to do is go to the art galleries in Westport."

"I know," I said through a wily grin. "You wrote about it in your personality assessment."

"Is that why you brought me here today?"

"I like to tailor my program to each individual person. My clients find greater success when they can find a way to relate to their assignments."

I grabbed one of the bottles of water as Ainsley nibbled on a cracker. "Interesting. So, what else have you got planned for my 'tailored program?'"

Shooting her a sly smile, I answered, "You'll just have to wait and find out." At that, I popped a grape into my mouth and gave her a wink.

The heat rose in Ainsley's cheeks, and I reveled in the fact that my grin was responsible.

She snickered through a sigh. "I can't wait until I learn to do that."

"Do what?" I asked.

"Be comfortable enough with myself to flirt as naturally as you do."

Busted.

What she didn't know, however, is that I *wasn't* comfortable and *nothing* was natural. I second-guessed every single move I made around her. It was as if all my years of transformation had disappeared within one minute of meeting her. This girl had me on the ropes.

"You give me too much credit," I said, playing humble. "It's all just smoke and mirrors. You'll learn that for yourself soon enough."

"Gosh, I hope so." She cracked the cap of her water bottle and took a sip before adding, "You know... I think I should tell you something."

"Shoot," I offered casually, even though I was feeling anything but. From the tone in her voice, I wasn't sure I was going to like what she had to say.

Her head was down as she picked at a white daisy on her skirt. "I know your website says all this stuff about confidence training, but I guess I didn't really believe it until I met you. I thought you were going to be a shallow jerk who specialized in making girls pretty, nothing more. I mean, how could you do all that you claimed over the course of only two months? But I'm starting to get it now. I'm starting to understand. Still seems to be too good to be true, however."

I couldn't help but smile at her "confession." I'd been gearing up to hear the worst, but of course this sweet girl wouldn't have anything truly negative to say. "I know my official title is 'Image Consultant' but yes, I'm more of a life coach. I help people find their confidence which in turn boosts their self-esteem, makes them more outgoing, better conversationalists..."

"And you really do all that in eight weeks?"

"I can do it in a lot less time than that, considering our starting point."

"Starting point?"

"You're already a knockout."

Ainsley had been so engaged with our conversation that she'd forgotten to be shy. Until now. Her eyes dropped again as she said, "I don't... Thank you, but you don't need to..."

"Look, Ainsley. Most of my program is geared toward helping a woman recognize her strengths, and we may as well get started on that right now. In just the few days since we started talking, I can already tell that you're sweet, and modest, and very brave, if you want the truth. A huge part of my job is to help you develop those qualities, highlight them for their fullest impact out in the real world." I took a sip of my water before continuing. "So, yeah. While I don't ignore the potential when it comes to internal beauty, my clients have always found the most success when I devote my resources to accentuating their *ex*ternal beauty, for no other reason than when a woman looks good, she feels good." I'd had attractive clients before. Hell, I wouldn't be doing my job right if every one of them weren't stunners by the end of my program. But none of them had started out with as much natural beauty as Ainsley Carrington. "The fact of the matter is that I don't think you realize how truly gorgeous you are already. I'll be working backwards this time."

There was no reason not to be completely honest with her. After all, it was my Number One rule, and she should be made aware of the power she already possessed. As crazy about her as I was, my attraction needed to place second behind her triumph.

Ainsley's lips tightened as she tried to restrain her smile. "I've... I've been told that I'm *pretty*. I guess I never saw what all the fuss was about." The most alluring flush crept up her cheeks as she met my eyes to add, "I mean, you must understand. You're essentially what people would call handsome, yet you don't seem to flaunt it."

"That's because I don't care about it." *Yes I do.* "I make the most of what I have to work with, but I can't really take credit for good genes." *Yes I can.*

"Being good-looking is hardly an accomplishment, you mean?"

"Exactly." *Unless you count the years I spent at the gym.*

"And besides, it shouldn't matter what a person looks like, right?"

If I didn't know any better, I'd swear Ainsley was trying to reprimand me. I'd been drooling over this girl from the first moment I met her, almost entirely due to her looks. As much as I tried to tell myself I was above surface beauty, it was a futile attempt to avoid acknowledging that I was full of shit.

Hell, I knew what a hypocrite I could be. I was just surprised to find that maybe *she* knew it, too.

CHAPTER ELEVEN

Week Two was all about observation. When Mia made that crack about the piano player at The Blue Bar, she had unknowingly had her first session with me without even realizing it. That incident is what made me think to go see that shitty band.

It was like she knew exactly how to do this; she just needed me to guide her in the right direction. There was no adjustment period for her. She just dove in. She just *got it*.

Mia Cruz was shaping up to be the easiest client I ever had.

I'd spent a couple days fine-tuning a program just for her: Intensive diet and workout schedule, maybe a crash course at Toastmasters, some trust-building exercises. She was great one-on-one; it was the crowds she wasn't comfortable with. So, a few tasks in some populated settings would surely play in down the line.

To start with, however, I figured the easiest outings would simply be in a relaxed atmosphere where she could remain fairly anonymous, which is why we were headed over to The North Meadow Rec Center to watch the guys play some pickup basketball. Talk about guys with confidence.

The courts were only a short distance from Mia's apartment, and it was a breezy Saturday afternoon. Perfect conditions for a good walk.

I nabbed a good spot out front of Mia's building, a glass-and-steel, rent-controlled monolith in the low nineties. I buzzed the button marked CRUZ and was immediately met with her intercom-garbled voice. "Coming!"

She must have flown down the stairs or something because I'd barely locked my car by the time she appeared at the lobby doors. Told you she was quick.

I shot her an impressive smirk, remarking, "Wow, you're fast."

She threw her hands out to her sides and exclaimed, "That's what they used to say about me in high school!" We both laughed until she added, "I would've invited you up but my place is a shithole."

From the looks of the exterior, I doubted it.

"Well, why don't you escape this 'shithole' for a little while and move into the hotel?"

Mia tied her hair into a knot as we crossed the street, saying, "Why? Luke, we've been through this. I live in the city, for crying out loud."

"I'm aware of that."

"So why bother with the expense of moving a few blocks away?"

Mia lived more than "a few blocks away." Native New Yorkers avoided Times Square like a guy in an Elmo costume avoids a shower, but for me, it provided the most convenient spot to set up a base of operations. Most of my clients were out-of-towners, so they were into the tourist thing anyway. Mia's apartment was fifty blocks and a world away. "Because I like to contain my victims. It helps instill full immersion in the program."

"Well, considering I'm only doing a *half* program, it makes more sense to save money where I can."

Oh yeah. That was another stipulation. I had to readjust my entire course to accommodate Mia's unique circumstances. Since she already had social skills, we were only going to work on her business acumen. Do some trust exercises. Get her used to being in front of a crowd.

She insisted she needed to take part in the spa day, though.

The rec center had a huge, twelve-court, outdoor facility where a person could normally find an unoccupied blacktop. Jared and his new buddies were already mid-game by the time Mia and I showed up. I'd brought him here last month during *his* second week, too, and he wound up becoming friendly with a couple of the guys. It's just who Jared was. He had the kind of personality that drew people to him. I'd been trying to convince him of that since the first day we met. Lately, he'd finally started to believe it about himself.

Mia and I took a seat on a nearby bench as I pointed to the copper-haired maniac who'd just stolen the ball. "That's Jared. He's one of my clients."

"Oh yeah?" Mia asked. "Cheaping out on me, Taggart?"

"What do you mean?"

She gave a huff before shooting me a side-eye. "Is it two-for-one day in Swan World?"

I couldn't help but chuckle. "I guess it is."

The fact is, I loved when there was crossover between my clients. The shared experience allowed them to bond and made for an unofficial little support group where they could bitch about me behind my back. Most importantly, of course, is that it allowed them to up their social skills.

Mia sat at attention as she watched the frantic blur of four very competitive guys trash-talking their way across the court. "So, I'm just supposed to sit here and watch these guys play basketball?"

"That was the general idea, yes."

"I'd rather be out there."

What? Was she serious? "With these guys?" I asked incredulously. "They're pretty tough, you know."

She cocked her head to the side and sassed, "So am I." When all I did was stare at her in stunned silence, she explained, "I have three older brothers. We play basketball."

The two of us were caught in a staredown until finally, I surrendered. "Alright, crazy. You wanna take on the big boys? Be my guest. It's your funeral."

Mia stood and put her hands on her hips. "You really don't think I can play, do you?" she asked.

"I didn't say that."

"What, you think I can't hold my own with those jockstraps?"

I raised an eyebrow and shot back, "I don't believe in using the word 'can't' with my clients."

She knew I was testing her, and it didn't take more than that for her to rise to the challenge. "Prepare to eat your words, Taggart," she said, pulling off her shoes and tossing them onto the bench next to me.

"Whoa. You're going barefoot? Your feet are going to get creamed!"

"Well if my *life coach* had mentioned what we'd be doing today, I'd have been better prepared with a pair of sneakers. I can't run in those!" she snarked, flipping a hand toward her abandoned sandals.

I was still laughing as she slipped through the chain link gate and into the court. "Got room for one more?" she asked, much to the surprise of the four men on the blacktop.

The guys halted their playing but immediately launched into razzing her for having the audacity to step foot on their turf. Mia was lucky that we weren't down at 4th Street. The games at The Cage were taken way more seriously and she wouldn't have been as welcome. These guys were merely screwing around.

You wouldn't know it by the hoots and hollers that greeted her from the first second she entered their realm, however.

The guy with the ball stepped right up to her, leered at her from head to toe, and offered, "You can play with me anytime, *mamacita!*"

Mia stepped even closer. "That's so romantic! I can't wait to tell our grandchildren how we met." Then she grabbed the ball from his hands and sank a three-pointer.

The guys just went nuts.

Jared waved me in. "Taggart! She can only play if you do. We'll get a three-on-three going. Come on!"

I wasn't very athletic when it came to most other sports, but my father and I had spent countless hours shooting hoops on our private court. I knew my way around a net enough to pass myself off as a decent player.

Mia, however, was killing it. She was quick. And her defense was harsh, man. All the guys were having a tough time getting around her. She wasn't afraid of a little rough-housing, either. Let's just say that if there was a ref officiating this game, Mia would've fouled out by now.

She was a force to be reckoned with. I mean, the guys were practically career pickup game professionals. The fact that she was able to hold her own was surprising, to say the least. Even more impressive when you consider she was barefoot.

Needless to say, the game got pretty heated. At one point, Jared went up for a shot, Mia was a bit overenthusiastic with her defense... and they both collided in mid-air. We all froze in shock as Mia was thrown to the pavement.

Jared was the first to snap out of it. "Oh shit I'm sorry!"

He crouched down next to her as I ran over in a panic. "Are you okay?" I asked, holding her head in my hands to check her pupils. What if she were really hurt? What if she had a concussion?

She sat up and inspected her elbow, waving us off with her free hand. "I'm fine."

I ran my fingers down her arm to make sure nothing was broken. "You sure?" I asked, still not convinced, but helping to haul her to her feet.

Mia dusted herself off, saying, "Positive. If you think a *cara mierda* like this is going to take me down, you're sadly mistaken."

Neither Jared nor I knew what the hell she just called him, but we both figured it was nothing good. We shared a shrug before I threw an arm around Mia's shoulders, busting her chops when I said, "Come on, Kareem. Let's get you out of here."

Thank God she was okay.

WEEK THREE: ASSURANCE

Etiquette training
Trust exercises

CHAPTER TWELVE

Even though my primary physician had sent my entire file ahead of me, Dr. Mandelbaum insisted we redo all my tests anyway. It had been about a year since my last full-round, and the doc wanted to see if there had been any changes in that time.

I was led into the first of multiple examination rooms, then subjected to an entire afternoon's worth of vivisection from there: MRI, PET scan, SPECT scan, blood work... not to mention the written forms thick enough to rival my personality assessment booklets. I was poked, prodded, examined. I was stuck with needles more times than a pincushion.

As bad as it sucked, it's not like I didn't know what to expect. I've done this numerous times before. I've been looked at, talked about, and passed off to so many "specialists" that today's visit barely registered. Nothing new to see here.

After every inch of my body had been scrutinized inside and out, I was ushered into a small office and asked to sit in a green leather chair until the doctor could come in and discuss my results. Take a tip from an old pro here and make sure you've planned ahead of time for this moment. Charge your phone, pack a snack, or hell, bring a book. Because you'll be able to get through the entirety of *War and Peace* in the time it takes for the doctor to step foot into that office.

"Mr. Taggart. Pleasure to finally meet you. I'm Dr. Mandelbaum." The doc breezed into the room, so I stood to shake his hand. He was about the same age as my father, which was weird, because he sounded a lot older on the phone. He was tall and fit, with a slight dusting of gray hair and clear blue eyes.

"Nice to meet you too, Doc."

"Thank you for waiting." I sat back down as he perched a hip on the corner of his desk and opened the large manila folder in his hand. He pulled a pair of glasses out of the front pocket of his white coat and put them on before speaking. "I've been looking over your stuff, specifically your SPECT scan. It's showing a profound lack of blood flow to the right temple and frontal lobe—"

"Where long-term memory is stored," I cut in. "Sorry for interrupting you, but I've heard it plenty before today. I already know there's no chance that my memory will return."

"*Little* to no chance."

"That's what I said."

"No. You said '*no* chance.' It's that 'little' I'd like to explore."

I'd been offered "solutions" before. I wasn't holding onto any delusions that he held the key to the right one. "Dr. Mandelbaum? I need to be honest, here. I only kept our appointment today to appease my old man. He's the one that's obsessed with getting my brain straight. I'm happy enough living for the future. I don't need to recapture my past."

"Now, son, if everyone had that type of attitude, I'd be out of a job. I've spent my entire career researching every possible way there is to treat my patients, and a handful of them have either trusted me enough or been just desperate enough to try them."

"If you're talking radical surgery here, I've already had about two dozen doctors tell me it won't do any good."

He smiled and crossed his arms. "What if I told you I've been experimenting with some *non*-surgical options for PRA?"

"I'd say I've already tried acupuncture, herbal teas are disgusting, and I'm not a praying man."

His lips pursed on a repressed smile as he explained, "You said you experience vivid dreams. That's a good indicator of effective neuro-activity. Your already existing lucidity will be an asset. I'd like to help you develop the part of your brain responsible for your dreams, give you some mental exercises to strengthen that ability."

"Mental exercises?" I asked, confused. "Isn't that like asking a one-legged man to spend some more time on the treadmill? I'm only working with a partial deck, here."

That made him chuckle. "No worries. What *is* there should be enough to get the job done," he said on a wink.

He picked up the phone on his desk and arranged for me to meet "Gia," the resident meditation guru on staff. As skeptical as I was, I was also intrigued by this guy's methods. I didn't meet too many doctors who placed much stock in alternative medicine.

Dr. Mandelbaum ushered me down the hall to a decent-sized room with earthy paintings and colorful fabrics covering the walls. Very hip, very new-age. Large windows that looked out onto a rolling lawn with a large fountain at its focal point. The lulling sound of Muzak merged with the unmistakable scent of patchouli incense, creating an environment of deliberate calm. It felt like church.

Gia herself wasn't at all what I expected. I was prepared to meet some wacked-out hippie but she looked... completely normal. Mid-thirties. Dark hair. Nice smile.

She had me lay down on the couch before walking me through some relaxation exercises. She told me the idea was to put my body to sleep in a way that would ensure my brain remained wide awake. She said it was kind of a self-hypnosis, the same technique used by method actors to prepare for a scene.

I was kind of afraid of "the scene" that awaited me.

You can't really blame me for being hesitant about delving into my brain. The nightmare of the accident's aftermath was bad enough without inviting the memory of the actual accident itself. Not being able to even recognize my own father—hell, not even recognizing *myself*—tended to incite a crystal clear panic, even if the cause behind it was a little fuzzy. The terror of not knowing where—or *who*—I was had always transmitted itself perfectly.

And now here was Gia, teaching me how to fight through the haze in an attempt to make everything even clearer.

I wasn't sure if I even *wanted* to regain what I'd lost.

CHAPTER THIRTEEN

"It's an escargot tong."

Ainsley pointed to the utensil in question as Miss Melanie nodded her head in approval.

We'd been at *The Etiquette School* for two hours already, but Ainsley only needed the first few minutes to make a favorable impression on her instructor. She'd already dazzled her teacher with her impeccable handwriting and unparalleled floral arrangement skills, but now she was seated at a table with a forty-piece place setting.

And she was killing it.

"Very good, Miss Carrington," Melanie gushed.

The Etiquette School was a relic of a lost time. Finishing schools had all but become extinct by the sixties, and for good reason. But a few survived, and thank God, because they were an integral part of my training process.

I'm not a caveman. Promise.

I only utilized charm school for the security it offered my clients. If a woman was already uptight to begin with, being thrown into a tizzy about table manners wasn't going to help her. The Etiquette School offered private, one-day workshops as a crash course in proper conduct. Posture, manners, decorating; a multitude of skills only a true debutante would need to master.

Miss Melanie waved "the waiter" over and had him place some soup in front of Ainsley. She picked up her outermost spoon and scooped it through the bisque toward the far end of the bowl before sipping daintily from its rim.

"Very good!" Miss Melanie said, practically beaming. "Mr. Taggart, it would appear you've brought me a natural."

Well, duh. I figured today would end up being a technicality, another check off the list. But I didn't realize that Ainsley had been playing the part of a refined society gal for so long that *every* aspect of etiquette was second nature.

After Ainsley displayed exemplary teacup-holding abilities and supreme bread plate comprehension, Melanie came to the same conclusion as I had. "I think we've got table manners down pat. Let's celebrate with a bit of champagne, shall we?"

The waiter came back out with a tray of filled glasses, and we each took one, making sure to grasp them strictly by the stem. Normally, I wouldn't bother with such formalities, but I did it correctly because I didn't want to be reprimanded by Miss Melanie. Ainsley, however, did it correctly because it was the proper way to do it.

Miss Melanie turned toward me and asked, "Would you care to make the toast, Mr. Taggart?"

"Of course," I answered before holding my glass toward the lovely blonde woman in front of me. "To Ainsley Carrington. May she find what she's looking for."

Melanie and I clinked our glasses and took a sip as Ainsley stood there with a serene smile plastered to her face. I thought for sure I would've tripped her up, but no. Of course she was aware that she wasn't supposed to drink after a toast made in her honor. I knew it. Ainsley obviously knew it. But Miss Melanie... Jesus. She was practically orgasmic about it.

She lowered her glass, proclaiming, "Bravo, Miss Carrington!"

Once Mel came down from her climax, she announced it was time to move onto appearance.

Smooth sailing, there.

Mel inspected Ainsley head to toe as if she were a show-pony. "Hair is healthy and shiny. Skin? Luminous. Makeup? Natural.

And your fingernails," she added, lifting Ainsley's hand to her face, "are flawless!"

What the hell was the deal with her fingernails? Who the hell even noticed such a thing?

Ainsley was flattered, though, smiling on a polite, "Thank you."

Mel beamed as she dipped her head toward her student. "But appearance is so much more than just what you look like, Miss Carrington. It's about how you carry yourself, conduct yourself, the body language you project." She tapped the back of her fingers under Ainsley's chin, commanding, "Head held high! Shoulders back!" Ainsley snapped to attention as Melanie added, "Now *smile*."

My jaw twitched as I attempted to keep myself from laughing. Poor Ains.

"Each person you encounter deserves the very best version of you," Melanie went on. "You must bestow dignity, no matter their position."

"Even if the guy's a dick?" I asked.

"Mr. Taggart, I'll thank you to mind your language in the presence of ladies."

"Sorry."

For the record, I wasn't sorry. It was too much fun to rile her up.

"Now," she went on, ignoring my attempt at levity. She grabbed a paper fan off a side table and fluttered it in front of her face. "Please observe."

Melanie proceeded to drop into an exaggerated curtsey, one of her wrists at an impossible angle at her side as the other moved the fan under her chin. She held the pose for a solid ten seconds before standing and slightly nodding to the both of us. "Some people might say that a curtsey is old-fashioned. I say that you must be prepared for any eventuality. What if you suddenly found yourself in the presence of royalty?"

"I'd realize I was in the wrong room?"

I couldn't help myself. I had to do it.

Miss Melanie bypassed the reprimand that time as she gave a playful snap of her fan against my arm before aiming it at Ainsley. "Your turn, dear."

Ainsley shot an uncomfortable look at me, causing me to shrug and wave a hand in her direction. "Go for it."

She sighed self-consciously before dipping into a practiced curtsey, her head bowed toward the floor, her skirt arranged in a perfect circle around her pretzeled legs. I suddenly realized she was embarrassed not because she thought she couldn't do it, but because she could do it all too well. To make her feel better, I broke out into applause, even going so far as to offer a hearty whistle.

Mel was just as impressed. "Model student!" she said, holding the fan across her heart. "Mr. Taggart, I do believe you're having some fun with me today. It would seem Miss Carrington is already quite proficient in all the social graces."

Ainsley stood, smiled modestly, and said, "Social graces, yes. Social skills? Not quite, I'm afraid."

Miss Melanie clasped her hands and bowed her head, dismissing Ainsley's concerns as she advised, "Good manners make good acquaintance."

I had to physically restrain my eyes from rolling at that one. Sure, Mel. All the most popular people got there because of their unparalleled knowledge of fish forks.

Melanie didn't see the pointlessness to any of this. Instead, it seemed she couldn't wait to see what other tricks her new pet was capable of. She was already off on a tear, gliding away as if she had roller skates attached to her feet. I shook my head in disbelief as I watched her make a few passes across the expansive room and back again, displaying the grace and posture she expected to see from Ainsley. "Here's an interesting fact: The way to tell a true lady is that she *floats* when she walks," she instructed, rolling her L on the word. "She's light as a feather. Mysterious. Elegant. *Poised.*"

A potential debutante might have found that "interesting fact" fascinating, but I sure as hell didn't.

In any case, this was all starting to seem like a colossal misuse of an afternoon. Ainsley had obviously spent years playing the well-bred lady, and Miss Melanie wasn't going to be able to teach her anything she didn't already know.

As soon as Mel was out of earshot, I dipped my head close to whisper in Ainsley's ear. *"I'm thinking this is a complete waste of time. Let's hop in my pickup and go get some corn dogs."*

Ainsley had to stifle her giggle as she nodded her head in agreement. *"I thought you'd never ask."*

CHAPTER FOURTEEN

I'd subjected Mia to a full two weeks' worth of workouts. There wasn't any noticeable change to her appearance yet, but I knew if she followed along with the regimen, she'd start to see the transformation soon enough.

She had repeatedly postponed our appointment with the nutritionist, and I was getting pretty pissed off about it. She claimed she already ate healthy, but come on. Her diet obviously had room for improvement. I was planning on making a point to nail her down about it after our workout tonight.

Mia threw her towel onto a nearby weight bench and put her hands on her hips. "So. Where shall we start the torture today?"

I laughed, then directed her to the treadmill. "Let's start off easy." Mia hopped onto the machine and I set the workout for twenty minutes of power-walking peppered with intermittent sprints. All week, I'd had her on a steady walking pace, but it was time to up the intensity level. "I'll be right there on the rowing machine if you need me."

The complaints didn't start until minute ten, during Mia's second sprint. She was sweating up a storm and breathing heavily as she moaned, "*Canto de puta!* I've been on this thing for an hour! This is inhuman!"

I chuckled as I came over to slow down her MPH and give her a pep talk. "You're doing great. I know it seems impossible now, but I promise, it'll get easier as the weeks go by. Starting an exercise routine is always hard."

She tried to catch her breath as her pace slowed. "Hey, I exercise."

The fuck she does. "Oh yeah? How often?"

"Often."

"Walking from the subway station to your office isn't exercise. Any steps count, but—"

"I *dance*," she interrupted. "So you can lose the smarmy tone, pal."

I wasn't trying to goad her, but if she *danced* as often as she said she did, she wouldn't be toting around all the extra poundage. "Dancing is good exercise. But even if you go out every Friday and Saturday night, it's still not enough. That's why we're here. I'm going to get you on a regular exercise routine. These pounds are going to fall right off."

She hit the button to slow down the machine but didn't bother to speak until it had come to a full stop. "Luke. I was perfectly willing to follow your instructions, to do what you asked of me. But there are a few things we should get straight right from the start." She took a swig of her water as I stood there, stunned at the change in her personality. The Mia I was looking at was not the insecure girl who had come to me for help. This was Career Mia, future Vice President of Manhattan Media.

It was pretty intimidating.

"A. I don't only dance on the weekends. In fact, I rarely go to clubs at all. I'm a sports bar kind of girl, so can it with your pre-conceived notions about me being some sort of Puerto Rican disco queen.

"B. The dancing I was referring to was Zumba. It's crazy exhausting, and I rock at it.

"And C. I wasn't complaining about my lack of stamina on this stupid treadmill. I could do this all day if I had to. The fact is, I'm only bitching because it's so *boring*."

She stepped off the machine and stood only inches from my face to deliver, "And lastly, you've got some nerve talking about my weight like it's a bad thing. I happen to *like* the way I look. I have no *desire* to be a stick. I'm healthy, I'm hot, and most importantly, I'm happy with myself just as I am. If you're not okay with that, then I don't see the point in working together anymore."

I was practically speechless and I felt like a complete dick. "Look, Mia. I wasn't trying to insult you. This is just my job. I assumed you were like my other clients. They all want to be made over."

"Not this client."

Man, was she *pissed*. It never occurred to me that she didn't want to lose weight. I mean, why would it? People came to me to be turned into swans. It was the name of my business, for fucksake. Hell, some of my clients had gone so far as to treat my program like it was nothing more than a fat farm. What better incentive to get into shape than by spending eight solid weeks alienated from their vices?

But Mia's anger made me realize that I shouldn't have assumed anything about anyone, especially her. Just because most of my clients wanted to change their looks didn't mean all of them did. She made it sound as if her excess weight not only didn't bother her, but that it was an asset. She'd never even mentioned anything about it before today, so why had I been so fixated on it?

It was confusing enough having to adjust my belief system with Ainsley. It was world-shattering to completely reconstruct it for Mia.

We were caught in a silent staredown for a minute until I finally caved. "I'm sorry. You're right." Her posture softened after that, so I kept going. "For what it's worth, I'll admit that I was wrong to make generalizations about you. Every person has their own unique set of circumstances, and I'll be sure to remember that from now on. Okay?"

The wrinkle between her eyebrows relaxed and her side-eye turned into a small smile. "Okay."

"Truce?" I asked hopefully. I held my hand out toward her, and thankfully, she didn't hesitate to shake it. "Good. Now what would you say to grabbing a drink?"

Her tiny smirk broke into a wide grin as she answered, "I'd say you're buying."

CHAPTER FIFTEEN

I had my father's driver pick up Ainsley from the city as I ran some errands, readying for the day ahead.

Our predetermined location was a non-descript warehouse along the waterfront in Greenhaven, a place I knew all too well. By the time the car pulled into the lot, I was more than ready to see her. I escorted her out of the car as her eyes went huge, taking in the sight of the sign out front:

NEW YORK GRAND
Ballroom and Dance Academy

"Dancing?" she asked, incredulously. "Luke, I don't think I've ever ballroom-danced in my life."

I smirked and explained, "Hence the dancing lessons, Ains."

If she noticed my inadvertent slip with the casual nickname, she didn't show it. "We're taking dancing lessons?"

"No," I answered. "I've taken enough of them to last me a lifetime. *You* are taking dancing lessons."

My father was almost obsessive with the way he raised me to be a "proper gentleman." He never wanted me to endure the snubbing from The Quality like he had. Along with the dancing lessons, I'd been subjected to years of crew, fencing, martial arts, and horseback riding, all of which were oh-so-useful in New York City.

The most abuse came from Miss Sabrina, my dance instructor here at The Grand. I was hardly a star pupil, but under the tutelage of that patient, scary woman, I managed to pick up a few good moves.

I also picked up a respect for dressing correctly for every situation, a mentality I displayed as I held up the box in my hands. I'd picked up a little something for Ainsley earlier in the morning, and she seemed delighted and surprised that the package was for her. I pulled the long, blue dress out of the box and held it up for her inspection.

"What's this?" she asked, wide-eyed.

"It's a dress, Ainsley. Miss Sabrina insists on appropriate attire while in her studio."

She looked down at her lavender blouse and matching, knee-length skirt. "Is what I'm wearing not okay?"

I'd already learned that *anything* she wore looked fantastic on her. "It's perfect. Just not for today."

I stuffed the gown back into the box as I led Ainsley through the metal doors and into the familiar formal space. The dilapidated exterior contradicted the extravagance contained within. The room was a gilded expanse of rich woods and elaborate, gold-leafed moldings. Turn of the century frescoes had been hand-painted on every paneled wall, crystal chandeliers had been hung from every medallion of the domed ceiling. Classical music was piping in through the speakers, lending even more magic to the breathtaking setting.

I put the box on one of the chairs against the wall and turned to gauge Ainsley's reaction, just catching the speechless "Oh" emanating from her perfect, pouty lips.

Before I could get caught up in the sight, a loud, echoing *"Bienvenue!"* interrupted our observation and directed our attention toward an arched doorway at the far end of the room. Miss Sabrina swooshed in dramatically—her arms in the air, her red, floor-length gown billowing as she crossed the expanse of herringbone floor—to come greet us hello.

She was one-of-a-kind, that one. Tall, thin, bottle-brunette, and a perpetually pinched face as if she were constantly sucking lemons. I'd been her student throughout my teen years, and immediately sought out her services once I started Swan, Inc. She was supremely talented, overly strict, and sometimes, downright rude.

I loved the hell out of her.

"*Bonjour, Mademoiselle,*" I answered, taking her hands in mine and double-kissing her cheeks. "Thank you for seeing us today."

"Zat accent needs some work, Monsieur Tag*gar,*" she snipped. Releasing my hands, she held them out to Ainsley. "And who is zis lovely *amoureaux* you've brought for me today?"

"Miss Sabrina, this is Ainsley Carrington."

Miss Sabrina's dark brown eyes went large as she held Ainsley's hands out to the sides for unobstructed inspection. "Oh, she is *étourdissant!* Simply stunning!"

Ainsley was clearly overwhelmed, but she managed to smile politely at Sabrina's gushing.

"But zis dress? It will not do."

I laughed as I pulled the lid off the box, presenting the blue velvet for her assessment. Miss Sabrina smiled in approval before clapping her hands together in two sharp snaps. "Okay then. *Viens maintenant!* Come! We either dance today or die a thousand deaths!"

I chuckled at Sabrina's flair for theatrics, though I didn't doubt her personal stance on the matter. Dancing was her life.

* * *

Dancing may have been Sabrina's life, but poor Ainsley had no idea how much it would become *her life*, too, at least for the afternoon. After changing into her new gown, she was subjected to some basic posture cues and body stretches. After that, Sabrina dove in headfirst.

It took about an hour before any of the steps that Ainsley carried out resembled dance moves, but after the initial awkwardness, the two of them were moving around pretty well.

I'd been watching them from my post at the edge of the dance floor, drunk yet again from the sight of Ainsley Carrington. The enthusiastic way her eyes would light up whenever she did something right; the charming way she apologized every time she missed a step.

"Pas d'excuses!" Sabrina would always admonish. "Just try again."

I was proud that I'd found Ainsley a "proper ballroom dress," and the long, blue velvet was swishing around her ankles with every step. Her hair was loose and hanging over her shoulders, the golden waves bobbing in time with the music.

She almost looked too beautiful.

I couldn't take it any longer.

I walked over to the both of them and tapped Sabrina on the shoulder. "May I cut in?" I asked.

Miss Sabrina didn't look surprised so much as put out. *"Non.* Too much work left to do."

Was she really going to let me just stand here like a spurned dope in the middle of the dance floor?

I kept the annoyance out of my voice to ask again. "S'il vous plaît, *belle dame...*"

My old dance teacher was no match for a compliment. But even though we both knew I'd won her over, she sighed and waggled a chastising finger at me. "*D'accord*," she responded with a bit of irritation. "*Bien*. But of course. I suppose I could use a cup of *café*." She relinquished her beleaguered partner's hands and I stepped into place, but not without a final warning. "*Confiance*, Mademoiselle Carrington. *Respirer!*" With that, she waved her palms in front of her torso and took a huge breath. "Remember to breathe!"

And then she turned on her heels and stalked off.

I shook my head at her retreating form before holding my hand out to Ainsley. "Shall we?" I asked.

Ainsley responded by slipping one of her palms into mine and dipping into a corny half-curtsey. "*Oui, monsieur! Bien! Respirer!*"

I chuckled as I pulled her into my arms and lightly spun her around the dance floor. "I think I could get used to you speaking French."

"Interesting. Because I don't think I want to hear anyone speaking French ever again."

I chuckled, amused at the mutinous tone in her voice. Ainsley was certainly in rare form today. It was a nice change from her usual reserved personality. It was great to see her finally having some fun with this whole thing. Hell, it was great that *I* was having fun.

We were posed in a standard box-frame, but still close enough that I could smell her. I mentally thanked my father for the years of dancing lessons, because I was able to keep step on auto-pilot while still drinking her in. Despite the abuse she'd been subjected to for the past two hours, Ainsley looked elated. Her smile was dazzling, her cheeks were flushed, her sparkling blue eyes were... pointed toward the floor.

"Stop looking at your feet. Look at me."

Ainsley raised her head tentatively, meeting my gaze with what could only be described as *annoyed curiosity*. I had to stop myself from laughing.

"Okay, good. Now let me see that smile again."

"Hey, lady expert," she snarked. "Don't you realize how much a woman hates it when she's told to smile?"

That time, I did laugh. "I have a feeling Miss Sabrina's bluntness is rubbing off on you." Ainsley had never challenged me so fervently before. "Maybe take it down a notch, yeah?"

The lightened mood allowed Ainsley to continue with her goading. "You sure are bossy today."

"Sorry. I guess Miss Sabrina is rubbing off on *both* of us." I quirked an accusing brow at her which made her giggle.

"Besides," she said, "I think I'm doing a pretty good job anyway. Don't you?"

"That I do." Before she could bask in my praise, I added, "*But* you could be the best dancer in the world. It doesn't count unless you can sell the attitude to go with it."

I guess she didn't find my backhanded compliment very flattering because she gave a huff and said, "Trust me, I'm starting to develop an *attitude* about this whole thing!"

I missed a step as I chuckled. Whether Sabrina was responsible or not, Ainsley had apparently begun to cultivate a bit of a rebellious streak. I liked it. I corrected our movements and elaborated on my point. "A man just asked you to dance. You should be acting as though there's no way he wouldn't have. No surprise, no eagerness. You need to play it cool. Gracious. Untouchable. Hard to get."

"You expect me to convey all that and still remember the steps?"

"Yes. More importantly, you should expect it from yourself."

I don't know what well of confidence Ainsey drew from, but there was a noticeable change to the expression on her face. Her lips quirked into the tiniest hint of a knowing smile as her eyelids relaxed, offering an artless seduction which almost knocked me off my feet.

Respirer.

I wanted to commend her efforts, but I didn't want to scare that look off her face. I was enjoying it too much. "*Trés bon*," I offered diplomatically, returning her flirtatious smile with my own.

Ignoring my lurching stomach, I continued to twirl Ainsley around the dance floor.

I was drawn to the curve of her lips—getting lost in them, if I'm going to be honest—and wondering what they would feel like against my own. Probably soft. Probably perfect. Heated breaths exchanging as I ran my fingertips across the smooth skin of her nape. I bet she'd taste as sweet as her flowery perfume.

Thank God we had a few inches between us because I had a raging hard-on from the thought. It was the first time in my four years at this job that I found myself grappling with my conscience.

Sure, there were a few ladies that I turned into fine-looking women. But by the time the program was finished, they were ready to try out their newfound confidence on the guy that they'd had their eye on before coming to me. It's why they enrolled in my course in the first place. The story was always the same: They were into some guy who wasn't into them. They needed me to teach them how to change that situation. And I did. In two short months, I transformed them into self-assured man-killers. Social. Beautiful.

Ainsley was different, however. She was already beautiful, so I had a full eight weeks to soak her in. But I had made the decision that absolutely *nothing* would happen between us until we were through working together, and I planned on sticking to it. She came to me for help, and help her I would, even if it killed me first. I owed her that.

Didn't mean I had to be happy about it, however.

I spun her out and reeled her back in, causing Ainsley's mysterious smile to turn into a full giggle.

Considering I'd just reinforced my vow to remain hands-off, the sight of her elated face was more frustrating than encouraging. Because of that, my voice was overly sharp as I directed, "Stop mooning at me. You're supposed to be playing hard-to-get, remember?"

Ainsley's smile was gone, replaced with a forthright glare. "And when did I ever give you the impression I *wasn't?*"

Maybe this assignment was going to kill me sooner than I thought.

CHAPTER SIXTEEN

For Mia's and my next exercise session, I let her drag me to a Zumba class. I figured it could count toward dancing lessons, because I knew damn well she'd give me a hard time about going to Sabrina's.

I was also trying to make amends for being such a horse's ass the other day, for assuming all my clients wanted the same thing. It's just that it was my experience that women wanted to be pretty. And feeling pretty, up until now, was always largely based around body weight.

But the thing was, Mia was already pretty. Maybe she wasn't typically "hot," but her self-image kind of compensated for that. It was refreshing, if I'm going to be honest. She knew what her body was capable of and seemed to be perfectly comfortable in the skin she was in.

And holy shit could she *move*.

I'd commandeered a chair in the back corner of the room. My original plan was to watch Mia for a few minutes and then hit the machines for my own workout. No reason to waste good gym time. But instead, I became mesmerized by Mia's dancing. I ended up staying for the whole session.

Every woman in that studio was working it, but Mia was owning that class. She swiveled her hips in time with the salsa beat, her hands and feet snapping in perfect choreography. Her moves were elegant and dirty and sexy and *real*. I couldn't get over it. This chick was born to dance.

When the class was through, Mia came over to me looking sweaty and elated. I tossed her a towel, giving her a wide-eyed, "Wow."

Her face broke into an exuberant grin as she answered in a breathless, "Told ya."

"No. You *showed* me. You looked incredible out there. Really, Mia. Not only that, you made it look fun."

"Well, maybe next time, you can join in and we can have fun together." Her eyes stayed on mine a beat too long, but before I could fully register it, she looked away.

"Hey. Why don't you shower up and get dressed. We still have an assignment on the schedule to get to."

She gave me a casual salute as she answered. "Yes sir."

* * *

It took us about an hour to make it out to Sleepy Hollow. Perfect timing. The sun had just set, casting an orange haze over the treetops and bathing the streets in shadow.

We parked in the gravel-and-dirt lot of Horseman's Acres, a real live produce farm located on the edge of Westchester County. Mia stepped out of the car and looked around at the rows of corn, the small petting zoo, the surrounding woods. "For the life of me, I can't imagine why you hauled me all the way out to a *farm*," she scathed.

"You'll find out soon enough," I shot back.

I led her to the large red barn on the far end of the lot. Inside was an active market—shelves along the walls stocked with homemade pies and jams, rows of tables filled with baskets of all the vegetables grown right here on the farm.

"There are about three hundred farmer's markets every weekend in the city. What's so special about this one?" she asked.

I couldn't help but smile as I answered, "This one has a haunted forest."

Seeing as it was barely September, the timing was a bit early for a creepy hike through the woods. But this town was made famous solely due to spooky shit. They celebrated Halloween year round.

"A haunted forest?" she asked through a curled lip. "Are you serious?"

"It's Trust Week, Cruz."

"So?"

"So, you agreed to this. You signed the contracts. That means you're going to have to trust me, trust yourself. Even beyond Week Three. Remember?"

She let out with a quick burst of air. "Fine."

We made our way to the front counter and bought our tickets. The pimply-faced teenager behind the counter advised us to, "Go out the side door and just follow the orange arrows into the woods. They'll keep you on the trail."

As we walked away, Mia squished herself against my side with a sarcastic, "Oooh this is soooo scary. Nothing says horror like fluorescent orange arrows."

"Stop being such a buzzkill, Cruz. I've been to this thing before. It's no joke."

"Are you scared?" she asked on a disbelieving laugh. "Big strong man like you afraid of a little—"

Just then, Michael Myers stepped out from behind a tree causing Mia to jump a mile.

"Cabron!"

I squeezed her hand a little tighter, trying not to bust out laughing at her reaction. "I thought you didn't scare easily."

"He caught me by surprise. That's all."

"Oh, is that all?"

I navigated us around the machete-wielding maniac and got us back on the path just in time to see the zombies creeping out from behind the trees. They surrounded us from all directions—jaws slacking, feet dragging—and while Mia would surely deny it, I felt her pressing closer against my side.

It's hard to keep your cool when you're shitting a brick.

We darted around the zombies and into the pitch black of the woods. The piped-in background noises got louder the deeper we ventured along the trail; howling, scratching sounds that made the hair on the back of my neck stand up.

We came to a "dead guy" hanging from a tree, his bowels spilling onto the ground where a ratty-haired, dirty woman was scooping them into her mouth.

"Okay, that's not scary. That's just gross."

Mia spoke too soon, because suddenly, a chainsaw buzzed loudly as Leatherface jumped out at us. That was enough to spook her properly. She grabbed my hand and we ran down the path into a little clearing... which was of course set up to look like a cemetery. We slowed down some once the ground became squishy under our feet. It felt like the earth was opening up underneath us and trying to suck us in.

Mia was hopping from one foot to the other as she let out with what was undoubtedly a string of curse words. *"Vete par carajo tu madre es en puta!"*

Man, she was really bugging out. "Mia! It's okay! Look, it's just a bunch of mattresses underneath some dirt and leaves. That's why it feels like you're sinking."

She attempted to catch her breath, and forced a nervous chuckle as if everything were fine. I knew that logically, she was aware that this was all fake. But if she said she wasn't freaked out, she'd be lying. "Just get me the hell out of here, okay?"

I couldn't help but chuckle. "Okay, okay."

She pointed out the orange arrows with one hand while holding onto my arm for dear life with the other. She calmed down some as we walked. Always on edge, but able to keep from jumping at every sound coming from the trees.

All was well, until we saw... The Clown.

He was standing ominously at the end of the path. A bloody-faced, sharp-toothed clown holding an ax. There was nowhere else for us to go but forward.

"Que. Carajo."

Even *I* knew she was asking *What the fuck.* "We have to walk by him to get out of here."

"No we don't!"

"Well, we could always go back the way we came."

"Not a chance!"

She was laughing, and we both knew the scary clown was nothing more than some college kid in a costume, but yeah. It was still creepy.

As we walked closer—slowly—the clown just stood there—watching us—as a litany of whispered Spanish prayers slipped from my companion.

Finally, I cut her off when I asked, "Wanna make a run for it?"

"No. Yes. *Padre santo que estas en los sellos ayuda me.*"

I pulled Mia tightly against my side, took a deep breath, and we went for it. The clown made a final lunge for us and only managed to clip my sleeve, but Mia screamed anyway. We were cracking up laughing as we sprinted the last few steps out of the woods, winding up back in the field in front of the barn. With the bright lights and people milling about, it was easy for her to shake off the last of her fear.

"I totally hate you for making me do that!" she chastised, smacking my arm.

"Fine. Hate me all you want. But the fact is, as scared as you were, you did it anyway. That's what I like to refer to as bravery."

"Vete a la mierda, cara culpa."

"I'm afraid to ask."

"I told you to fuck off." She looked rather proud of herself as she added, "And then I called you an ass face."

CHAPTER SEVENTEEN

Jared and I had become pretty close throughout this adventure. I didn't get too many male clients as it was, but I'd never had one that I related to so much. Kinda sucked that he lived all the way out in Ohio, because our association had all the markings of turning into an epic friendship.

I've already told you that I didn't have many friends growing up. And believe me, I'm more than willing to take responsibility for that; the situation was of my own making. Hell, even as an adult I found it really hard to let anyone in. I guess when you've spent years trying to overcome the loser inside, you can sometimes forget that you're not one.

But it was hard to keep my walls up around Jared. He was just a genuinely nice guy. There was no artifice there, no ulterior motive. He just wanted to be the best version of himself and assumed everyone around him was already without flaw. It made me want to live up to his high opinion. I suppose that's what drew people to him. It was easy to be friends with someone who already liked you.

We had a meeting at Toastmasters later in the day, so we decided to kill our wait time by heading over to the driving range out in Jersey to hit some golf balls. We set up in two adjacent stalls and left each other to work on our swings.

It was unusual for us to spend so much time together without talking, but then again, I wasn't exactly feeling like my usual self. I didn't get much sleep last night. Even my newly effective, tried-and-true relaxation exercises were proving no match for my overactive mind. My thoughts had been plagued with a crisis of conscience, and I spent the better part of the early morning hours trying to work it out. I wasn't having much luck, and my brain didn't have much room left to concentrate on the task at hand.

Needless to say, my game had seen better days.

"What's the problem today? You seem distracted."

Jared's observation broke through my musing. I tried to play it cool as I teed up another ball and asked, "Oh yeah?"

"Yeah. You're not normally this quiet. Everything okay?"

"No."

When I was met with Jared's patient glare, I decided to just confess. I swiped a hand through my hair and took a deep breath. "I think I'm falling in love with one of my clients."

It was the first time I'd allowed myself to put my feelings in just such terms before, and saying it out loud only confirmed what I feared to be true.

"It's not me, is it?" he asked, completely whiffing on his swing.

"You're pretty damn cute, but no," I answered, laughing.

Jared took another chop at the ball before asking, "Just so I'm clear, we *are* talking about Mia, right?"

That stopped me in my tracks. "What? No!" *Why the hell would he think that?* Mia and I had gotten pretty friendly lately, but *friend* was all she'd ever be. "No, I meant Ainsley."

"Who's Ainsley?"

Who's Ainsley? Ainsley was only the sweetest most beautiful girl I'd ever met in my life, that's all. No way I was gonna gush about all that to Jared, though. I already felt like a complete sap. "You'll meet her next week," I said instead, swinging my club and sending my ball hurling across the green.

"Is she hot?"

That made me snicker. "She's... perfect."

Jared had taken to hacking away at his ball. "So, what's the problem? You must find yourself in this situation all the time."

That one threw me enough that I couldn't concentrate on my swing. I lowered my club to the ground and crossed my hands on top of the grip. "What do you mean?"

"Well, these women are your personal pet projects. It's the *Pygmalion* syndrome. You fall in love with your creation."

I'd always been proud of what I was able to turn these women into but I never fell for any of them. "No. This is a first for me."

"Well, how do you normally handle this stuff? Like, with a regular girl?"

"I don't."

His club froze in midair as he looked at me in disbelief. "Are you trying to say you've never had a girlfriend before? I'm starting to think I should be asking for a refund, here."

"No. I've had girlfriends, just no one serious. I've never been in love with any of them. I've never been in love *at all* before."

There went my attempt to hang onto my cool.

"Well, why would you," he said on yet another unproductive swing.

"Huh? What do you mean?"

"Well, look at you. If I had the looks and the money and the game that you do, studmuffin, I'd never settle down either. I'd be too busy banging every hot chick I met. Why do you think I took this course?"

I crossed my arms and raised an accusing brow in his direction. "Please tell me after all I've tried to teach you that you're not just looking to get laid."

"No, man. Of course not," he laughed. "I did this for me first and foremost. I'm down ten pounds. My arms are starting to develop actual muscle. I'm feeling pretty great about it. But I'd be lying if I said I wasn't looking forward to testing my new self out on the ladies."

I snickered as I teed up my final ball. "Well, let's go hit the bar and see what we can do."

CHAPTER EIGHTEEN

"That's it. Nice and easy."

Ainsley and I were in the parking lot of an abandoned strip mall for today's assignment. She was behind the wheel of my Aston Martin, attempting to give it a little more gas. The car lurched for a second until Ainsley slammed on the brakes—hurtling me toward the dashboard—and I threw my hand out to stop myself from crashing through the windshield.

The car started to roll as she turned toward me to ask, "Oh no! Are you okay?"

"Brake!" I yelled, causing Ainsley to floor the gas again, until she realized her mistake and slammed the brakes instead. At least I was prepared for the abrupt stop that time. "Put the car in park. Please."

She did it, amidst profuse apologies. "Oh my gosh! I'm so sorry! Why can't I do this?"

"You *can* do this. Don't be so hard on yourself. It's not easy to learn something new."

"It doesn't look nearly this difficult from the backseat."

I chuckled at that one. Ainsley had been pampered her entire life, been driven everywhere she ever needed to go. It probably never occurred to her to learn to do it herself. If it had, she realized there was no need.

In any case, our little driver's ed mishap was the first relaxed moment I'd had all day. I'd spent the past hours in her presence freaking out over my "love" realization, and had reverted to my default mode of "strictly business" because of it.

"Well," I explained, "that's why I arranged this lesson. It's good to learn how to do things for yourself."

"Good how?"

"Self-sufficiency equals self-esteem."

She pursed her lips, eyeing me skeptically. "Mmm. Hmm."

"Would you like to try again?"

But instead of putting the car in gear, she continued staring at me. Her curious blue eyes were making me nervous, so I broke the gaze to redirect my attention toward the radio. I was absently flipping through the stations when she called me out. "You're acting weird today."

It was the truth, of course, but I didn't want to admit it. "How so?"

She ran her hands over the steering wheel and shrugged. "You've been very... *businesslike* all day."

That I had. I was too afraid of letting my emotions slip, so I compensated by going in the completely opposite direction. But instead of cool and casual, I was coming across as a robot. Guess she noticed.

I forced a smile and tried out a joke. "I'm a business*man*. See? I've got the suit and everything." That made her giggle. "Besides," I added, babbling through my nervousness, "you're not paying me to goof around."

She turned toward me and shot back, "I *like* when you goof around." Her eyes lingered on mine for an extra beat, causing my pulse to speed up.

Shit.

"Yeah, okay, good to know," I said. "Sorry. Guess I'm just having an off day."

"I also like it when you flirt with me."

Wait. What?

I was speechless at that bit of news, and could only stare at her in shock. "You do?"

"Yes. It makes me all nervous in the most amazing way. Like I'm scared and excited and intrigued all at the same time."

"It does?"

"God yes."

Holy shit. Was this really happening? I found myself inching closer toward her side of the car, staring at her lips as I said, "Well then maybe I should keep it up."

Keeping it up wasn't going to be a problem. It had been "up" since the start of this conversation.

We were locked onto each other's eyes, my heart hammering in my goddamn chest... because I knew I was going to kiss her. I didn't even think about it, didn't try to talk myself out of it. I couldn't hold back anymore. I was going to knot my hands in the back of her golden hair and pull her face to mine, slip my tongue between those gorgeous, full lips and unleash all the pent-up desire I'd had for her since the first minute I met her. Sweet and soft for as long as I could stand it, then rough and unyielding until the two of us burst into flames.

I swallowed hard as my hand raised on its own to touch her hair. But before my fingers could even make contact with a single strand, she said, "It helps pull me out of my shell. It shows me what sexy is supposed to look like. I've been taking mental notes to use all these lines on Blake."

I could practically hear the record scratch. "Wait. What? Who's Blake?"

"Blake Atwood."

My eyes tightened as I took in the name of one of the city's most prominent real estate developers. I knew who he was of course, but I couldn't quite understand what he had to do with this conversation. "What about him?"

Her eyes found the hands in her lap as she explained, "I told you I was husband hunting, remember? Our parents are friends. I've had a crush on him since we were fifteen."

Fuck!

Here I'd been, assuming if I could just bide my time, Ainsley would be mine for the taking at the end of our eight weeks together. But she only came to me because she wanted my help to land another guy. Not just husband hunting in general, but a specific fucking guy.

Even still, Atwood wasn't going to be an easy catch. The guy was a known playboy, confounding when you take into consideration that he was an absolute tool bag. But when you ran with the rich and the powerful, the babes were never far behind.

I finally snapped back to attention and was able to find some words. "Blake Atwood? Really?"

"I know it sounds stupid. I just… We just have so much in common. Honestly, we'd be perfect together! He just doesn't know it yet."

"Well then he's a fool."

The thought of a finite deadline for our time together used to fill me with impatience. Now, it was causing an inexplicable pang in my stomach. I didn't like the idea of having to say goodbye, and I sure as hell didn't like the idea of handing her over to another guy when I did.

The realization hit me hard; a sucker-punch to the gut.

How the hell did I fail to see it coming?

CHAPTER NINETEEN

I woke up sicker than a dog on Sunday morning. Probably nothing more than a nasty cold, but it was enough to incapacitate me. I was barely able to roll over and pick up the phone.

Mia was being a pain in the ass about taking the course at Miss Melanie's, so I'd been secretly plotting an alternative plan for this morning. But now there was no way to carry out the surprise.

"Mia," I mumbled into the phone. "I'm so sorry, but I'm going to have to reschedule our appointment."

"You sound like shit."

"I feel like it, too." *For more reasons than one.*

"Awww," she busted. "But I was so looking forward to learning how to be a *proper lady.*"

Against my better will, I found myself snickering. "It's not just salad forks and pinky popping," I defended. "The right school will also train you in *business* etiquette."

"I know how to shake hands and look someone in the eye. I know not to pick my teeth with the expense report in the middle of a meeting. I know these things already, Luke. I've told you this."

"Well, in any case, you wouldn't have had to go anyway."

"What do you mean? Giving up on me already?"

"No," I chuckled. "I was going to swap out your day at finishing school for breakfast at The Russian Tea Room instead."

"Oh, man! I would've loved that!"

"I figured as much."

"It sucks that you're sick."

"Sure does." As if on cue, my body heaved with spastic coughing.

Before I could apologize, Mia said, "Hey. Why don't I come over? You obviously need someone to look after you."

It sucked that she was right. Of course my father had chosen *this* weekend to take one of his rare business trips, and I didn't feel comfortable asking any of the help to play nursemaid to me. Besides, I was a grown man, for godsakes. I could take care of myself.

I got myself under control and shot back, "No, Mia. I'm fine."

"You're not fine! What's your address?"

From any other client, the question would have seemed bizarre. But ever since that trip out to Sleepy Hollow, Mia had started to feel less like a client and more like a friend I was helping out. Well, I guess in the case of today, she was trying to help *me* out.

There was a bit of back-and-forth, but since Mia wouldn't let it go, I finally caved and gave up the info. If she wanted to risk getting the plague, I wasn't going to stop her. Not that I could. That chick normally did whatever the hell she wanted anyway.

I managed to drag myself down the hallway to unlock the side door, then into the shower before getting dressed and sinking back into my bed. I got pretty tied up in a *Walking Dead* binge—appropriately enough—but it was only a couple hours later that there was a knock on my bedroom door.

"Come in!" I yelled, the sheer exertion of which had me coughing all over again.

Mia breezed in, took one look at me, and snarked, "Wow, you look great."

"Save the commentary, Cruz. Have some respect for the dead." I blew my nose and threw the tissue in the garbage pail. "Guess you found the place okay."

"Yeah. It was pretty easy. Well, I mean, I took an Uber," she answered, scanning her eyes around my bedroom. "I think I went to the wrong door, though. Unless you forgot to unlock it. Anyway, I rang the bell and your *butler* let me in."

"William isn't a butler," I defended. "He's an *estate manager*."

"Oh for fuck's sake like there's any difference."

I chuckled through a cough as Mia made herself comfortable in the wing chair next to my bed. She dropped a big cloth bag at her feet before smoothing her hands over the fabric of the chair. "This is some house. Makeovers must pay well."

"It's not mine. I live here with my father."

She raised a questioning eyebrow at me. "And how old are you?"

"Twenty-eight, wiseass."

She pulled off her beige poncho and draped it over the back of the chair. She was wearing a matching beige top underneath. Damn. I was really looking forward to introducing some color into her monochromatic wardrobe. "Twenty-eight. And you obviously make a good living for yourself."

"Yeah, so?"

"Sooo why not get your own place?"

I snickered to myself as I answered, "Because my father thinks keeping an eye on me is the only reason I stay alive."

When Mia's face scrunched, I gave her the short version of my life story. "When I was twelve, I almost died. Nasty-ass car accident. Dad feels safer keeping me close." I pulled my hair back to show her the scar on my forehead. She leaned in closer to inspect the pale line as I added, "The place is big enough that it's like living on my own anyway. We could easily go days without bumping into each other."

"Do you?"

I couldn't help but grin. "No. Never."

Mia returned my grin with a warm smile of her own. "So," she started in, changing the subject, "How are you feeling?"

Like shit. Like a fucking heartbroken idiot. I pulled a tissue from the box and blew my nose. "Like my own body is trying to waterboard me."

"Congested?"

"Yes. Head and body aches, runny nose. And these tissues suck."

"Well, lucky for you I brought provisions." She grabbed the bag at her feet and started rifling through it, pulling out a cavalcade of seemingly random items and placing them on my nightstand one by one. "Nyquil. A quart of chicken noodle soup from Dean and DeLuca. Gatorade. Lots and lots of Airborne. And..." she shoved all the stuff out of the way to present me with the final item. "A box of Puffs Plus so you don't shred your nose."

"Wow, thanks. Looks like you thought of everything." I dove for the soup and popped the lid, grateful that Mia thought to bring a spoon.

She paused her unpacking to gauge my reaction. "How is it?"

"I *think* it's good... Too bad my taste buds are so screwed up. Want some?"

"No thanks. I grabbed something before I came."

How could she know this is exactly what I needed today? I was already feeling better. "I can't believe you brought all this stuff over. Really. Above and beyond, Cruz. It was really cool of you to come take care of me. Thanks."

"Just take it off my bill," she said on a shy smile. "Besides, I didn't even show you the best part yet." She reached back into the bag and pulled out a stack of DVDs. "I brought some movies! I've got Heart-Shaped Box, Unleaded, and Swayed."

I couldn't help but notice the common theme between all three of her chosen films. "You a Trip Wiley fan?"

"Who isn't?"

I tried to be cool as I said, "No, he's a good actor. I guess I just didn't realize you were into blond guys."

"I'm into *that* blond guy!"

My stomach kind of sank when she said that. Which caught me off guard, to say the least. I didn't know where the pang was coming from. What was the big deal? So she had a crush on an actor. Lots of people did. I didn't know why I was getting so caught up over it. I guess maybe because I looked nothing like the guy, and to tell you the truth, maybe I was a little jealous.

She tossed the movies onto the bed with a shrug and dove back into her bag. "I also brought Some Kind of Wonderful and The Princess Bride."

I could only roll my eyes. "Really?"

Mia hugged the boxes to her chest. "Only The Most Romantic Movies Ever Made!"

Her exhilaration made me laugh, and I almost choked on my spoonful of soup.

She added the boxes to the pile on the bed and continued, "Aaaand, since we have to improvise on my etiquette training, I was also able to dig out an old copy of," she pulled her hand out of the bag with a flourish and held the DVD out toward me. "Dat-da-da-dahhhh! My Fair Lady!"

That made me chuckle. I guess she found a way to do her assignment today after all.

"I'll leave the rest here for you to marathon on your own, but I figured you'd want us to watch this one together. These are my own copies, so take care of them."

She hopped off the chair and slid the DVD into my Playstation. I fiddled with the remotes to get the movie started as Mia made herself comfortable back in the chair.

I was looking forward to having something else to distract me from my misery, but I guess it was hard to stay focused on a movie I'd already seen before. My head had been consumed with thoughts of Ainsley and Blake Toolbag Atwood since yesterday afternoon, and the sudden lack of conversation between Mia and me had me thinking about it all over again. Over the past twenty-four hours, I'd worked myself up into quite the frothing rage. I didn't say much throughout the first half of the movie, resorting to absent, one-word answers until she finally gave up talking to me altogether. I'd almost forgotten she was even here.

That was, until she said, "I would totally fuck Professor Higgins."

The declaration knocked me right the hell out of my moping. "What?"

"You heard me."

I gaped at her in shock. "Are you serious? He's such a weenie."

"What can I say?" she shrugged. "I've got a thing for smart guys."

And blond guys. And redheads. And guys who wear masks and rescue princesses. In other words, guys who were nothing like me. What did that say about the type of guy *I* was if I wasn't even good enough for a girl like her? "You've apparently got a thing for *lots* of guys."

"What's that supposed to mean?"

"Nothing. Just forget it," I said, a little more forcefully than I intended.

"It's not 'nothing.' Jeez. What the hell crawled up your butt today?"

"I'm sick."

She grabbed the controller and hit pause before turning to face me. "It's more than that. You were nice when I first got here, but to be honest, you've been a bit of a dick ever since."

If she was looking for my full attention, that got it. I'd been distracted and short-fused all day, stewing in my own jealousy about Ainsley and projecting it onto Mia. I didn't feel too good about that.

I sighed, finally raising my eyes to meet her gaze head-on. "You're right. I'm sorry."

But instead of accepting my apology, she continued to stare me down. "And?"

"And what?"

"And are you going to tell me why?"

I ran a hand over my hair and shook my head at my lap. I didn't know if I'd be crossing some line by bringing my personal problems into my professional life. It seemed I'd been doing that a lot this week, first by falling for Ainsley in the first place, then by confiding to Jared about it. Top it all off with the fact that I'd allowed Mia to come here and play nursemaid, and Jesus. You'd think I didn't even know where the lines *were* anymore.

Mia was looking at me expectantly, waiting on my answer. Crossed lines or no, I became aware of my current reality: She deserved an explanation, she was volunteering to be my sounding board, and to tell you the truth, I kind of needed all the help I could get. "Fine. Look, I'll tell you what's going on but only because I need a woman's opinion on this."

"Gee, thanks. I feel so special," she said, rolling her eyes.

"I didn't mean that. I'm just... I'm just glad you and I have become friendly enough that I can tell you this kind of stuff. I don't have too many other people I can talk to."

She seemed to like the sound of that as her face broke into a small, proud smile. "Okay, lay it on me."

So I did. I told her all about Ainsley. From the first moment I met her, to the agony during every moment since. I told her about Rule Number Two and how I'd never date one of my clients while we were working together. I told her I didn't think I had enough time to wait until our eight weeks were up because Ainsley had already set her sights on Blake Sperm-Face Atwood. I talked and I talked while Mia listened intently, nodding her head, measuring my every word.

I actually felt relieved at having purged the situation from my brain. It felt great to be able to trust her with this.

When I was through, I looked at her and said, "So that's it. I just don't know where I am with this whole thing." I was waiting for some Dalai Lama-type enlightenment from her, some perfect female wisdom to make sense of this whole mess.

"Huh," she finally said, raising her brows. "I guess *you* like blondes, too."

Definitely not the reaction I was expecting. I snickered as I said, "Correction: I *like* blondes. I *love* this particular blonde."

Mia's eyes went wide. "Wait. You really think you're in love with her? After only a few weeks?"

"How long is it supposed to take?"

"I don't know. Good point. I guess when it's right, it's right. Right?" Her face fell as she mulled it over.

I was flattered by her reaction. Kinda sweet that she was taking my stupid love life to heart. I couldn't contain my smirk as I asked, "So, what do you think I should do?"

Mia bit her lip and gave a shrug. It felt like an eternity before she finally looked up to meet my eyes. "Sorry to say, *mamoa*. But I think your only move here is to tell her."

WEEK FOUR: POSITIVITY

Dental visit
Smiling practice, eye contact

CHAPTER TWENTY

After forty-eight hours of soup and about a dozen Airborne tablets, I was feeling a hundred times better than I had over the weekend.

I'd done a lot of thinking the past two days, an easy enough activity in which to indulge, seeing as I was confined to my sickbed the entire time.

Mia had given me some good advice to chew over, and chew it I did. I came to the same conclusion that she had. She was right. I needed to step up my game.

I was about to break Rule Number Two.

I wouldn't normally even consider it, but Ainsley wasn't just any normal girl.

The fact of the matter was, I needed to get her to fall for me. Not an easy thing to do when I was so hellbent on keeping things professional. But I'd started to think that maybe if I played things just right, she'd realize she wouldn't have to go "husband hunting" after all. Maybe she'd realize that the perfect guy was right in front of her this whole time.

Don't get me wrong. This sure as hell isn't me saying that I was looking to get married—hell no, not a chance, not going to happen. I'm just saying that if push came to shove, I *might* be open to the idea of at least thinking about it.

Maybe.

Possibly.

But first things first.

I had to get her to fall for me before she could get Atwood to notice her. And I couldn't very well do it without breaking a few of my hard and fast rules. Desperate times called for desperate measures.

I'd been a mooning dope for weeks. That wasn't me. I'd done a ton of work on myself to turn into the hot, confident guy I am today, and yet I'd never let Ainsley see past the surface. My carefully cultivated persona. My default act. Within one minute of meeting Ainsley Carrington, I'd reverted back into the loser geek from my past, second-guessing every move that I made. When I wasn't acting like a fawning idiot, I was playing robot, and I couldn't even decide which was worse.

Enough was enough. It was time to get serious. It was time to play the game.

It was time to break out... Bruce.

Now. Before you can laugh at me, I'll explain that I'm fully aware that Bruce is a stupid name for an alter ego. But in my defense, I came up with it when I was fourteen. Bruce Wayne was the Jekyll to Batman's Hyde, and we all know how much I liked to think of myself as Batman.

As a superhero, he was a total badass, but Bruce Wayne was the ladykiller behind the mask. Dude was smooth when it came to the chicks, and I needed all the inspiration I could get if I was going to make Ainsley mine.

She liked it when I flirted? Fine. She was going to get the full force of Lucas Taggart in all his swaggering glory. I knew how to turn wallflowers into confident women, but I could also reduce them to puddles of mush, too. Bruce had the power to make that happen. By the time we were through, she wouldn't even remember who the hell Blake Clownstick Atwood was.

"Great job, Ains," I said as she released the lat bar.

She slumped forward on the workout bench and took a few deep breaths. I tried to play it cool as I straddled the bench behind her and gave a friendly massage to her shoulders. "You worked hard today. You're going to be feeling this one tomorrow."

She sat up a bit straighter and turned her head to look at me over her shoulder. "Mmm. I'm already feeling it now."

Thankfully, there were a few inches between us on that bench. My voice dropped to ask, "You ready to hear about this week's homework?"

Ainsley nodded as she swallowed hard, clearly affected by my smooth delivery. *Way to go, Bruce.*

I stopped rubbing her shoulders and gave her ponytail a playful tug. "Eye contact. You need to practice. At any time you need to speak to someone over the next forty-eight hours—I'm talking waiters, front desk managers, any person you pass in this very lobby—you will do so while making eye contact."

She turned sideways on the bench to look at me. "Okay. I think I can do that."

"I know you can." I lowered my voice, somewhere between an authoritative tenor and a hoarse whisper as I met her gaze. "Start making it a habit. Look at people when you're speaking to them. Recognize that you're worthy of their full attention."

"I don't like full attention. Full attention allows someone to see every flaw."

"Your *second* assignment," I amended immediately, "will be to make eye contact with *yourself.*"

"Pardon?"

"You will spend a full five minutes in front of the mirror every day looking yourself in the eyes."

"Like, just staring at myself?"

"No, not just staring. You will find at least one good thing to say about the person looking back at you. And you'll write that thing down in your journal." I slid closer as Bruce swiped a strand of hair behind her ear. "There's plenty of good to see. You just need to open your eyes."

Ainsley tried not to fidget as she stammered, "Okay. I can do that."

I chucked her under her chin. "Atta girl."

She broke our gaze to grab for her towel. "Can I ask you something?"

"Anything," I answered, shooting her a wink.

"Are you sure you're over your cold? Your voice is really scratchy today."

Shit. I cleared my throat and answered, "Uh yeah. Just some residual aftermath, I guess."

"At least you sound better today than you did yesterday." Her focus dropped to my lips as she added, "You'll get over it soon enough."

Doubt it. Just the sight of her half-lidded eyes staring at my mouth was enough to shred me. What the hell was going on here? I was supposed to be taking the upper hand today. With one sultry look, Ainsley had completely turned the tables on me.

Screw the smooth talking. I could barely find *any* voice as I said, "Okay. I think that's enough for one day."

Thanks for nothing, Bruce.

CHAPTER TWENTY-ONE

I'd been doing my relaxation exercises pretty regularly. Thus far, they hadn't been doing much good. I wasn't able to bring back any profound memories, but it kept the nightmares at bay and helped me to fall asleep a little easier every night, so I kept up with them.

But this morning, I had another vivid dream. One I'd never had before. I thought that maybe there was a chance that it was a memory.

I got myself ready and headed down the hall to the kitchen. My father was in his usual spot at the table, reading *The Wall Street Journal*, his dark hair the only part of him not hidden behind the newspaper.

"Hey Pop?"

"Yeah?"

"I uh... I had another one of my dreams this morning."

My father put down his paper and finally met my eyes. "You okay?" He knew that my dreams were normally kinda fucking traumatizing whenever I had them.

"No, not that one," I said, putting his mind at ease. "This was a new one. It felt the same, though. Like it was a memory, you know?"

He did know. I'd explained the phenomenon to him years ago. Sometimes, my dreams were just dreams. Other times, they offered glimpses into my real life. It didn't happen often, but when it did, I could always tell the difference.

"Oh?" he asked, eyeing me curiously.

I leaned back against the counter and tapped my fingertips on the granite. "Did we have a dog when I was little?"

"A dog?"

"Yeah. A German Shepherd."

He gave a snap to his newspaper and redirected his attention toward it. "No. I haven't had a dog since I was five. Why do you ask?"

"Well, I saw one in my sleep. I was rolling around on a red rug with a German Shepherd. I just didn't know if it was a dream or a memory."

He snickered as he said, "You must have fallen asleep watching *Lassie*."

"That's a collie."

"Rin-Tin-Tin, then."

I tried to contain my smirk as I shot back, "You know, Pop, it's two-thousand-sixteen. They actually make some shows in full color these days."

He didn't even look up as he hurled a croissant at me.

I caught it, laughing as I took a bite. "I gotta run. Thanks for breakfast."

* * *

"I cant kalk ih ih hing in."

Mia's mumbling pulled my attention from the gum-disease poster I'd been inspecting. Gross.

I turned toward her prone form, lounged out in the dentist's chair, her mouth in a plastic brace. "What?"

Her eyes rolled as she yelled, "I CANT KALK IH IH HING IN!"

I finally comprehended what Mia was trying to tell me. "You're not *supposed* to be able to talk with that thing in, dopey."

Mia let out with a frustrated huff as I settled back into my chair in the corner of the office. I pulled out my phone to play some Virus Buster, trying to kill some time.

Mia, however, didn't have much patience for silence. "I'n ored out a ny nind."

"*You're* bored?" I shot back. "I'm the one who has to sit here and watch your teeth get whiter."

"Are ay?"

I craned my neck in an attempt to take a look at her mouth. It was hard to gauge any changes while her teeth were glowing purple under the ultraviolet light. "I can't tell yet."

Ever since last weekend when Mia came over to take care of me on my deathbed, our dynamic had drastically changed. For the better. There was always an easy camaraderie between us, but now we shared a special friendship, too.

I didn't beat myself up too badly about it. Yeah, I may have crossed over some invisible, self-imposed line, but who cared? I liked having her around. I'd grown accustomed to her face, as it were. We were comfortable with each other. Maybe it was because I didn't automatically think about taking her to bed every minute. I don't know. I'd never really had a real friendship with any woman to compare, but if all those goopy romcoms on my television were to be believed, the sex thing usually got in the way.

That's not to say that I *never* thought about it. I'd taken her Zumba class for the first time last week. It was embarrassing; I was barely able to keep up. But watching Mia's hot dancing was worth the humiliation. She was right—we definitely had fun together.

Actually, we had fun no matter what we did. She even made hanging out in this stupid dentist's office entertaining. Yeah, I was still upset about Ainsley but I could compartmentalize like nobody's business. Plus Mia helped to keep me grounded about the whole thing. A godsend while I was already stressed out about keeping so many other plates spinning in the air. I had Jared's final week to prep for, Mia's and Ainsley's fourth. I had follow-up appointments with Dr. Mandelbaum to schedule in between tasks and working out with all three of my clients, plus I had to meet with two new ones in the coming weeks.

If I ever switched jobs, I could easily add "juggler" to my resume.

But right now, I had to get Mia out of that chair so we could make it to our next appointment in time. Her office was closed for two days due to Rosh Hashanah, so it was nice being able to tackle some of our assignments during the daytime without her having to give up her entire weekend.

She never seemed to mind, though.

* * *

We pulled up in front of WPZU studios in Brooklyn. The place was nothing more than a boring, squat, concrete cube with a huge antenna tower surrounded by a dirt lot and a chainlink fence.

I cut the engine as Mia stared out the front windshield. "You keep bringing me to these decrepit shitholes, and I'm going to be asking for a refund."

I snickered as I exited the car, came around to her side, and held my hand out toward her. "Wouldst the lady be so amiable as to accompany me into said decrepit shithole?"

She laughed and shook her head as she slipped her hand in mine and exited the car. I walked her toward the entrance and buzzed to be let in.

"What is this place? What are we even doing here?" she asked.

"Patience, m'lady. You'll find out soon enough."

We were cleared for entry, so we pulled the heavy steel door open and stepped into the lobby, a bare-bones space with a few cheap chairs and bad lighting. A gum-snapping twenty-something occupied the front counter, her jean-clad legs crossed on top of the desk as she played on her phone. She blew a bubble in Mia's direction and asked, "You here for the interview?"

Mia had no idea how to respond, so I answered for her. "She sure is."

"Good. Harry was getting pretty bored back there. He's in the studio. Straight toward the back."

Mia waited until we were halfway through the building before asking, "Interview? I already have a job, remember?"

"Of course. Just not one that requires you to *smile the entire time*."

She looked about ready to pull the jugular out of my neck. "What the hell is this, Taggart?"

I didn't get a chance to answer, because Harry had come over to greet us. "Four o'clock! Right on time. You must be Mia Cruz." Harry shook Mia's hand enthusiastically as I tried not to bust out laughing. "And you must be Luke?"

"Sure am, Harry. Nice to meet you."

"Thank you both for coming in. So, Mia," he directed toward my unsuspecting client. "I'm hoping Luke has already filled you in about our hiring timeline. We're merely putting out some feelers right now. You're aware that the job won't be available for a few more months, yes?"

"Uh, yes. Of course," she answered convincingly.

"Sadly, our Marnie will be leaving us in the spring to have her baby."

"Oh, won't that be nice."

I had to stifle my laugh at Mia's professional tone. She had no idea what she was in for.

"Your agent here has already told me all about you, so why don't we just get down to it?" Harry led us toward the soundstage, a collection of lights and cameras angled toward a large, blank backdrop, asking, "How long have you wanted to be a weather girl?"

Mia caught a glimpse of the green screen on the camera's monitor, and finally put two and two together. And God bless her, instead of running screaming out of the building, she played along. "Oh, ever since I was a little girl. I've always been fascinated by... uh... *rain*."

"Well we certainly get enough of it here in New York, right?" Harry said, heading for one of the cameras.

It was about that time that Mia reached a stealthy hand over and pinched my arm, whispering, *"I'm going to kill you,"* through her teeth.

I gave her a friendly shove toward the set. "Maybe later. Right now, you've got some weather to report. Don't forget to smile!"

She shot a dirty look at me but took her place in front of the screen.

The next half-hour was the most entertaining thirty minutes of my life. Since Mia mentioned her love of *rain*, Harry had her dress in a yellow raincoat and matching hat, then handed her a red umbrella.

She endured Harry's lighting tests and blocking instructions with a friendly smile plastered to her face, but any time he looked the other way, she'd aim death glares at me. Once the cameras started rolling, however, she morphed into the epitome of professionalism. She hit her marks and read every word off the teleprompter like a champ. Fucking hysterical. Even better once she really got going.

Mia flashed her newly-whitened smile as she pointed to the screen behind her, "...and then on Sunday, prepare for the clouds to go away. The sun will be making a welcome appearance, so make sure you soak up the last of those summer rays!"

In an act of pure inspiration, she went off script to ditch the umbrella and toss her hat in the air à la Mary Tyler Moore before shooting a dazzling grin at the camera. "Time to lose the rubber boots and put on your fancy schmancy shoes! I'm Mia Cruz for WPZU. Have a great weekend, everyone!"

It was physically painful to hold in my laughter. Seriously. I thought I was doing some major internal damage.

It wasn't until we were back in the car, buckled up, and engine started that Mia spoke to me. Even then, it was only to offer a single word. "Don't," she warned, stuffing her purse at her feet.

My lips had been clamped together for a solid five minutes, so it was difficult to allow any words to escape without cackling, but... "Fancy. Schmancy. Shoes."

That was it. That was all it took. The dam broke.

We both exploded in a burst of hilarity, the two of us literally holding our sides as we cracked up.

"You jerk!" she admonished once she found her voice. "I can't believe you made me do that!"

"*I* can't believe you *did* it!"

She swiped a finger under her eyes and said, "Contract be damned. You owe me *huge* for this one! You'd better figure out a way to pay me back."

"Oh, I know it," I shot back, putting the car in gear. "I'm prepared for you to make my life a living hell until I do."

CHAPTER TWENTY-TWO

In order to take advantage of all that smiling practice, I arranged for Ainsley to take part in a custom photo shoot. It was another two-for-one day in Swan World, as Jared would be the acting photographer.

He'd shown me some shots he'd taken over the years just for fun. Photography had always been a passion of his, but only as something to do to pass the time. He'd never pursued it as a career. Until now. He'd spent the past twelve years fighting his way up the corporate ladder, making bank, and convincing himself he was content with his lot. Once he was fired, however, unemployment forced him to take stock of his life. He started thinking about a career change, and he'd come to me for the confidence makeover needed to strike out on his own.

I was more than happy to hire him for his first paid gig.

I rented out some equipment and arranged a studio space for Jared to do his thing. The place was owned by a past client of mine, so she had no problem with letting us take it over for the day. The "studio" was actually her apartment, a hip loft in SoHo—brick walls, exposed pipes, floor-to-ceiling windows— and I was grateful to Samantha for letting us use it.

Ainsley was posed on a wooden bench against a rented white backdrop. She was clearly nervous, so we figured we'd start with some simple head shots to get her into the right frame of mind. Jared did a great job of easing her into the shoot, cracking jokes and putting his subject at ease.

"You're getting off easy," he teased, moving the camera in closer. "For *my* smiling practice, he made me audition for a toothpaste commercial."

Ainsley and I both laughed as Jared snapped the shutter. Yeah, his audition was pretty funny, but I was only laughing because his comment reminded me about Mia playing weather girl the other day.

It was pretty cool watching Jared in his element. The guy really knew his stuff. I felt a bit of pride that my training had brought it about.

"How we doing, Ains?" I asked.

"Oh, just fabulous, thanks."

That made me chuckle. I knew it was tough for Ainsley to be the center of attention, but after only a few minutes, she was already starting to come out of her shell.

Jared lowered his camera and asked, "You think you're ready to do a few full-body shots yet?"

Ainsley stood up and held her hands out to her sides. "As I'll ever be."

Our original plan was to do a head-to-toe body mural, but I didn't think Ainsley's modesty would permit her to be photographed in nothing but a thong, no matter how much paint was used to cover her up. Instead, she wore a fitted bodysuit and jean shorts, and Samantha concentrated her artwork over top of her clothes. She did a cityscape across her midsection, then expanded onto her skin to add some famous New York landmarks in an interlocking collage across the rest of her body. It was colorful and original and really looked terrific.

I guess the camouflage allowed Ainsley to really get into the shoot, because she was able to concentrate on poses that best showed off the artwork instead of merely feeling like *she* were the focal point.

Jared took a dozen pictures before he lowered his camera and furrowed his brows. "Wait. I just had a brilliant thought."

As it turned out, his genius idea was to take the shoot outdoors. Perfect. It was a gorgeous day outside and the natural light could only be an advantage. The three of us climbed out the window and navigated up the fire escape to the roof, hauling just the barest essentials along with us—Jared's camera, the rented light umbrellas, and a folding chair.

Jared set up near the exposed pipes of a rusty heating unit, and the setting served as a perfect backdrop for the cityscape painted on Ainsley's skin. The fresh air really freed her up, too. She was able to relax and get into the spirit of the assignment, moving her body into elaborate poses as Jared snapped away.

"I think you missed your calling as a model," I joked as Ainsley giggled.

"Yeah, right."

"Don't pay any attention to him, Ainsley," Jared said. "You're doing great." He shot me a look over his shoulder, waggling his eyebrows, busting my balls. For the most part, he'd played it cool all day, and for that, I was grateful. I was worried about being exposed. But aside from a whispered, *Holy shit* when I first introduced them, he didn't say anything about it at all. In fact, neither he *nor* Samantha made mention of my blatant flirting. They knew damn well that the extra attention wasn't part of my job description, but thankfully, they didn't call me out for it.

After all, Bruce had a job to do, too.

"Hey," I said. "I'm just happy to see you've been doing your smiling homework."

Ainsley huffed. "Homework? I did *extra credit*. I've been doing so much full-time grinning, my cheeks are sore!"

She couldn't possibly have appreciated the double-entendre of her statement as she chose that moment to turn her back to us, showing off the reverse side of the mural. I, however, appreciated the view of her "cheeks" quite a bit.

She put her hands to her hips and looked over her shoulder, flashing a dazzling white grin that would rival any Miss America contestant.

"Beautiful!" Jared exclaimed. "Hold it. Right there. Perfect."

He moved in close and snapped a few face shots before allowing her to break the pose.

She shook out her hands and slumped her shoulders with a, "Phew! Hey, Luke. Forget about modeling. It's a lot harder than it looks!"

I crossed my arms and perched a hip on the perimeter wall. "I said you *could* be a model. Not that you *should*."

She shot me a look out the corner of her eye as she leaned against the wall next to me. She'd not only gotten comfortable with all the flirting I'd been indulging in but was learning how to play along.

God help me.

"Yeah, well, maybe we both have hearing problems. I said I *liked* art, not that I wanted to *be* art!"

"A more beautiful masterpiece there never was," I teased, trying not to smirk. My lips twitched anyway, causing her eyes to roll at my cheesy line.

"It's going to take three showers to wash all this paint off my body," she said, holding her arm out for my inspection.

I arched an eyebrow at her. "I'll be happy to offer my services in that department."

"Luke, you're so bad," she said, slapping my chest playfully.

Just as things started to get interesting, Samantha joined us on the roof, carting a basket filled with water bottles. "How's it going up here?"

When Sam first came to me, she was a skinny little pixie of a thing. Funny as all hell and totally adorable. She had just moved here from New Jersey and was having some trouble acclimating to the city. Plus, after years of living as an artist and spending her life in overalls, she didn't really have much fashion sense. She took my course not only to learn how to dress, but to gain some New York City know-how.

"Pretty damn good, Sammy," I answered. "Thanks again for letting us use your place."

"Yeah, it's perfect," Jared piped in. "Check it out." He held his digital camera out for her inspection, and Sam didn't waste any time looking through the fruits of today's labor.

Ainsley took advantage of the break, grabbing two of the bottles from the basket and handing one to me. "Today was fun!"

"I'm glad you think so."

"I didn't think I had it in me."

Had it in her. Heh heh.

"I did. And what happened to all that positive thinking you were supposed to be doing this week?"

Her eyelids lowered expertly as she took a sip from her water bottle, teasing me. "Don't worry, Luke. I've been doing *all* my homework." Just when I thought I couldn't get worked up any more than I already was, she flicked a few droplets of water in my direction wearing the flirtiest grin I'd ever seen.

Holy shit. I've created a monster.

WEEK FIVE: AFFIRMATION

Say yes
Let go of inhibitions

CHAPTER TWENTY-THREE

"It's Bikini Day."

Mia and I had been walking through midtown, but she stopped dead at my pronouncement. "Bikini Day?"

It took all my effort to keep from grinning. "Yes, ma'am."

We resumed walking again, Mia letting out with, "Do you mean 'bikini' literally? Like, that's why you sent me to your little friend to 'take care of any unwanted body hair' yesterday?"

"I'm invoking our 'trust rule,' here, Cruz."

"Fine. You're the boss." She rolled her eyes before adding, "But I'll have you know that your wax girl is a sadist."

I was laughing as I stepped off the curb, and that's when Mia grabbed my hand. Before I had a chance to wonder what was happening, she pulled me backwards just as a flash of yellow zoomed past. *Holy shit. I almost got hit by a cab.*

"Holy shit! You almost got hit by a cab!" she shrieked, holding a palm across her heart.

Whether she was too freaked out to realize or she was simply being over-cautious, she didn't let go of my hand. I didn't mind. It was nice.

I led her into *Barney's,* and sure enough, my personal shopper was already standing sentinel at the top of the stairs waiting to greet us. Corinne was middle-aged, thin as a rail, and a total class act. She and I had been working together for years.

"Good morning, beautiful!" I greeted as we jaunted up the wide staircase. Corinne's blush turned as burgundy as the dyed bun on top of her head at my compliment. "Corinne Cavanaugh, please meet your next victim, Mia Cruz. Mia, Corinne."

"Good morning to you both. Are we ready for Bikini Day?"

Mia sighed and answered, "No. I'm still in denial that this is even happening."

Corinne smiled graciously before liberating Mia's hand from my own. "Luke, go help yourself to some coffee, then meet us at the dressing room in about an hour."

Barney's had an entire alcove set up for any beleaguered husbands to cool their jets while their wives racked up the credit cards. There were worse places to kill time. The room had brown leather couches, a TV, and a coffee bar, plus a wall of sporting magazines and newspapers. You know, men stuff.

The two girls disappeared into a sea of designer racks as I made myself comfortable in the Men's Lounge. I considered doing some shopping of my own, but I had a feeling I'd best stick around.

That notion was confirmed about twenty minutes later as I heard a kerfuffle coming from the dressing room. As I made my way toward that section of the store, the voices became clearer.

I stopped outside of the door just as Mia huffed, *"But I LIKE the black one!"*

With the patience of a saint, Corinne explained, *"I'm sorry, Ms. Cruz. I'm under strict orders. No beige. No gray. No black."*

"But black is more... conservative."

"Sweetheart, it's a bikini. There's nothing conservative about it, regardless of its color."

"Yeah, no kidding. Look! The girls are barely contained in this thing."

I heard the exasperated sigh coming from my client, and assumed those beautiful brown eyes were only seconds away from shooting flames. I figured I'd better step in to get Corinne out of the line of fire. "Mia? How's it going in there?"

She grumbled as Corinne cracked the dressing room door and slipped out. "Well, we zeroed in on the perfect suit, but Miss Cruz isn't quite feeling it."

"I wanted black!"

"No black, Cruz."

Corinne and I shared an eyeroll before she encouraged, "It really is a fantastic suit. Luke will agree with me. Come out and see for yourself."

"No."

"C'mon, Mia," I said. "There's no one else out here."

"There are floor to ceiling, three-hundred-and sixty-degree mirrors out there!"

"That's kinda the point."

She grumbled something unintelligible but finally stepped out of the dressing room. And when she did... My. Heart. Stopped.

The bikini was an iridescent aqua, shimmery and alluring, attractive as all hell. The shiny fabric hugged her full hips and accentuated her curvy chest, visible even though she had her arms crossed over herself, concealing most of the view.

I finally found my voice enough to comment, "My God, Mia. You look…"

"Like a deranged mermaid?" she finished for me, throwing her hands out to her sides and allowing me a better view.

"No," I laughed, trying to maintain my cool. "Like a beautiful one."

I pointed to the mirrors on the wall, and Mia turned to look for herself.

She rubbed a palm across her stomach, pushing at the rounded skin, sucking some air into her lungs to flatten her abdomen. She rolled her eyes and exhaled before attempting a different tact. She assumed a straighter posture, pulling her shoulders back and forcing "the girls" up and out.

Mia's head cocked to the side as she put her hands to her hips, her ponytail bobbing across her shoulder. "Huh. I guess this isn't *that* bad." She gave a half spin and peeked over her back. "And it kinda makes my butt look okay."

I'd been trying to keep my eyes off her luscious ass, but it was nearly impossible. *Okay* was an understatement. "Fuckin' yeah it does."

Both women turned to gape at me in unrestrained shock.

Shit.

"I meant... That's what I was trying to tell you before. You look great."

Corinne shooed Mia back into the changing room to get dressed, and then we did a little extra shopping. I settled up the tab for the suit—plus a matching coverup, beach bag, and a pair of "you-owe-me-bigtime-for-this-so-I'm-buying-these" shoes— and then we headed out for the rooftop pool at the Marriott Marquis.

The Marriott's roof deck was one of many hot spots in the city. Famous faces mingled with not-so-famous ones, and there were always plenty of each to be found. I'd reserved a private cabana for the day, but we wouldn't be spending much time in it. Today was all about being seen.

Mia is going to hate it, I thought, smiling to myself.

Taking over half of an entire city block, the deck was humongous. Four separate bars were stationed at each corner of the expansive pool; hundreds of lounge chairs and couches and tables filled the spaces in between. There was a retractable roof to turn the space into an indoor venue during the winter, but in

September, it was still warm enough for open-air sunbathing, which was our order for the day.

As Mia took in the view, I directed her toward our cabana and told her to get into her new suit.

She was decidedly not happy about it. "Wait. I thought the exercise was to put on a two-piece. You didn't say anything about me having to wear the thing in public!"

"Just exactly what was the point in buying a new suit if you're never going to put it on, Mia? It's Affirmation Week. Saying yes to things. Being open to adventure, remember?"

"Sure, if by 'adventure,' you mean 'suicide mission!'"

"What happened to the body-confident woman who reamed me out three weeks ago?"

"She'd be a lot more body-confident in a black one-piece."

I laughed. "Trust rule, Cruz. You look fantastic in that thing. I promise you'll be fine. Just think Caddyshack."

"What the hell?"

"I thought you were the eighties movie expert. Please tell me you've seen that one."

"Yeah, of course I have. But what does it—"

"The pool scene with the hot blonde everyone was into. Think you can do that?"

Her eyebrows rose as her face melted into a sly smile. "I can try."

"That's the spirit."

I set up shop next to the pool, laying out our towels on a couple of unoccupied lounge chairs before taking a seat in one of them, waiting for my turn to get dressed. When I heard the exaggerated smack of canvas hitting canvas, I turned my head to see Mia standing in the open flap of the cabana door in a model pose—hand on hip, fingers under her chin, eyes pointed skyward.

She was only joking around, but I was too impressed to laugh. The girl knew how to make an entrance.

She must have tapped into her inner Lacey Underall, because she came strutting out of the cabana looking like an absolute maneater. Head held high, straight posture, an alluring sway to her hips as she sauntered toward me. She stood at the foot of my chaise and untied the sheer sarong around her waist, dropping it onto my feet with a smirk before dipping a toe into the water.

Damn. She said she was going to try, but she did a whole helluva lot more than that. She was positively killing it.

I could barely take my eyes off her, and I noticed I wasn't the only man on that rooftop who wasn't able to look away. She took the long way around the pool, and then climbed up the ladder to the diving board. Mia looked like a goddess up there. Untouchable. Alluring. Sexy as all hell. She pulled the tie from her hair allowing that thick, black mane to tumble over her shoulders, raised her hands over her head... and dove in.

Holy shit.

She emerged near my feet and threw her arms over the edge of the pool. "So," she said, trying to keep her smile at bay. "Did I do okay up there?"

I planted my feet on the ground on either side of the chaise and leaned forward with my elbows on my knees. "No," I answered. "You fucking *destroyed* it up there."

Next thing I knew, my pants were soaked as Mia splashed me, laughing proudly.

CHAPTER TWENTY-FOUR

For our next task, Ainsley and I headed to the sports complex out in Jersey. She was nervous on the ride over, and I had to remind her to stop fidgeting.

"I just don't understand why you won't tell me where we're going."

"Because it's a surprise. Don't worry, you're gonna love it."

When we pulled up in front of the Shermer Heights Training Facility, Ainsley was skeptical.

When I announced that we'd be figure skating, she was aghast.

"Figure skating?"

"Yes ma'am."

Ainsley aimed an incredulous look at me.

Guess she didn't love it.

"C'mon. It'll be fun," I said, hopping out and coming around to the passenger side. Her face still looked unconvinced, but she took my hand and let me escort her out of the car.

The Shermer Heights Training Facility was a humongous sports complex. There was a full-size ice rink, turf football field, and batting cages inside, plus three baseball diamonds, a soccer field, and a driving range outside. The driving range shared a border with the country club's 18-hole golf course. It's where I'd taken Jared to hit some balls the day I confessed that I was in love with Ainsley.

And now, here she was, right here with me.

I'd brought a bunch of clients here over the years for indoor rock climbing, sky diving, you name it, and after all those visits, I'd reached a point where I was dealing directly with the manager. I knew him pretty well.

He knew we were coming today, so he was right there at the front desk to meet us as we entered the lobby. "What's up, Luke?"

Wyatt McAllister was in his late thirties, but he didn't look it. I guessed the active lifestyle allowed him to retain his youthful appearance. He had overgrown sandy-brown hair, a scruffy jaw that just screamed *extreme sports*, and a tanned, weathered face that he wore as tribute to his outdoorsy existence. Plus, the bastard had a charming-as-fuck grin that belonged in a Clif Bar commercial. He was a solid dude.

"Hey Wyatt. This is Ainsley."

"Nice to meet you Ainsley," he said on a toothy grin. "Ready to channel your inner Michelle Kwan?"

Ainsley smiled politely but answered, "Not really!"

Wyatt chuckled as he walked us through the cavernous, active facility toward the rink. Past the basketball courts, past the indoor bike-and-board park. "Don't worry. Robin will take good care of you. You're gonna have a blast."

He opened the heavy glass doors to the rink, and we were greeted with a burst of cold air. And right there was Robin, out on the ice, twirling up a storm. He waved when he saw us, and executed a tight, three-sixty spin in midair before nailing a perfect landing.

Ainsley took one look at the guy and asked, "I'm not going to be doing *that*, am I?"

Wyatt and I laughed as Robin skated over to the edge of the rink. "Hello, Ainsley." He took her hand and kissed it, saying, "I'm Robin. I always like to personally introduce myself to my victims."

Ainsley sighed. "*Victims.* Well, that certainly makes me feel better."

Wyatt teased, "Don't sweat it, Ainsley. This will only hurt a little."

"Besides, Wyatt's trained in first aid," Robin said.

I piped in to add, "And CPR if I'm not mistaken, yeah?"

Ainsley looked from me to Robin to Wyatt then back again. "Oh, you boys are just hysterical. You should take this show on the road. You could probably make millions."

The three of us cracked up as I threw a consoling arm around Ainsley.

"Speaking of the road," Wyatt said. "I've got to hit it. You guys good?"

I gave him a high-five and said, "Yeah, I think we're all set. Thanks, Wyatt."

"No problem. Hey, say hello to Jane for me, will ya?" He waggled his eyebrows as he backed toward the door, finally giving us a wave as he made his exit.

I just dropped my head and snickered as Ainsley asked, "Who's Jane?"

Robin and I shared a knowing look as I explained, "She was a client of mine a few months ago. Wyatt and she... uh..."

"Okay. Got it," Ainsley interrupted, saving me from having to spill all the details. And thank God, because she'd probably pass out if I told her some of them, including the fact that they had sex right here on the very ice we'd be occupying in a few minutes.

After Ainsley and I changed into some skates and an extra layer of winter clothing, we headed out onto the ice. I wasn't the strongest skater, but at least I had the advantage of having done it a few times before. This was a first for Ainsley.

She held onto the wall in a white-knuckled death grip, trying to find her footing.

"Don't fight the ice," Robin advised. "Trust your feet."

Ainsley rolled her eyes as she snipped, "The *ice* is slippery and my *feet* are strapped to two razor blades!"

I laughed. I couldn't help it.

"It's not funny, Luke! I've never done this before!"

"I'm aware of that," I said on a raised brow. "It's why we're here. Affirmation week, remember? You need to say yes to things, do something you've never done before."

"Yeah, well, I've never punched anyone in the teeth, either, so maybe I could just do that and call it a day."

"No violence on my ice," Robin admonished. "The only contact I want to see is while you're dancing."

Ainsley's mouth gaped. "I can't even stand on these things and you expect me to dance?" she asked incredulously.

"I know it seems impossible, but I promise, I'll have you looking like an old pro before this day is through."

Robin wasn't lying. Even though it took a few hours, Ainsley had not only learned to skate well enough to stay on her feet, but we were presently in the center of the ice, working on an actual routine.

Robin had partnered with her to go over the move a dozen times. Now he wanted to see what it looked like as an observer. "Luke? Step in here and be me for a minute. Take her out for a spin and I'll watch, yes?"

Ainsley put her hands to her hips to ask, "What am I, a used car?"

When Ainsley was distracted by fear, her unfiltered personality slipped through. Kind of like how Mia only swore in Spanish. Both were hilarious to see.

I positioned myself behind and slightly to the side of Ainsley, then took her gloved hands in my own. I placed one on her waist and held the other out to her side. The nearness made me dizzy and caused an electric current to race along my entire spine.

Bruce placed his lips closer than they needed to be to ask against her ear, "You ready?"

"No."

I chuckled against her back. "You've done this a million times with Robin. You're going to need to trust yourself."

"Kind of hard to do."

"Trust *me*, then."

The tension left her body at my words as she let out a foggy breath and leaned into me. Her scrunched brows softened as she focused on my lips before allowing those mystifying blue eyes to meet mine. "Okay."

From the feel of her body melting into mine to the guileless look in those gorgeous blue eyes, I almost couldn't take my next breath. I was pretty sure my heart stopped beating, but I was able to shoot her a smirk and respond, "Good."

Our locked eyes were interrupted by Robin's voice. "Okay! Once around. Just like I showed you, Ainsley."

I gave her hands a reassuring squeeze and then we were off. Ainsley made sure to forge ahead with a steady pace just like Robin had shown her. Which was a good thing, because I didn't have to spend the entire time trying to coordinate our strides. We didn't necessarily make a graceful pair, but we weren't so bad that we'd be laughed off the ice, either.

"Wonderful!" Robin gushed. "You think you're ready to expand the frame?"

I gave Ainsley a quick, reassuring hug before extending my arms, allowing some space between us. I was worried that she'd waver without the support of my body behind her, but she did great.

I kept my voice low and purposely calm. "That's it. Slow it down. Nice and easy."

Robin was a bit louder with his commentary. "Way to go, Ainsley! Okay. Let me see the turn!"

She flicked a brief look of panic at me, causing me to reassure her. "C'mon, Ains. We got this."

"Oh God. Okay."

I raised our hands above Ainsley's head and crossed them as she turned toward me. It wasn't pretty, but she'd done it. "Yeah, Ains! Check it out!"

She was biting her lip in concentration, trying to stay on her feet as she skated backwards, but she was able to meet my eyes with an enthusiastic smile. Her ponytail was bobbing around at the top of her head, her cheeks were flushed, her eyes were sparkling. She looked vibrant. Exuberant. Euphoric.

Beautiful.

* * *

After we'd ditched the skates and changed back into our regular clothes, we thanked both Robin and Wyatt for the lesson before heading out to the parking lot. I opened Ainsley's door to usher her into the car, but before she took her seat, she put a hand on my forearm.

"Luke, wait."

After all those hours of extra clothing between us, I was stunned by the skin-on-skin contact. I swallowed hard before asking, "Everything okay?"

"Better than okay." Her face split on an elated grin as she added, "I haven't thanked you yet for everything you're doing for me. I already feel like a different person."

"Don't change too much," I teased. "I kinda liked the original one."

She snickered demurely before shaking her head at me. "I know you did. And it means the world to me." Her hand slid slowly up the length of my arm until her fingertips played at the edge of my golf shirt. "Thank you."

Her eyes met mine in that half-lidded stare she'd recently learned to project, and it took all my strength not to back her against my car and plant my lips on her.

Fuck. I trained her too well. The beautiful version of Ainsley was heart-stopping. The shyness was intriguing. The sweetness was endearing. But Ainsley *flirting* was the deadliest incarnation of all. With her grateful eyes staring up at me, our hands on each other's skin, it would be so easy to just lower my head and kiss her.

I was mentally warring with myself about it, so much so that I hadn't realized I'd stepped closer toward her obliging form. My hands automatically wrapped around her waist as hers slipped around my neck; my head lowered on its own. Before I could bring my lips in for a landing, however, she buried her face against my chest and gave me a good squeeze.

A hug.

Jesus Christ, a fucking hug.

Terrific.

I squeezed her back, finally finding my voice. "You're welcome, Ains."

"I just can't thank you enough."

Sure you can. Nakedly.

We pulled away from each other as I said, "Hey, don't go giving me all the credit, here. *You* did this too, you know."

Who the fuck am I fooling? I did this to myself.

CHAPTER TWENTY-FIVE

"I really don't like this."

It was now the second time Mia had expressed her reluctance to carry out tonight's assignment. She was supposed to be reciting a report on any subject of her choosing, but she'd been stalling for time since we got here.

We were in a private back room at *Roebling*, a bar-slash-restaurant in the heart of midtown. It was only us back there, but the space opened up to the main bar area where there was a crowd of about fifty or so enjoying their Friday Happy Hour. Mia wasn't digging the extra bodies within earshot.

"That's kind of the idea, Cruz. You're not *supposed* to like it." When she did nothing more than shoot a dirty look my way, I said, "You're supposed to be letting go of your inhibitions this week. Learning how to not give a shit."

She grumbled but didn't argue my point, which I interpreted as capitulation, unwilling as it may have been. "But why is *he* here?"

Jared perked up at Mia's acknowledgement. He was clearly happy that she was aware that he existed, and didn't seem to care that she was annoyed by it. "Extra body," I said. "I'm easing you into your fear of crowds with a small, safe audience."

"Safe," she huffed. "I'm still nursing the bruises he gave me on that basketball court."

"*You* crashed into *me*," he defended.

"You both crashed into *each other*," I clarified. "Besides, Jared's on Week Seven. He just had his makeover and we needed a place for him to show off his new look."

"Yeah, so hurry up with this thing. I've got some ladies to hit on."

Mia rolled her eyes. "Great. So you get to kill two birds with one stone, he gets to annoy some unsuspecting women, and I get to be humiliated in front of the entire world!"

I raised an eyebrow at her. "A bar full of people is hardly the entire world. Besides, they're in a completely separate room from us and they're not even paying attention. They wouldn't give a crap even if they were. C'mon. You got this."

Mia gave a huff in her seat, but her scowl had disappeared as she grumbled, "Fine." After an extra pause, she stood at the head of the table and cleared her throat. "Welcome, everyone. My chosen topic for our discussion this evening will be *Misogynist Themes in the Movie 'The Princess Bride.'*"

Jared and I couldn't contain our laughter. When she shot us both dirty looks, I explained, "We're not laughing *at* you. Promise!"

She stood a bit straighter and launched into her report, a scathing tirade against the patriarchy while still justifying the awesomeness of the story.

The cautious looks she kept shooting toward the oblivious bar crowd became less and less frequent as she spoke, ultimately allowing herself to throw her all behind this task. She talked about "arranged marriages" and "warmongering males in power" before softening her argument to commend the "*real* men" of the story—even managing a bonus Fezzik impersonation—and when she was through, Jared and I broke into applause. I was glad that I'd taken the time to watch the DVDs she'd left for me last week—and crap, I had to admit, *The Princess Bride* was a really great movie—because it helped me appreciate her report even more.

Mia wrapped up her presentation with a silly curtsey as Jared immediately took the opportunity to split for the bar.

I clapped a congratulatory hand on her shoulder as she plopped down on the chair next to mine. "Great job, Cruz."

"Thank you."

"See? Confidence while public speaking is all about preparation. You knew your subject matter well, so I have to imagine it was easy enough to report about it, right?"

Mia ignored my assessment and instead commented, "*Dios mío*, you smell good."

The change of topic caught me off guard. "Yeah? Thanks."

She moved her face closer to my neck and took a big whiff, exaggerating a euphoric roll of her eyes. "Lemme guess. Clinique Chemistry."

"Yeah. How'd you know?"

She sank back into her chair and crossed her legs, waving me off with a flip of her wrist. "They were my account last year. God, I love that stuff. Gets me all worked up and sweaty."

"I've seen you sweat. Right now, you're merely glistening."

"It's the panic."

I was starting to think it was her. Mia had such an inner awesomeness about her, it made her *glow*. "No. I think it's just *you*." That made her smile as I added, "You are going to make some poor bastard insane one of these days."

"I'm sure you mean that in the most complimentary way possible."

"Of course. I mean, you'll drive him crazy, too, but..."

"Gee, thanks."

She knew I was only busting her chops. "Besides, once I'm through molding you into the perfect woman, you'll have your pick of 'em. There won't be a guy alive who'll be able to resist you." I nudged into her but she didn't nudge back.

Instead, her eyes tightened as she scrutinized me. "I don't need to be perfect. And I think you're selling the entirety of the male population short."

The abrupt change in our conversation's tone threw me. I sat back in my chair and furrowed my brows. "What do you mean?"

"Well, you said yourself that you need more than a pretty face. Yet you assume every other man on the planet only cares about looks."

"No, I don't." Not *really*.

"Yes, you do!" she said, flicking a hand in my direction. "Why else did you start this whole image consulting thing? You're playing Frankenstein with these girls in the hopes that they can land some guy and validate your abilities."

"Whoa. Hold on. That's not what I'm doing."

"Isn't it?"

"Well, it's not *all* I'm doing." I didn't know where any of this was coming from. I had a proven track record. My methods worked. "Yeah, okay, so maybe I make girls pretty. But I'm doing it purely for the confidence boost. Are you going to try and tell me you don't *feel* better when you *look* better?"

"Of course I do, but—"

"And does looking pretty take anything away from the person you are inside?"

"Well, no…"

"*Which*," I went on before she could get in another word, "I'll remind you is only half of what I do, here. The whole point is to teach these women confidence."

"It doesn't change the fact that you think they'll catch a man with their newfound attributes. One, who the hell says that the end-all be-all of a woman's happiness lies in the acquisition of a man?"

"*They* do," I smirked. She knew it was the truth. The majority of my clients came to me because they wanted to snag themselves a *Mrs.* title.

"And *two*," she continued, ignoring the undeniable fact I'd just presented, "you seem pretty damn sure of yourself that you and you alone are the best judge of what does and does not constitute attractiveness."

"Hey. You should see some of my past clients. When I get through with them, they're *universally* hot. Not just to me."

"What the fuck does universally hot mean?"

I could tell Mia was getting pissy with me. I shrugged off her attitude and answered her question. "You know damn well what it means. The kind of girl that's so hot that *everyone* thinks she's hot. The kind of girl that breaks through a guy's 'type' because of it."

"Like who? Give me an example."

"Marilyn Monroe," I shot back without hesitation.

"She's dead. Gimme another one."

"Ann Margret."

"Then or now?"

"What do you think?"

"Mm hmm. Anyone from this century?"

"Jennifer Lawrence."

She weighed my response as she regarded me with skeptical eyes. "Oh, I see. I'm sensing the pattern here. Caucasian girls with blonde hair are universally hot."

"Ann Margret's a redhead."

"You know what I mean. Someone like your little crush Paisley—"

"Ainsley."

"Whatever. Someone like Little Miss Whitebread-Blonde-All-American is considered the ideal. But someone like say, Sofia Vergara isn't?"

"No, she is."

"Salma Hayek?"

"Her, too."

She smirked in spite of herself. "Yet you didn't even mention either of them. Are you trying to backpedal with your racial preferences or are you simply trying to humor me?"

"Neither. I know what you're trying to do, here, and it's not going to work on me. I can find a universally hot chick in every color of the rainbow. *Race*," I scathed, "has nothing to do with it."

"Oh, so, you're just *personally* attracted to white girls with light hair."

I hadn't really ever thought about myself as having a "type," but Mia was right. I did tend to favor blondes. "I guess," I admitted. "But that's not to say they're the only ones I'm attracted to."

"Have you ever slept with a *trigueñita*?"

"I don't know what that is."

Mia's wide, impatient eyes glared at me as she waved her hands down her sides, silently indicating *a girl that has brown skin like me.*

"No," I answered automatically. "I guess I haven't."

Instead of chastising me like I expected, her eyes met mine in a half-lidded, seductive stare. She leaned in a little closer and ran a hand along my thigh, and I almost leapt out of my skin as the unexpected contact made my throat go dry. I was too stunned by her hand on my leg and the look on her face to speak, but thankfully, Mia's voice cut through the silence. "Then you have no idea what you're missing out on."

Holy shit.

My cock actually twitched in my jeans at the sound of her sultry voice, but before I could even register what the hell was going on, she sat back in her chair and started laughing her head off.

WEEK SIX: IMPLEMENTATION

Utilize training in real world
Start conversations in social settings

CHAPTER TWENTY-SIX

I personally chauffeured Jared to and from his third and final session with the therapist. Today was the first time I'd seen him in four days.

The thing is, I normally remained hands off during the final week of my program. My clients needed to practice their new persona on their own, without me standing over their shoulder. Plus, the therapy sessions were merely a very condensed version of a full psychoanalysis. They needed to fully commit in order to get the most out of the few sessions offered. My hope was always that they'd continue with their therapy on their own. But even after only a few sessions, they're feeling ready and able to take on the world. That's when I showed back up to help celebrate how far they've come in only two short months.

Jared and I headed to his new favorite restaurant in the city. We had an appointment at the sports facility to go bungee jumping tomorrow for his Final Task, but tonight, we just wanted to celebrate over a couple of burgers.

He was happy that our training was through, but not so thrilled about having to leave the city. "New York is amazing," he said over his beer. "I'm thinking of moving here permanently."

"Wow. Really?"

"Yeah. I've been talking to Samantha ever since that photo shoot at her apartment. She's got some friend named Livia that runs a pretty big deal photography studio out in Jersey, but she's looking to expand her reach in the city. I don't know. I guess I'm feeling optimistic that it could turn into something. I checked out a couple apartments this week."

"That would be awesome. It would be great to have you around."

"I bet you say that to all your clients."

"No, actually," I said meaningfully. "I really don't."

Jared understood where I was going with my statement, but in true guy form, neither one of us dwelled on it.

"So, hey. How's it going with the blonde?" he asked, changing the subject.

I shrugged. "It's not, yet. I can't do anything about it for a few more weeks, so I'm trying not to think about it." *Yeah, right.* As if I've thought about anything but her for the past month.

"Well, I'll tell you who I wouldn't mind waiting for, and it's that Mia. Holy shit that chick is smokin'."

"We're just friends."

"I know," he said on a sly grin. "Which is why I'm guessing you won't mind if I take a crack at her?"

I almost took a crack at his *head* for suggesting it. But instead, I pulled out my phone to text him her number, saying, "Sure. Go for it. It'll be entertaining as all hell to watch her eat you alive."

Jared waggled his eyebrows as he popped a fry into his mouth. "One can only hope.

CHAPTER TWENTY-SEVEN

Mia's "breaking the ice" task was set to take place at my favorite sports bar. I drove to her apartment to pick her up before hauling the both of us down to the village.

We chatted about her work for a few minutes, but Mia was obviously intent on continuing our conversation from the other night. It was like she'd been busting at the seams to get back on the subject as she asked, "So. Did you nail Paisley yet?"

"Ainsley," I snickered. "And no. I already told you, I won't until we're done working together."

"Yeah, but you also told me that you've stepped up your game recently. What happens if she bites and your eight weeks aren't up yet?"

I flashed back to the other day at my car after our ice skating lesson. I never even thought about it. I was going to do it. Afterward, I'd been able to appreciate that nothing had happened between us. There's no telling where things would've led just from a simple kiss.

My resolve had been strengthened since then.

"Well, she'll still be my client until the end of October. I guess I'll have to wait."

"Are you really going to have the strength to turn her down?"

I pulled up to the curb about a half block from our destination. "Trust me, I'll be able to hold out."

I got out and came around to Mia's side, but she didn't wait for me to escort her out of the car. "Oh sure," she said, slamming the door shut. "The girl you're crazy about finally falls for your bullshit, and you're going to tell her to wait twelve more days, or six, or three until it's official before banging her."

Mia seemed unusually pissy about the situation. I didn't know why she suddenly had a problem about it. "Why do you care so much?"

"I don't," she stammered. "I just find it fascinating."

I put a tentative hand at the small of her back to lead her down the sidewalk. "Well, maybe you'll find *this* fascinating, because to answer your question, yes. I'm telling you, it'll be a piece of cake. I can wait."

"What, are you getting so much great sex from every other woman in this city that you can hold out indefinitely?"

"Not indefinitely. A few more weeks."

"But *how?*"

"Because I've already held out for twenty-eight years, for godsa—"

Oh shit.

Shit.

Shit.

Shit.

How the fuck did I just say that out loud???

We both froze on the sidewalk as Mia aimed an incredulous stare at me, her eyebrows raised in accusation. "Is that part of the men's program?"

"What?" I asked in an attempt to buy time. *How the hell am I going to get out of this?*

"Is that a 'tip' you reserve for your male clients? To tell women they're virgins? Does that help them get laid quicker?"

The jig was up. I considered lying just to get out of having to admit the truth, but I'd be breaking the number one rule of my program. I was already venturing into some pretty gray area with Rule Number Two, and I had to maintain *some* standards for myself.

159

Didn't make the news any easier to confess, however.

"No. I'm uh… I'm actually…"

"You're really a *virgin?*"

God, I always hated that word. "Yes."

"As in, you've never had sex with another human before."

"That's traditionally the definition of that word, so yes." Mia gaped at me in shock, unsure whether or not to believe me. "Please stop staring at me like that."

"I just… I don't know what to say. How does something like that even happen?"

I swiped a hand over my face. I was kind of hoping she'd drop the subject, but I could tell that it was merely wishful thinking. "Pretty much because it *doesn't* happen."

She jutted a palm in my direction. "But look at you! You're a hot, confident guy. I've seen you in action, dude, and you've got game."

"Thank you?"

Her eyes widened in alarm as a sudden revelation came to her. "*Dios mio*, do you think you might be gay?"

I knew she was only trying to help, but she was totally on the wrong track. I chuckled as I answered, "Definitely not."

"Then what's the problem?"

As humiliating as this conversation was, I couldn't help but grin. Mia and I were comfortable with one another. It allowed me to be a little lighter about the whole thing. "I could tell you but it would undermine my entire marketing angle. If my clients ever knew…"

"I can help you!" she blurted out, throwing her arms in the air. "Who better to work on your marketing angle than a marketing *expert?* C'mon. You need to discuss this." When I continued to hesitate, Mia crossed her pinky finger over her heart and held it out to me. "Pinky swear. What happens at McGee's stays at McGee's."

I gave her a long, hard look out the corner of my eye before linking my pinky with hers, then turned to go inside, Mia trailing on my heels. I flagged the bartender down and ordered two shots of Jaegermeister.

"I don't drink Jaeger," Mia said through a scrunched face.

"They're both for me. If you want me to talk about this, I'm going to need to drink my way through it."

She clapped in victorious glee as I downed my two shots and then ordered us a couple of beers. It wasn't until we were settled in at a booth in the back that I finally spoke again.

"Okay. So, you remember I was in that accident when I was twelve."

"Hard thing to forget."

"Well, afterwards, I was sent to a boarding school upstate. I'd missed so much classroom time that my father thought I'd have a better shot at catching up if I was 'fully immersed in a scholastic atmosphere.'"

"Your father sounds like he'd be fun at cocktail parties," she snarked.

"No, he's cool. Just took my education more seriously than he ever did his own." I took a sip of my beer and continued. "I was a scrawny little thing, made even scrawnier from the months lying in a hospital bed. You'd think some schmancy private school would afford a more sheltered environment, but really all it did was allow for the assholes to pick on the weaker kids within a vacuum. I was bullied almost every single day of middle school. I couldn't wait to come back to Westchester and start over, but high school was no different."

Mia's eyes softened, and I started in again before she could say anything pitying out loud.

"But I was smart. I studied. Made good grades. Got into a good university. It wasn't until sophomore year of college that I thought to make myself stronger—mentally as well as physically. I worked out hard; I studied even harder. By junior year, I'd completely transformed. Finally, the girls started to notice."

"Where'd you go?"

"Georgetown."

"Nice school."

"Yes, it was."

Mia sighed and rested her elbows on the table. "So you didn't start dating until you were... what? Twenty?"

"'Dating' is a relative term."

"How so?"

"Because I've never really had a serious girlfriend."

She looked at me as if I'd just stripped down naked and broke out into a dance on the table. This conversation was almost as embarrassing. "So like, you've never even, you know..."

"I'm not a monk, Cruz. I've done stuff with girls before. Just not... that."

"But again... You haven't really explained what happened."

"What *didn't* happen." When Mia did nothing but roll her eyes, I said, "I told you, I was shy. And scrawny. I had zero game."

"Yes, but that was high school. You said you transformed yourself after that. You turned into this and you still never dated anyone in college?"

"Not really. By then, the persona ran too deep. I wasn't used to girls noticing me. Once they finally did, it took me years to figure out a way to work it."

"But you've been out of school for... what? Six years now? What are you waiting for?"

"The right girl."

There was an uneasy silence between us until I cleared my throat and added, "I was a late bloomer but I still had a hard time believing I *had* bloomed. It's difficult to shake off that voice in your head, the person you once were." I snickered, my face dropping to my shoes as I added, "Week Eight is normally devoted to this entire subject, by the way. My clients inevitably feel like whole new people at the end of this. They need to learn how to deal with it."

"I highly doubt that you're able to instill that in your clients in eight weeks when you haven't even learned how to deal with it after eight *years*."

She was right, of course. Take away the fancy suits and the cultured veneer, and I was nothing more than an empty shell. "To tell you the truth, I'm still learning."

"To tell *you* the truth, I kinda want to fuck you right now."

The comment caught me off guard and I almost spit out my beer. I knew she was only screwing around, though. The fact that we were friends was actually what made this completely awkward situation less so. Our eyes met for a beat before I broke, just cracking the hell up.

Mia laughed and added, "You're not really my type, but wow. I think I could get past that just for the chance to deflower you."

CHAPTER TWENTY-EIGHT

Dave and Buster's was an adult arcade out in the Palisades. Basically, it was a place to relive your video game youth while drinking booze. It was a little cheesy, but a good place to go for an easy way to socialize. All that background noise from the pinging video games, tons of people milling about... It was impossible not to interact with your fellow humans in a situation like that. There were plenty of opportunities to strike up conversations with strangers, which was the focus of today's assignment.

Ainsley's task tonight was going to be to play some games and talk to whomever was occupying the machine next to hers. Easy, right?

I figured it would be a blast.

Problem was, Ainsley didn't have much video game experience, so she spent most of her time preoccupied with how awesome everything was. She was currently obsessed with Ms. Pac Man.

I watched from a safe distance, waiting for her to get to work. Soon enough, a young kid took over the Galaga machine next to her, and it wasn't long before the two of them were chatting it up.

Not exactly the type of conversation I had in mind for this assignment, but it was a start.

They moved over to pinball, and I was just about to step in and remind her that tonight wasn't about befriending ten year olds.

Finally, a better prospect took over the machine next to her. Mid-twenties. Decent-looking guy, but not too handsome that he'd be unapproachable. I mean, he had a fucking ponytail, for godsakes.

Perfect target.

I kept waiting for Ainsley to talk to him, but she and her new little friend were too tied up in their competition for her to notice. After Ponytail gave up and moved on, I went over to have a little chat. We were down at the half, and it looked as though my team was going to need a little pep talk from the coach if we wanted to win.

"Ainsley."

She didn't look up from the machine and simply replied, "Hey Luke!" The lights pinged as she sent her ball soaring up a ramp. "Oh, Luke. This is Kyle."

Kyle gave a half-hearted nod in my direction. "Whatsup, man?"

"Not much, *man*," I said back, trying not to laugh in the kid's face. I put a hand at Ainsley's back and asked, "You ready to take a break?"

"Yes. In a minute." She bit her lip and continued with her game.

"Okay. When you're through, come meet me at our booth. Our food is probably waiting for us."

It was only a few minutes later that Ainsley slid into her seat, an elated expression on her face.

"What?" I asked.

Her smile grew even wider as she held up a handful of tickets. "Look how many I won!"

She was so happy and excited, there was nothing to do but laugh. "That's great, Ains. But it's not really why we're here, right?"

"I know. But I'm having a good time."

"I'm glad you are." I couldn't help but grin at her enthusiasm. It was cool to see how much fun she was having. Every day, there was something new and fascinating to discover about her. I mean, I knew she'd grown up rich and sheltered, but how could I have assumed she'd never played video games before? I grew up under similar circumstances, but my Playstation was like a lifeline throughout my teen years.

We scarfed down a couple of burgers before it was time for Round Two. "Okay," I said. "This time, try and talk to some *adults.*"

She laughed and shot back, "Yes, sir!"

I watched from afar as she took over the Ms. Pac Man again, and it wasn't long before Kyle came and found her. I allowed a few minutes for those two to hang out, but when it looked like she was getting a little too comfortable with the situation, I stepped in again.

"Having fun?" I asked.

"No!" she exclaimed, as her last life fizzled out before her eyes. "But I made it to the fourth board! Look at my score!"

I chuckled, but didn't let her adorable face distract me. We bid our adieu to Kyle as I led her toward the center of the arcade. "Okay. I think it's time for some air hockey."

"I've never played air hockey."

"It's easy. No skill necessary. Find someone here and ask them to play you." She gave a shrug and started to walk off as I added, "*Not* the ten-year-old."

I had to restrain myself from laughing as I watched Ainsley's shoulders visibly slump. Poor girl. Thought she was getting off easy.

Turned out, I was the chump who'd be having the hardest time with this assignment. Ainsley walked up to the first man within her sights and asked him to play. It just so happened that the guy was too handsome for his own good. He seemed more than thrilled to have a beautiful stranger talking to him, and readily agreed to a game, even going so far as to insist he pay.

She made me proud with the way she smiled and joked as she thwacked the plastic disc across the table, really giving it her all.

Or maybe she was genuinely enjoying this dude's attention.

He was really laying it on thick, making a point to explain how to play, exaggerating his heartbreak every time she scored on him. *Take it down a notch there, Slick.*

I was proud of Ainsley for doing so well, but I wasn't digging the fact that this guy had been so receptive to taking the bait. I moved a bit closer to keep a better eye on the situation, and okay, yeah, maybe I was trying to eavesdrop.

Just in the nick of time, apparently.

"Oh my gosh," she said. "Am I actually winning?"

"The game *and* my heart, beautiful."

Ouch. I physically cringed from his corny line, but I almost dropped dead when he said, "Hey. Maybe you and I could go see some *real* hockey sometime."

That did it. It was time to step in and shut that shit down.

"Hey, Ains. How you doing?"

"Great!" she answered on an elated grin.

I nodded at Slick. "How's it going?"

"Good," he answered. "You know, except that your girl here is kicking my ass."

Better her than me, I thought. But instead of going caveman, I reveled in the fact that he'd just referred to Ainsley as "my girl." I liked the sound of that.

I snickered and shot back, "Yeah. She kicks my ass, too."

Ainsley bit her lip as she smiled up at me, and it was all I could do not to pull her toward me and bite that lip for her.

She finished her game with Slick and we both shook his hand. Mission accomplished. She'd completed enough of her assignment for one day.

Now it was *my* turn to play. "Wanna challenge the master at Gunfight at the OK Corral?"

She smiled as she answered, "Well, if you're such a master, I don't really stand a chance now, do I?"

I chuckled. "It's just point and shoot. I'm thinking you can handle it." *After all, you've been using my chest as target practice for the past six weeks.*

"Okay," she agreed. "But I'm getting pretty good at all these games. You may regret calling me out."

"Hmmm. Aren't we getting cocky."

"I'm getting confident. Not cocky," she shot back. She took her place at the machine and pulled the gun from its holster. "I know *you* can't tell the difference, but trust me, there is one."

Holy shit! Did she just bust my balls? "Did you just call me cocky?"

She gave a coy shrug, trying to hide her smile. "If it walks like a duck..."

I almost busted out into a full-on laughing fit. The "insult" was far outshined by the pride I felt for her in that moment. Ainsley was totally getting it.

The ball-busting was a major turning point which continued as we trash-talked our way through the game.

"Got you, Blondie! Take a seat."

"Oh please. Lucky shot. You suck at this."

"You kiss your mother with that mouth?"

"You can kiss my ass with yours."

Ainsley's use of the word "ass" had me sputtering out a laugh. I thought I was going to pass out. Holy hell was that funny. Who knew she had it in her?

"Obscene language from such a pristine girl," I snarked.

I waited for her to reply *I'm not that pristine*, but she only smiled in response.

Okay. I know it wasn't a direct quote, but I should have known that Ainsley wouldn't have gotten my Breakfast Club reference regardless. But dammit. That was a perfect line for this situation. I'd have to remember to tell Mia later. She'd appreciate it.

Once the game was over, I checked the score and said, "Damn. I wish we bet money on this game."

Ainsley shot me a side-eye. "No fair. I think my gun was broken."

"Excuses, excuses," I teased.

"No, I'm serious. Check it out for yourself."

I was skeptical, but swiped my card through the slot to cue up a single-player game. Ainsley aimed her gun and took a bunch of shots, only landing a few targets.

"I don't think it's the gun," I said.

I moved to stand behind her and reached my arms around hers, grasping her hands with my own. And okay, yeah, I leaned in just a little and pressed my front against her back as I helped her aim correctly. She not only let me do it, but her elated giggling made me think she was *enjoying* it.

It was like my greatest junior high fantasy come to life.

CHAPTER TWENTY-NINE

Tonight's assignment was an easy one. After our Zumba class, Mia and I showered and headed over to her apartment.

I was there to help her rehearse Buttercup's monologue from *The Princess Bride*. The plan was for Mia to recite it in the middle of Central Park next week, right there on the big rock at the edge of Strawberry Fields. The idea was to not give a shit about what anyone thinks and to pull off the Band-Aid when it came to public speaking. The back room at the restaurant was a good start, but now she needed to perform in front of a larger audience.

We'd culled the book version of the story for a monologue because the movie didn't have any long, sprawling one-woman speeches. Mia was pretty disappointed about it, but didn't really feel as passionately about any other subject matter. That's when I remembered the source material, and stopped off at The Strand to pick up a copy of the book. It was a really great speech. Lots of corny, lovey-dovey moments for a hopeless romantic like Mia to indulge.

We'd made ourselves comfortable on her big, beige sofa to go over the transcript. Her apartment was nothing like I had expected. It wasn't the dilapidated postage stamp she had made it out to be, and was actually a decently-sized space. Well, for New York, anyway. Aside from a short hallway that led to her bedroom and bath, the place was comprised solely of a living room and kitchen. There was no room for a table and chairs, but there wasn't really a need for them; her kitchen had a long island with four vinyl stools. It also had red walls, one of those cool, retro, cast-iron stoves, and a matching white fridge.

Which, apparently, was empty.

She'd been procrastinating for the past hour. Instead of reading the damned monologue, she spent her time doing anything but. Fidgeting with the stereo, pacing around the floor, retrieving drinks for me... and now she was getting exasperated by her fruitless quest for a snack.

She slammed the fridge door and sighed, "There's nothing to eat here and I'm starving. Let me take you out for some dinner."

"Mia, we're supposed to be—"

She waved me off with a flip of her hand. "We can work on my speech after we eat. I can't even think about being productive on an empty stomach. C'mon. I know the perfect place."

So it was about fifteen minutes later that we were stepping out of a cab in front of *Samara's Cuban BBQ* up in Harlem. From first impressions, it was a block party masquerading as a restaurant. Situated on a huge lot between two brick tenements, the entirety of the restaurant was outdoors; twinkle lights draped across the span between the neighboring buildings creating an open-air canopy that gave off a soft glow. Mismatched tables and chairs were surrounded by a perimeter of barrel-grills, the smoke and steam of the cooked food wafting toward the sky.

I didn't know what was cooking, but it smelled fantastic.

Mia took a deep breath and smiled. "You are in for a treat."

I knew she was right as she directed me over to one of the grills. The chef was a dark-skinned woman with an infectious smile who wordlessly held a couple chicken wings out at the end of her tongs as we walked by. *Free samples. Alright.* Mia and I munched on them as we made our way to an empty wrought-iron table, one of only a few that were left unoccupied.

She clapped her hands over her head. "Shots, por favor!" she ordered good-naturedly. The waiter didn't hesitate—nor did he ask what kind of liquor we wanted—as he plunked a couple of shot glasses and a carafe of something red on our table.

Mia poured us a round of drinks before holding hers out in a toast. "To friends, lovers, and everything in between."

"*Salud*," I replied on a smirk.

We didn't even look at a menu much less put in our orders before a tray of ribs were placed on our table.

"Okay then," I said. "I guess we're having ribs?"

Mia laughed as she chomped into one, barbecue sauce staining her cheek. "Not just ribs. The best ribs you'll ever eat."

It only took one bite for me to agree. The meat just fell off the bone and practically melted in my mouth, a perfect blend of smoke and seasoning with just the slightest bit of burn. "Oh man, you weren't kidding."

Mia smiled proudly as she poured us another round. "I never kid about good food."

* * *

The music was jamming. Hard to believe three guys were able to create so much noise. The sound blended with the spicy scent in the air, creating an energetic atmosphere which all but guaranteed a great night. Plus, Mia was always fun to hang out with. We ate, we talked... we did a lot of shots. I lost count. If this kept up, I was going to have to call a Dryver to get me and my car home tonight.

"Oh hey, I forgot to ask you," Mia slurred loudly, trying to be heard over the music. "Did you give my number to Jared?"

"Yeah. I hope that was okay," I said, pouring us another round.

"Yeah. It totally *WAS NOT!*"

I laughed, surprised to find that I was relieved. "What's the problem? You guys got along great the other night. I thought you two could—"

"Luke. I'm not interested. Yes, he seems nice, but I like him as a friend. You know," she said, as her voice took on an edge, "like you and me."

I didn't understand the bite in her words. "What's that supposed to mean?"

Mia downed another shot and waved at me to do the same. "Nothing. I just meant that we have a great time together. Probably because we don't have to worry about any of the sex stuff. I mean, I'm a career gal who's obsessed with her promotion, you're a virgin who's obsessed with Paisley—"

"Ainsley. And I'm not obsessed."

"Dude. You so are."

"Obsessed is a strong word."

She slapped her hands down on the table. "You're saving your virginity for her!"

My eyes bugged as I snuck a peek at our surrounding area. Thankfully, it didn't seem as though anyone was paying attention. "Christ. Is it really necessary to *yell?*"

Mia dismissed my question and continued with her attack. "You like to think you're so damn sexy. You and I both know you've got nothing to back it up."

"What the fuck, Mia?"

"Relax. I just meant that being sexy is just that. Emitting sexual vibes. Insinuating that you *want to have sex*. You never do, so..."

173

I didn't care how much sense her explanation was making. The truth was, I was still stinging from her inadvertent insult. "You don't think I'm sexy?"

"No. But if it's any consolation, I think you're smoking hot."

"Same thing!"

"Not hardly. In fact, you being a virgin actually explains a lot."

"Jesus. Stop throwing that word around. How so?"

"Well, you've always remained hands off with me." She smirked as she added, "Most guys don't have such self control."

"I've remained 'hands off' because we're friends. Also, you're a client."

"Hasn't stopped you from flirting with Paisley."

"Ainsley. And you know damn well I've been a perfect gentleman with her since Day One." *Until last week, anyway.*

"Maybe that's the problem." When all I did was look at her in confusion, she said, "The first day we met, I thought you were a total smoothy. You were flirty and sexy. But as soon as I signed up as a client, you turned all business on me. That's good, because it enabled us to become friends without the whole sex thing getting in the way. It worked out for us, but I can see why it would be a problem for you and your little blonde-girl crush."

"Hey. Bruce has been on the job for two weeks now."

"*Bruce* isn't getting you anywhere. Besides, do you want a girl to be attracted to your alter-ego... or you?"

I started to understand what Mia was trying to tell me. I'd played the poser, the professional, the coach, and the mysterious billionaire. Where had it gotten me? "You're right. I haven't exactly been putting myself out there."

"Hell, you've even held part of yourself back with me, and we're friends! I mean, I don't even know if there *is* a sexy guy underneath the statue."

It was almost as if she were testing me, seeing if I'd rise to her challenge. If that was the case, then bravo, because her comment had me stewing. Before I could change my mind, I grabbed her hand and pulled her out of her chair. *Challenge accepted.*

I led her to the dance floor with enough gusto and blind purpose to lead Mia to ask, "Okay, Kevin Bacon. Are you trying to dance your frustrations away?"

I ignored her *Footloose* jab and shot her a smirk, pulling her against the length of my body as I said, "Nah. I just figured it was time to put some of our Zumba skills to good use."

She seemed to like the sound of that, smiling as she let me move her around the floor.

I had a pretty good buzz going from all those shots, so Mia must have been flying. It was only a few minutes before we were both sweaty from the hot lights and vigorous dancing.

And, you know, because she was currently writhing against my cock.

Her body pressed against mine in a perfect fit, our dance moves synching together in practiced harmony. I had a hard-on but I didn't care if she felt it. I wanted her to feel it. Maybe it was all those drinks or maybe it was just a matter of salvaging my pride, but I wanted to unleash everything I had on Mia. I wanted her to see me as a goddamn man. I wrapped my arm around her waist and pulled her body tighter to mine as I shot her a seductive smirk, daring her to play along.

Her wide-eyed look of shock melted into a half-lidded glare. She buried her face against my neck, her fingertips feathering over my nape, the slightest caress against my skin, her breath at my ear. She smelled incredible. A mixture of heat and sweat blended with her natural citrus scent, and it turned me on more than I cared to admit.

Her fists knotted into my hair as payback, a deliberate seduction. I guessed she wasn't going to let me have all the fun. Her cheek brushed across mine as she pulled back to gauge my reaction. Jesus, we were officially drunk, but everything about this just felt too good to protest. Our eyes locked in a heated gaze, neither one of us willing to break the spell.

What the hell is going on here?

The fog of drink combined with the dizziness of my accelerated pulse, creating a dreamlike haze in my brain, an intoxicating concoction that was proving impossible to resist.

Screw it. This is happening.

Without fully realizing what I was doing, I grabbed her hand and darted us over to a more private area behind the building, immediately backed her against the wall, and slammed my lips on hers.

She let out with just the slightest gasp of shock, and Jesus, the sound tore through my chest as I kissed her even harder. It felt good, though. *She* felt good.

Her muscles relaxed as she melted into me, and feeling her just give herself over to the moment turned me on even more. My heart was beating an unsteady rhythm in my chest; my arms were shaking; my cock was harder than I thought possible.

I tightened my arm around her waist, hitched her leg higher, and circled my hips against hers, pinning her to the wall with my body. She was clearly not expecting me to retaliate so eagerly, but she didn't stop me.

Thank Christ.

The world disappeared as I felt her tongue licking my lips, causing me to meet her open mouth with my own. I couldn't stop the humming in the back of my throat as I devoured her, tongues and limbs tangling, causing me to lose my mind.

Holy shit.

She stood on her tiptoes and pressed her tits against my chest, welcoming my attack, spurring me further.

My hand slipped under her skirt on its own, massaging the soft flesh at the back of her thigh as my tongue buried itself in her mouth, the rock-hard bulge in my jeans writhing against the thin silk of her panties. I didn't even realize that I'd started pounding my body against hers.

Totally clothed.

Totally making out.

Totally. Fucking. Hot.

I didn't ever want this feeling to end.

CHAPTER THIRTY

My brain felt like it was splitting in two the next morning. My entire body felt groggy. My mouth was dry.

I shuffled into the kitchen and slammed down a handful of Tylenol along with a huge glass of orange juice just to get my day started, but wound up slinking back into my bed immediately after.

I couldn't get back to sleep, though.

Last night's madness with Mia kept rolling around in my mind. As hot as that kiss was, I was fairly certain it was a one-shot deal. We were drunk and feeling pretty loose, and I guess she was just tossing me a mercy hookup.

I really hoped we hadn't crossed some imaginary line that would prevent us from maintaining our friendship, however. I'd come to rely on her not only as a sounding board, but as an oasis from the stress.

Our friendship was awesome.

So was that kiss, though.

I couldn't imagine there'd be a problem. We just got drunk and screwed around a little. I didn't have a ton of experience to know for sure, but people do that all the time, right? It's not like it had to mean anything. It's not like Mia was going to be crazy-embarrassed or angry or awkward because of one drunken kiss.

Right?

I decided to give her a call just to be sure.

"Morning, Cruz."

Her voice sounded even more out-of-it than mine. "Mmm. What time is it?"

Shit. I didn't even think to check the clock before I picked up the phone, but I did it now. "A little after ten." *Phew*.

"How much did we drink last night?"

"Too much."

I could hear her rustling around on the other end of the line before her sultry, sleepy voice replied, "Worth it. Last night was *fun*."

"Yeah. Yeah it was." My brain flashed back to a few of our crazier moments from the night before, and my boxer briefs got a little tighter. *Get a grip, Taggart.* "Hey, so, uh..." I didn't know how to bring up the subject. "We're uh, we're cool, right?"

"Well yeah. I mean... wait. What?"

"I just want to make sure we're on the same page about... us."

She perked up a little as she joked, "Are you asking me to go steady?"

"No. Don't worry," I laughed out nervously. "Just the opposite, in fact. I wanted to make sure we're still friends."

There was an extra beat of silence before she repeated, "Friends."

"Yeah. We don't want what happened last night to change anything between us, right?" Mia didn't say anything, so I filled in the quiet. "You and me... We're good together. We're good friends. I don't want to lose us over this. Plus, you know, we still have to work together."

"Sooo, you're saying you want to go back to business as usual."

"Well, yeah. I know I don't have a lot of experience, so I didn't want you to think that our... you know, what happened between us... I just meant I wasn't going to turn into some lovestruck idiot or something. I figured I'd ease your mind about that."

"Suuure," she said flatly. Guess she must've been even more hungover than I thought. "Consider my mind eased. Hey look. I've got to go. Can we talk about this later?"

"I have an appointment with Ainsley later."

"Of course you do," she sighed. "I guess I'll just see you tomorrow."

CHAPTER THIRTY-ONE

Every Saturday was Open Mic Happy Hour at *Caroline's Comedy Club* on Broadway. I loved the Comedy Night part of our training. It usually served as a major turning point in a client's transformation. Plus, it was always a fun time.

Ainsley and I had a table right near the stage, front-and-center to see the show. Caroline's was a great place to catch any up-and-comers, and there was always a chance that a more established, famous comedian would decide to pop in to do a set.

Like today.

Ainsley and I had been watching the show, finding ourselves mildly entertained by the budding comedians who commandeered the mic.

In between, we were treated to Bob, the resident MC.

Bob hopped up onstage as the applause from *The Amazing Julian* died down. "Whooo! Let's give it up for Amazing Julian! He did a great job, didn't he?"

Bob told a few jokes before announcing, "Now boys and girls, we interrupt our regularly scheduled programming to bring you a real treat. One of our Caroline's graduates happened to pop in today, and I think if you cheer loudly enough, we can convince him to come up here and do a set." All eyes scanned the room, looking to see who he could be talking about. "Ladies and gents, let's hear it for Jay Mohr!"

No way!

Jay took the stage amidst a rousing round of applause, and within minutes, showed all these wannabes what real comedy looked like.

I snickered at his spot-on Christopher Walken and Norm MacDonald impersonations. Had my first laugh when he talked about his days on Saturday Night Live. But when he told a story about taking a bunch of drugs and driving into the city in his friend's Firebird, I lost it.

I could barely breathe, holding my sides and trying not to fall off my chair.

Ainsley, however, was wearing a scowl. I couldn't really ask her about it until after the set, though.

Jay wrapped up his act and hopped down off the stage. As we clapped, I turned to Ainsley and laughed out, "Oh man! That was hysterical! I'm still trying to catch my breath."

She gave a shrug and sipped her drink.

"You didn't seem to be as entertained…"

"There's nothing funny about taking drugs."

Okay there, Buzzkill.

"Sometimes comedians make up stuff for their shows."

"I guess."

Man. I'd been feeling guilty about the "fun" Mia and I had last night, but even without the makeout session, we tended to have a great time no matter where we went. Here was Ainsley who couldn't even muster up a chuckle at a professional comedian. It was a stark contrast.

I soon realized that maybe lack of humor wasn't the problem.

Bob had resumed with the open mic show, and we were subjected to three snoozer comedians in rapid succession.

The expression on Ainsley's face throughout was seemingly serene but I could recognize panic when I saw it. The longer the show went on, the more I felt her recoiling at the idea that her number would be pulled next. We'd worked on her routine all week—and the jokes were good—so her fear was more about getting up on that stage.

Maybe "fear" was an understatement.

The poor girl had turned white and she was currently wringing a napkin in her hands.

"You okay?" I asked.

She turned horrified eyes toward me. "I think I need air."

"Yes. Okay. Yeah, let's go outside for a minute."

We excused ourselves as inconspicuously as possible before heading for the door. Once outside, Ainsley took a huge breath and started pacing back and forth on the sidewalk. "I can't do this."

"Don't say can't."

"Fine. I *won't* to do this."

My brows drew together as I asked, "Why not? There's nothing you can't do if you just—"

"Luke! You're not listening! I said I'm not doing this and I meant it! Why would you even put this on my schedule?"

"It's a great exercise."

"Wrong. It's a great way for you to parade your trained monkey around on that stage!"

She was totally freaking out and I felt really bad about it. My intention was to help her step out of her comfort zone, not to completely terrify her. "Okay, calm down, Ains. It's okay. You don't have to. I'd never force you to do anything you weren't comfortable with."

She huffed at that. "As if you could. *I* make my own decisions. *I* say what I will and will not do. Got it?"

Her defiance was out of character, but I was proud of her for speaking her mind.

"Yeah. Yes. Sure. Hey, c'mere." I pulled her toward me and wrapped my arms around her. She just really needed a hug right then, an opinion that was confirmed as I felt her shaking like a leaf in my grasp. Shit. "I'm sorry. You going to be okay?"

She sniffled as she pulled out of my clutches. "Yes. I'm sorry for wimping out." Her eyes met mine to add, "And for yelling at you."

Her apology was enough for the both of us to shake off the drama of the past minutes and share a snicker as I put an arm across her shoulders and walked us toward my car.

As disappointed as I was that Ainsley wasn't going to go through with tonight's lesson, at least something good came of it. She would never have dug her heels in so adamantly six weeks ago. She may have "failed" at her task, but her willingness to stand up for herself was progress.

I wrote the night off as a success.

WEEK SEVEN: RENOVATION

Clothes shopping
Spa Day
Haircut
Makeup lesson

CHAPTER THIRTY-TWO

Holy Hell, this woman's fingers are a gift from the gods.

I'd talked Mia into the dual massage, figuring it would be fun. So, we were currently lying side by side on our respective tables as our therapists pounded our backs into a pulp.

Mia was a squealer.

It was pretty much the first sound I'd heard out of her all day. She'd been in a mood all morning, and I wondered what was up.

Rather than hound her about it, I figured it would be better to just leave her to her thoughts. She'd come to me when she was ready to talk. Until then, I couldn't imagine a more relaxing place to either work out some issues or forget about them altogether.

The *Luna Spa* was a kickass Zen den in the heart of Hell's Kitchen. It was a miracle that they were able to offer a peaceful atmosphere, considering Times Square was only a few feet outside their door. But Luna Spa must have had triple-thick insulation in their exterior walls or something. Aside from the background noise of some new age music and trickling water, the whole building was *quiet*.

There was something kind of crazy—and hot—about being naked in a roomful of women except for a thin towel. I kept trying to catch Mia's eye to share a laugh about it, but she had her face permanently embedded in the donut hole of the table. I couldn't stop thinking about the two of us dancing the other night. Things had gotten a little fucked up. Fucked up, but incredibly hot.

Thank Christ I was lying on my stomach.

Fortunately, Mia was acting like it hadn't even happened. Maybe when you've slept with enough people, a simple dry hump on a dance floor didn't register. I wouldn't know.

In fact, she was pretty much ignoring me altogether.

When our hour was up, we walked together toward the locker rooms. She was either chilled out from such a relaxing massage or she was giving me the silent treatment. I felt I'd waited long enough to find out, and asked, "What's up with you today?"

I was expecting an aloof shrug, maybe a benign excuse.

I wasn't expecting to see tears in her eyes.

"Just don't do it," she pleaded. "Don't let Ainsley be your first."

Definitely not the conversation I was expecting. "What? Why?"

She sighed and ran a hand over her hair. "Because your first time should be with someone you love."

It was cool that she was concerned about me, but I couldn't understand why she was getting so emotional about it. And besides, "Who says I don't love her?"

"*You* do. With everything you've told me, and especially the things you don't. You only think you're in love with her because she looks perfect. I just... I just think you should wait. Really think about it. You've waited twenty-eight years. Do this right." I was caught off guard, and couldn't understand why Mia would be opposed to me finally getting laid. She seemed to enjoy it, why shouldn't I? "You said you were waiting for the right girl. What if she's the wrong one?"

"Mia. It's... nice and all that you find this so important. Really. I guess I just don't understand why you're getting so upset, though. Is this... Do *you* have regrets about some of *your* decisions?"

"No. I don't regret a thing. And stop talking at me like I've slept with half the city."

Her comment lightened the moment for both of us. Once we reached the ladies' locker room, I threw an arm around her shoulders and squeezed her against my side. "I'm not. And look, there's no need to freak out. I'm going to be fine."

My reassurances brought a small smile to her face. "Okay. You're right. It's not my place to say." She leaned into me for just the briefest second before stepping out of my grasp. She started to head toward the door, but stopped before opening it. Clasping her robe closed with a fist at her throat, she turned back toward me. "I just want you to be happy. You know that, right?"

I shot her a wink and grinned on my reply. "I do."

CHAPTER THIRTY-THREE

I couldn't stop staring at Ainsley as we walked the few blocks over to Barney's. Today was New Wardrobe Day, and the plan was to pick out a few new staples to match her new look, plus settle on a killer dress to wear out for our celebratory dinner tonight. Based on what she already looked like this afternoon, however, I figured I'd be dead before then.

She always looked great, so the reveal after her makeover yesterday didn't provide the shock that I normally got from my other clients. It simply enhanced her beauty. Her golden blonde hair was sporting some new platinum highlights, and a heavier hand was used on her makeup. She must have been paying attention during the tutorials, because she managed to recreate the look herself today.

Guess she liked it.

What *I* liked, however, was her decision to wear a pair of skinny jeans. She had them paired with a white silk top and a fitted black leather jacket. The look was pretty lethal. I hoped Corinne would nudge Ainsley into picking out more outfits like it.

"Hey Sandy," I teased. "I'm kinda digging this badass look you've got going on today."

"Sandy?"

"Sorry. Bad Grease joke." When she looked at me blankly, I explained, "Your outfit. It reminded me of the end of the movie." Ainsley's face scrunched in confusion. "When she shows up all made up... wearing a leather jacket..."

"Oh, yeah," she said as the lightbulb finally clicked on. "I guess I haven't seen that in a while."

Yeah, maybe you haven't seen it in a while but it's Grease, for fucksake, I thought to myself. Who doesn't remember that scene? It was one of the major inspirations behind me starting my business!

I shook off my bewilderment by the time we reached the corner, and absently reached my hand out to hers as we crossed the street. I hadn't even realized I'd done it until I felt her fingers thread through mine, and I was kind of stunned by how receptive she was.

It felt good, walking down the street on a random Wednesday with this gorgeous girl on my arm. I was crazy about her and could hardly wait for next week to tell her how I felt. I started to wonder what the hell I was waiting for in the first place.

Maybe Mia was right. Maybe I just needed to tell Ainsley how I felt. What difference would waiting a few extra days make? What did I have to lose? It's not like I'd made so much progress doing things my way. If I was just honest, if I just told her, she'd know for sure. *I'd* know for sure. No more games. No more act.

Hell, I knew she liked me. She told me flat-out weeks ago that she thought I was good-looking, and she hadn't missed too many opportunities to flirt with me since then. Now it was just a matter of officially getting this ball rolling. *I* was the one who kept bringing everything to a screeching halt.

In that moment, everything became crystal clear. I'd been dancing around my feelings for this woman for weeks, trying to work every angle to get her to fall for me without ever crossing any lines.

But screw it. Mia was right. It was finally time to cross the big one.

I needed to roll the dice. Take the chance. Make the play.

I had to tell her.

Now.

"Ainsley?"

We both looked up at the sound of a male voice, and there, standing on the sidewalk in front of us—with the worst goddamned timing in the world—was none other than... Blake Atwood.

"Blake!" she said in surprise. Her eyes immediately went wide at the unexpected sight of her crush standing in front of her.

But then, almost as quickly, her training kicked in.

My jaw gaped as the expression on her face relaxed into a flirty, seductive glare. I'd been on the receiving end of that look a few times over the past weeks, and from the shock on Atwood's face, I could tell I wasn't the only one who lost my shit at having it aimed in my direction. She put a hand to her hip and slithered, "It's been a while, huh? You look great."

Atwood did a double-take, trying to figure out what the hell was happening. "Wow, Ainsley... You look... different."

"I hope that's a good thing," she shot back, not missing a beat.

Her eyelids lowered expertly. Her coy smile was delivered perfectly.

Atwood was tongue-tied as he looked her up and down, completely lost in his quest for the most appropriate way to respond.

Don't ask me why, but I bailed the bastard out. "Hi, I'm Luke Taggart," I offered, holding out my hand.

I don't even think Atwood was aware that I was standing here until now. He blinked a couple times in my direction before meeting his hand with mine. "Blake Atwood. Nice to meet you."

He looked from me to Ainsley and then back again, trying to gauge whether or not we were a couple, the unspoken question playing out across his face.

Ainsley answered it. "Oh, Luke is my..." she aimed pleading eyes in my direction before inspiration struck. "Luke is my friend from Botany Club! We just had a floral arrangement lesson."

Floral arrangement lesson? Yeah, great save there, Ains. Now I look suuuper cool.

Atwood aimed a toothy grin at her. "You and your flowers, Ainsley. You haven't changed one bit."

"Oh, I think you'd be surprised," she shot back, striking just the right note. Jesus. It was torture having to watch her direct all that cultivated sex appeal toward another guy. My own creation was going to be the death of me. "Maybe we should go out and discuss it. Are you free for lunch?"

Free for lunch? She was already asking him out? Fuck! *Don't say yes, Atwood. Do NOT say yes. Do. Not. Say—*

"Yes, as it so happens, I believe I am," he answered, a bit too cat-who-ate-the-canary for my taste. "In fact, I know the perfect place. My driver is parked right around the corner." He raised an eyebrow at me to add, "Lou, will you be joining us?"

Well, didn't I feel like the third wheel. How the fuck did that happen? I was looking forward to spending the day with Ainsley, but by the pleading look on her face, I could tell that she was silently imploring me to let her bail.

The invitation was only extended my way anyway because I was standing right there. It was the chivalrous thing to do, even if he and I were both well-aware it was an *un*vitation. But if I was going to return the gentlemanly gesture, the only choice on the table was to decline.

I knew this.

So did Atwood.

In fact, it looked like he was counting on it.

Just because my brain knew the right thing to do didn't mean my fist wasn't just itching to bury itself in this guy's smarmy face. It was so unfair. I fell for Ainsley even before she turned into the sex kitten standing before him today. Hell, I was the guy that turned her into one! And now this pretentious goon was going to reap the benefits?

This. Totally. Blows.

"Actually," I said, sounding more agreeable than I felt, "I have somewhere I'm supposed to be and I'm already running late. Thanks for the offer, though. Pleasure meeting you." I held out my hand and Atwood shook it as Ainsley bit her lip, trying to hide her grin.

"I'll call you later," she said.

"Yes. Yes you will," I practically warned.

I was numb with shock as she kissed me on the cheek.

It was the first "intimate" contact between us.

And I felt nothing.

CHAPTER THIRTY-FOUR

I kept Mia company while she was imprisoned under the hair dryer. I hadn't originally planned to spend my entire day at the salon, but I couldn't do another minute alone in my house. I hadn't heard from Ainsley since Blake Cocksplat Atwood whisked her away for their little lunch date yesterday, and it was driving me fucking insane, waiting to talk to her about it.

Hanging out with Mia was a good distraction. And thankfully, her mood from the other day seemed to have dissipated. The two of us had returned to a semblance of normalcy over the course of our morning, so much so that she was back to her old, bossy self.

"Hey, Luke? Can I bother you to grab me a magazine or something?"

She'd just gotten her highlights done, so her hair was wrapped in foil spikes that stuck out in all directions over her head. She looked like a hot, female Hellraiser.

"Yeah, sure. Which one do you want?"

"I don't care. Something with a celebrity on the cover. I need to catch up on my gossip."

I went over to the magazine rack and scanned the available titles. I bypassed *People* and *Entertainment Weekly* in my quest to find something a bit more tawdry... Aha! I pulled down a copy of *The Backlot*, then delivered it to Mia along with a cup of water.

"Oooh! A rag mag! Thanks!"

I shook my head as I snickered, "I figured that one was right up your alley."

She lowered the magazine and met my eyes. "Well, how else am I expected to find out which Kardashians are fighting this week?"

I didn't get a chance to bust her chops about it, because just then, my phone started buzzing. I pulled it from my pocket and checked the number.

Ainsley.

I don't even think I excused myself before darting out the side door to answer it. "Hey."

"Hi Luke!"

Christ. The blissful sound of her voice almost killed me. "I was wondering when I'd hear from you."

"I'm sorry I haven't been in touch. Blake and I..."

Blake and I. Shit. I didn't need to hear the details. "So, I guess things went well yesterday."

"Very," she sighed, and the sound tore right through my fucking chest. "You would have been so proud of me. Things went so well at lunch that we wound up having dinner, too."

"That's... great. Truly, Ainsley. This is fantastic news." *Not.* "So, you landed your man."

"I did. Thanks to you."

Yeah. Thanks to me. Jackass that I am.

"Oh, no. You did this all on your own."

"Yes, but I never would have had the confidence to open my mouth in his direction, much less flirt with him in the first place if it weren't for everything you've taught me. Even if I could have, I would have been lost during any further conversation. Talking with him now is... practically effortless!"

"Wow, great. That's really... you know... great."

Say 'great' again, dickhead.

"He's coming by any minute to take me out again today. I almost can't believe that this is really happening."

Me either.

"That's awesome, Ainsley. I'm really, really happy for you."

I'm really, really full of shit.

"So, I guess I just didn't want you to wonder about me when I didn't show up tomorrow."

I'd been so caught up in my own pity-party that it took an extra second before I could register what she'd just said. "Wait. What? What do you mean?"

"Blake was supposed to go to Syracuse on some business yesterday. When he ran into me, he postponed the trip until today. He asked me to go with him. I guess I'm trying to say that I won't be able to finish Week Eight."

Shit. There it was.

I'd been hoping that things wouldn't go so hot yesterday, but obviously, I was kidding myself. Things between those two were apparently progressing at an alarming rate, because he'd already asked her to go away with him. Yeah, okay, fine, it was only upstate New York, but still. I fucking created this femme fatale and now she was going to be turning all that charm and seductiveness on some other guy? *You're welcome, Atwood.*

"So I guess this is goodbye then, huh," I stated. There was no reason to question what was happening here.

"Yes. Well, hopefully not forever. I'd like us to keep in touch."

Sure, pal. Maybe I can help you plan the wedding. Hell, why not lop off my balls and throw me in a bridesmaid dress while you're at it?

There was an awkward pause between us as I tried to come up with the right thing to say. *I'm in love with you. Don't go.* But instead, I wimped out and wrapped up the conversation. "Yeah, of course. I guess until then... Good luck."

"Thanks, Luke. I'll talk to you soon, okay?"

"Yeah, sure."

I stared at the phone as if it were an alien object in my hand. The time log showed that our conversation had taken three minutes and forty seconds. Just a little under four minutes for my entire life to implode.

Record time.

I shoved my phone back into my pocket and went back to Mia, still stuck under the hair dryer.

"Your other woman?" she snarked.

"Yep. But she's not mine anymore. She decided to drop out in her final week of training."

Her jaw dropped. "What? Why? This is the fun part!"

I shrugged. "Guess she already got what she came for."

"Huh?"

"Blake took the bait."

If I didn't know any better, I'd almost say it looked as though she were trying to hide her elation. "Oh, man. Are you okay?"

No. I'd been trying to focus on the pride of a job well done. I'd given Ainsley the skills and the confidence to put herself out into the world and land her successful, boring, dream man. Hell. Maybe they'd get married and have eleven kids. Maybe they'd live happily ever after. She would never have any reason to challenge him and he would never find the need to question her devotion to him.

I wish I could say I was totally fine about it. But damn. It really stung.

"No, Cruz. I don't think I am."

* * *

I had to suck it up and pull myself together in order to make it through our dinner date. Mia and I had settled on *Ocean* as the venue for her to show off her makeover, and yeah, thanks for the reminder, but I was already all too aware that this restaurant was the very place where I'd first laid eyes on Ainsley.

Super choice. Great thinking.

Neither one of us was in the mood for a full meal, so we grabbed a high-profile table near the bar figuring we'd be satisfied enough ordering off the apps menu.

Mia was really feeling her new look. Her jet black hair had been streaked with some chocolate highlights before being cut in long layers, and the thick curls fell over her shoulder in an alluring cascade. The real kicker, however, was her outfit. She was wearing a knockout red dress with a plunging neckline that suited her so well, it seemed as if it had been designed just for her. But even the prospect of all-night-cleavage wasn't enough to jog me out of my mood. I ordered our food and downed a few drinks and tried to keep up my end of the conversation. My head was in a fog, and I was merely going through the motions of a pleasant night out.

Mia noticed.

"How's the tartare?" she asked, eyeing up my plate.

"Good, I guess. Want some?"

"No thanks. I'm still working on my conch." I think I grunted in response, causing Mia to continue the conversation without me. "*How is it, Mia?* Oh, really good, Luke. Thanks for asking."

I smiled in spite of myself. "Sorry. I guess I'm not such a great date tonight."

I was thinking that she'd understand and let my comment lie when instead, she placed her hands on the table and stared me down. "Alright, Taggart. Enough, already. You really need to stop moping about it."

"I'm trying."

"No, you're not trying at all. You never did."

I lowered a brow at her leading statement. "What the hell is that supposed to mean?"

"You *never* tried! You never put yourself out there to Paisley."

"Ainsley!"

"Who gives a shit!" She sighed as she swiped a hand over her hair. "You know, I was willing to sit back and let you try to win your *trophy*. I thought it was what you wanted, so all *I* wanted was to see you happy. But now I know I was wrong. I should have stepped in sooner and stopped you."

"Stopped me from what?"

"From making a huge mistake."

I snickered bitterly as I shot back, "I've made a whole lot more mistakes than just one."

"The point is, you never told her how you felt. And now you're going to mope around forever because she didn't love you back?"

"It *just* happened, okay? It's still raw. You don't know what I'm going through. You don't know what it's like to be in love with someone who chooses someone else."

"Don't I?" Her squinted eyes met mine in a hard stare, but she didn't elaborate. "And for the record, you never loved her anyway."

"Excuse me?"

"You never loved her. You were *infatuated* with her. Lust isn't love."

The look on my face was bordering on sneer. "I find it really interesting that you think you can tell me how I feel."

"I don't think it. I *know* it. I know you better than you know yourself, Luke. You're conceited and kind, frustrating and fun. Your heart is usually in the right place but your dick is always pointed in the wrong direction. And the thing is, if you weren't so busy chasing after your dream girl, you would have been able to see what was right in front of you this whole time. Because that's the thing. Dreams are only that. They're not real."

I was so tangled in my own gloom, I couldn't decipher where she was going with her diatribe. "Way to kick a guy when he's down, Mia. Can't you see I'm miserable about this? Why are you trying to twist the knife? Why are you getting so pissy about this?"

"Because, *estúpido*, I'm here! I'm real! And I like you, you *pendejo!*"

"Pen day ho?"

"ASSHOLE!"

My jaw practically dropped to the floor. *No need to start hurling insults, pal.* "Whoa. I like you too. What's the problem?

Her brows scrunched before her eyes broke from mine. "The problem is that I think I... I more you."

"You *more* me?"

"Yeah. And it kinda sucks that you don't more me back."

Whoa. Where the hell was this coming from? Mia and I were friends. That's it. Nothing *more*.

I didn't know what I was supposed to say, and just stared at her, speechless.

Mia took one look at the stupid confusion on my face and said, "Just forget it. Forget I even said anything. I'm going home."

WEEK EIGHT: INTROSPECTION

Therapy
Final task

CHAPTER THIRTY-FIVE

I lay in bed that night, unable to turn my brain off.

Too much had happened over the course of the past twenty-four hours. In just one short day, I'd been ditched by Ainsley for another guy, turned into a heartbroken wuss, and got drawn into a fight with—well hell, let's just call her out for what she is—my closest friend.

Mostly, though, I was thinking about Mia.

I couldn't understand where her anger was coming from. She was acting more like a jealous girlfriend than simply a girl friend.

Because she *mores* me.

That little nugget was a bit of a surprise. When did she start having feelings for me? If I'm going to be honest, I have to admit that yeah, of course we'd had our moments. That kiss was fucking hot. Even before then, I'd found myself attracted to her a time or two, but it didn't *mean* anything. She was just, you know, like a great person or whatever.

I mean, it's not like I could be immune to her existence. It's not like I couldn't see how awesome she was. Mia was a blast to hang out with and she had an incredible sense of humor. She was sweet and attentive, bossy and wisecracking. She was gorgeous, obviously, even before the new hair and makeup, but it was her personality that made her truly beautiful. The way she carried herself. Her sexy brown eyes. The seductive way she danced. Her sultry grin.

Of course I noticed those things. How could I not?

She'd become my salvation in the past weeks. I was grateful to have her in my life. There were a few times when I'd open my appointment book, see her name on my schedule, and smile like a total dork, excited to know I was going to see her that day.

But just because I looked forward to being with her, and we had a great time whenever we were together, and I trusted her above anyone else, and she was funny and beautiful and totally fucking amazing in every single way...

Wait.

I sat up in my bed, my pulse racing. I put my hands to my head and gave a shake to my skull, physically attempting to knock some sense into my brain. But it was too late.

The revelation hit me hard, a sledgehammer to the face.

I leapt out of bed and paced the floor, feeling my entire world tilt on its axis.

Mia was right. I never loved Ainsley. How could I claim to love someone who had me overthinking every single second in her presence? I always had to be on around her, measure my every word, watch my every move. I was a babbling, stammering toolbag around her, never myself, never at ease... and why? Because she was *pretty?* We had nothing in common beyond that one, superficial trait. No wonder she wasn't into me. I was full of shit.

Not like Mia. Mia was cool and fun and *real*. Even more, *I* was real with her. I'd never been more myself than when the two of us were together. There was no ego, no act.

Just me.

Just us.

Holy fuck I'm an idiot.

I'd been unknowingly breaking Rule Number One for weeks. I'd been dishonest. Lying to myself as well as my clients. Chasing after Ainsley when I should have been falling in love with Mia instead.

And I had.

I knew that now.

It took me until right this very minute to see the truth.

I'd wasted all that time falling in love with the wrong girl.

I liked to think of myself as a con man, if only as a play on words. I taught confidence, get it? But the title fit me better than I ever realized. I was a fucking fraud of the highest order. I was a fake and a phony and an empty shell of a man.

Mia knew it.

And she wasn't afraid to call me out for it.

And she mores me anyway.

My brain was racing as I tried to figure out my next move. An apology was in order, that was for damn sure. Fact was, I was planning to go straight to Mia's apartment first thing in the morning to let her know I was wrong.

I could have called, but the selfish truth is, I was too afraid of the conversation going badly. What if Mia had already given up on me? What if I was too late? So, instead, I wimped out, lay back down, and used my relaxation exercises to help me settle my mind and go to sleep.

I wanted one last night to pretend that she still loved me before she told me to go fuck myself.

CHAPTER THIRTY-SIX

I'm in the backseat.

It's nighttime. It's raining.

Mom.

Dad.

Me.

Singing along to "Fly Away."

Rain slamming against the roof of our car. Loud.

Staring out the front windshield. Hard to see. But I know we're on the road that winds around the lake. The lake where Dad took me fishing last summer.

It's late. It's dark. No one's fishing today.

No one's driving today. Except us.

And I guess that one other car. We're the only ones on the road.

"That truck's driving a little too fast for this weather."

Headlights coming closer... filling the car with light... too bright...

I woke up gasping, feeling like my heart was going to explode out of my chest.

I knew what scene was coming next and I was thankful that my body woke me up before the vignette could play out. I knew every second by heart anyway. Me, lying on that road, bloody and bruised and not knowing who the hell I was.

This latest nightmare was the first time I'd ever remembered anything *before* that moment, however.

And I knew it wasn't just a dream. I knew the vision was real.

But I couldn't figure out why Katherine would be in the car. She left a month before the accident ever happened, didn't she? Besides, the woman in the passenger seat had dark hair. Not blonde.

The logical side of my brain was battling with the truth, the truth I was trying to deny. The stomach-churning reality was that I *knew* that was my mom and dad in my dream.

Thing was, the woman in that car wasn't Katherine… and the man wasn't Frederick.

I whipped off my covers and barreled down the hall wearing nothing but a pair of flannel pants and blind fury. I slammed my fist against my father's door—two sharp booms that echoed throughout the hallway—before tearing into the room.

My father was already on his feet, standing in the middle of his dark bedroom, looking half-asleep and completely baffled. "Luke? What are you doing? It's one o'—"

"Who are you?"

"What? Are you sleep wal—"

"WHO THE HELL ARE YOU?"

His brows tightened in bewilderment. "I'm your father. I'm—"

"My father had gray hair."

The air left the room as his eyes went wide, staring at me in shock, incomprehension, and something else I couldn't quite identify. It wasn't until he sank down onto the couch at the foot of his bed that I was able to put my finger on it:

Guilt.

His eyes met mine in disbelief. "How do you know that?"

He didn't try to deny it. I had to give him that much. "I had my dream again." He nodded his head in understanding. He knew which dream I was talking about. "But it started *before* the accident this time."

He shook his head at his feet, a beaten man. "Okay. You're looking for the truth. You're entitled to it." He ran a hand over his face and met my eyes before taking a deep breath, coming clean. "I adopted you, Luke. Sixteen years ago."

"You *what?*"

"I filed the papers a year after the accident, although I wanted to do it much sooner."

"But..." I couldn't verbalize all the questions running through my mind. *He wasn't my real father? How did he know me? Why did he adopt me? What happened to my parents?*

"I was driving home from a meeting out in New Jersey. It was raining, just pouring buckets. It was hard to see, and I was on a dark, empty road. And then... lights. Still, unmoving lights. An accident. It must have just happened; there was no one else there. Just a truck turned on its side and a smashed-in car. I pulled over and called nine-one-one from my car phone, then got out to check the damage. The truck driver wasn't badly hurt, but from the looks of the car, I didn't think I'd find anyone alive. I wouldn't know how to help them if I did. I told the truck driver to stay still and couldn't do anything but wait for the ambulance to get there. And then I saw you."

That was the part of his story I knew all too well. "Lying in the road."

"Yes."

"And you came over to me."

"Yes."

"And you called me 'son.'"

He shook his head at his feet. "I did."

"So, then what? I blacked out before the ambulance got there."

"So then the police came and confirmed that your parents..." *were dead*, he left unsaid. "The ambulance loaded you up, and I went with you to the hospital. I don't know why. I just saw you there, banged up and bloodied... no family... and I just couldn't let you go through what was to come on your own. Fifty-eight hours and two surgeries later, you were alive, but just barely. You woke up... and you just... *looked* at me. I'll never forget that moment, Luke. You looked at me with fear, but also... recognition. And the first word you said after all those days asleep... You woke up and you looked at me and you asked, '*Dad?*'... and I just melted."

I had no recollection of the memory, but apparently, it was a big moment for him. "But you weren't my dad. You didn't think to correct me?"

"The doctors didn't think your memory loss was going to be permanent. They told me to just let you think whatever you needed to think for the few days until you could remember on your own."

"But I never did."

"No." He brought his fingers to his head, massaging his temples.

"And all that time in the hospital, you never thought to tell me I wasn't really yours?"

He dropped his hands and looked at me with a mixture of remorse and awe. "Oh, but you were, Luke. I knew as soon as I saw your face that you were my son. I fought it, though."

"You *fought* it?" I had no idea what the hell he was trying to say.

"Why do you think I sent you away to that boarding school? Yes, you needed to catch up with your studies and Wentworth Academy was the best school around. But the real reason was because I needed to separate myself from you. I didn't *want* to love you. You weren't mine to love. As more time went by, I realized... I realized maybe you could be."

"But why did you keep the truth from me?"

His tone changed from placating to defensive as he lurched to his feet. "You were recuperating! The doctors didn't want to shock you while you were healing. You assumed I was your father and I let you believe it, thinking you'd remember the truth in a few days' time. I always planned to tell you the whole story once you started getting your memory back. But you never did! Days turned into weeks. Then months. Then years. After all that time passed, it just seemed pointless to bring it up. By then, you were my son."

I dropped to the easy chair, too overcome by all the new revelations to stay on my feet as my head dropped into my hands. "Oh God. My parents died!" It was both heart-wrenching and frustrating to mourn the loss of two people I couldn't even remember.

"Yes. I'm sorry, Luke. I've always wanted to be able to tell you how sorry I was that they were gone."

I'm an orphan. A twenty-eight-year-old orphan. I was able to acknowledge that much, but I was still having some trouble putting the puzzle pieces together. "So all that stuff about my mother—Katherine Warren—you just made up a human for this story?" I'd spent years staring at her picture, wondering why she left, if she'd ever come back to us.

"No. Kate was—Kate was very real. She used to call me *Rick*," he said on a sad chuckle. "And as far as I know, she's very much alive."

Not that it mattered. The woman I'd believed to be my mother all these years was just some random person from his past. Well, maybe not *that* random. "You were in love with her."

209

"Yes. She was the love of my life. I fell for her almost immediately, but she was married."

"Wait. She was *married?*"

"You can't choose who you love, Luke. We couldn't fight what we had. Besides, Ken and she were over long before we..." He trailed off before he could finish his thought. Thank God. I didn't need to hear the details about their fucked-up life. I was still reeling from trying to figure out my own. "She eventually left her husband and two kids behind to be with me."

I was in shock from the whole conversation, but that last bit put me over the edge. "She had *kids?*" I asked, stunned and disgusted.

"Yes." He made his admission not with pride, exactly. More like determination. A willingness to own it. "I loved her. Lord knows I tried not to, but I did."

If they were so goddamned crazy about each other, then where the hell did she go? "What happened to her?"

"I already told you the truth about that, even if I adjusted the dates. We spent almost four years together until she disappeared." He looked up at me, his eyes pleading. "In nineteen eighty-eight."

"Same year I was born."

"Yes. Unrelated, of course, unless you count the fact that while I was at my most miserable, I had no way of knowing the joy that was awaiting me, that my son was being born. It just took a dozen more years before I could meet him."

"But you said she left right before the accident." Then again, I guess he'd said a lot of things that weren't true.

"She may as well have. The twelve years between her leaving me and me finding you are all a daze. I threw myself into my work. I concentrated on building this house. Aside from that, I didn't allow myself to think, refused to feel. It's like I was dead all that time and only came back to life once I found you."

"So that's the real reason why you hardly talk about me as a little kid? Why there are hardly any baby pictures of me around the house? Because you didn't even *know me* until I was twelve?"

"I've made up stories and shielded you from the truth, and for that, I'm so, so sorry. I wasn't trying to deceive you. The longer it took for you to heal, the more elaborate the stories had to become. I've lived in fear of this moment for the past sixteen years."

His explanation had me firing up all over again, trying to make sense of this whole thing. What the fuck kind of soap opera bullshit was I dealing with here? How was this my life? "So, let me get this straight. If I never had that dream tonight, you would've just let me continue living a lie for the rest of my life?"

He slapped a palm to his chest, his eyes beseeching, his voice raw as he bellowed, "I'm not the bad guy here! I'm not the villain! I tried every way I could think of to help you remember on your own. Why do you think I never stopped researching doctors, made you go to new ones all the time?"

As angry as I was, I couldn't deny that fact. He'd never given up hope that I could get my memory back.

"But how were you able to keep it a secret?" I asked.

He looked at me as if the answer were obvious. "I moved you an entire state away. Who was going to tell you?"

"So you're saying there wasn't anyone who knew me *anywhere*? How is that even possible? Didn't I have any family? Friends who looked for me?"

"Your parents didn't have any siblings. You only had one grandmother still alive in a nursing home who didn't even know who *she* was much less would she know who *you* were."

"I didn't have any friends?"

"I was told you were a shy kid. Your parents kept to themselves, too."

My parents. I had a mother and a father who raised me for twelve years... and I didn't know a single thing about them. "Tell me about them. Anything you know."

He sank down onto the couch again and clasped his hands. "Your father was an insurance rep in the city. Your mother was a high school English teacher at a private school in Norman, New Jersey. It's where you grew up."

"What were their names?"

"Matthew and Janet."

Matthew and Janet. Matthew, my father. Janet, my mother.

I had a sudden unquenchable thirst to find out every detail about their lives. "What else do you know about them?" I was hoping he would have an entire history to share with me, a culled trove of information to help me understand where I came from.

But instead, his shoulders slumped as he shook his head at his feet.

"You don't know anything, do you," I scathed. "You couldn't even be bothered to find even one person who'd be able to give me their life story? *Not one person?*"

"I needed to pretend they never existed. It's what I had to do in order for the two of us to move forward."

I looked at him, waiting for him to continue. When he didn't, I asked, "What was *my* name?"

He took a deep breath and finally met my eyes. "Lucas Atticus Mason."

CHAPTER THIRTY-SEVEN

There was only one person in the world I needed right then. The only person who would care enough about me to help me get through this.

Who *cared*, anyway.

It was close to three in the morning by the time I pulled up in front of Mia's apartment building. I went to her front door and buzzed, hoping against all hope that she'd answer. It took four tries, but finally, I heard the garbled scratch of her intercom as a sluggish voice asked, "Hello?"

"Mia." I didn't say anything more than that. I didn't know *what* to say. "Please," I begged as an afterthought, feeling like my knees were going to give out from under me.

She didn't respond, and in the excruciating silence that followed, I leaned my forehead against the wall and placed a flat palm against the speaker.

Please.

Finally, without another word, the front door buzzed. I launched myself inside and headed straight for the elevator, cursing the slow trek up to the twentieth floor.

By the time I turned the corner to her apartment, she was standing in the open doorway, her arms crossed against her chest, a scowl on her face. "Luke, it's the middle of the—"

Her words were cut off as I wrapped my arms around her waist and collapsed into her. I didn't even realize I was shaking until I felt her hands resting against my shoulders.

The anger left her voice as she asked, "What's going on? Are you okay?"

"*No.*"

"Luke..." she said, warily. "You're scaring me."

I pulled back to look at her, to explain myself. I knew I looked like a beaten man. I didn't care. "I'm so sorry about tonight at the restaurant, about everything *before* tonight, for not seeing it sooner. You've been right in front of me this entire time, and I didn't..."

Mia's face was a mask of concern. She seemed confused about my apology, but more focused on my red-rimmed eyes. "Luke..."

"I need you, Mia. And I just..." I knew I was coming off as selfish, but my head was too fucked up right at the moment to care. "I just need to be with someone who gives a shit about me right now, okay?"

Her expression softened as her eyes teared up. "Okay."

At the sound of that one, capitulating word... I broke. I wrapped my arms around her and buried my face in her neck, bawling like a kid who'd just wiped out on his bike. The pain was just as bad. No pride, no ego. Just Mia's arms around me, smoothing down my back, her soft voice whispering in my ear, "It's okay, Luke. It's okay."

She closed the door behind me, offering some soothing shushes against my hair until I took half a step back to pull myself together. *Friend* Mia was looking back at me, and I didn't know if I had the right to ask her to be anything more.

I could barely see her through the blur of tears but maybe it was better that way. I didn't want to wait for an invitation on her face that I knew wouldn't be there. Before I could talk myself out of it, I lowered my lips to hers.

She didn't stop me. She welcomed my invasion, kissing me back, slowly, gently, sweetly as her hands went to the back of my neck. Her lips were soft—softer than I anticipated—I don't know why I was expecting anything different. I guess maybe because I hadn't been expecting anything at all.

Her kiss was a cure, draining the questions from my brain and absorbing the pain from my heart. And I took and I took and I took until the ache disappeared from my chest, until the hurt dissolved into the ether.

Our mouths opened for one another and I swept my tongue inside, tasting her sweetness, coming unglued. I slid my hands down her hips and pulled her toward me, claiming her, consuming her. I couldn't get close enough to her. This gorgeous, infuriating woman.

I hadn't even realized I'd been walking her backwards toward her bedroom until we were in the middle of the hallway, Mia's hand reaching behind her for the doorknob. We both knew damn well what was going to happen on the other side of that door.

"You're okay with this?" I asked.

Her liquid-chocolate eyes met mine to answer, "Yes."

"But I was such an ass."

"Yes, you were."

I placed a hand at her jaw, swiping my thumb over her cheek. "I want to make it right. I don't know what I can tell you to make you believe me."

"So, show me, then."

She opened her door as her body melted against mine and I kissed her again, tightening my arms around her. My heart almost exploded as her hands slipped down my chest and pressed against the front of my pants.

I knew she was passionate but I never dared to dream what it would be like to have that passion unleashed on me. I never wanted anything so much. We both collapsed onto her bed, and I tried to kiss her with tenderness but I just couldn't hold back any longer. I rammed my hips against hers, almost passing out from the sweet friction of her body writhing under mine.

I tore my lips from hers to ask, "Are you sure you want to do this?"

"Yes. Are you?"

"Fuck yes."

The next moments were an agonizing blur: Her sultry voice and her melted-chocolate eyes and the lemon-scent of her skin and the feel of her hands in my hair, and I wanted—no, *needed*—so we struggled out of our clothes until we were laid bare, no pretense, no act, and everything looked so perfect. She was all woman. A real woman, not just some picture in a magazine. She had enticing curves and toned muscle and soft flesh, every inch of which felt amazing under my palms.

I touched, I tasted, I licked. So sweet. Everything was so sweet. I had my mouth against her breast and I needed to tell her and my voice spoke without permission, "I more you."

Her eyes went wide. "You do?"

"*So* much more."

She grabbed me by the back of my hair and pulled my face to hers, smiling through our kiss.

Her hand went to her nightstand drawer and *I want I want I want* and it was more than I could stand, so hard as her palm wrapped around me, and I was scared and nervous and didn't know if I could do this right.

And then oh God *just like that, just like that*. So hot and wet and tight and...

"*Que rico tu te seintes.*"

I didn't know what she said but she sounded amazing saying it.

"*Dame mas.*"

216

We were writhing and moaning and I guessed that was a good thing and I was dizzy and bursting but I wanted to give her more, more, more.

"*Asi mismo, asi mismo, asi mismo.*"

And I was slamming into her and I could barely breathe and my head was swimming but Mia felt so good and *I need I need I need.*

I buried my face against her neck and she whispered in my ear as she put her hands on my ass and pulled me in deeper and oh fuck it was *too much too much too much.* Half-words and prayers and begging and pleading until we both screamed and our world exploded in a blinding white light behind my eyes.

Every inch of my body was on fire. Every breath of air was stolen from my lungs. I wrapped my spent arms around her and pulled her close, coming down, getting our racing hearts under control. We lay like that for a minute, touching each other's skin, panting, laughing, dying.

Mia was smiling like a loon as she buried her face against my chest and giggled, "I guess you're not a virgin anymore!"

"I love you, Mia."

She pulled back to look at me, her eyes wide, disbelieving. "You what?"

"I love you. I'm an idiot for not seeing it sooner. Because I know you love me, too." When she opened her mouth to protest, I cut her off with, "Maybe you're not *in* love with me, but I don't care. It doesn't matter. I'm in love with you and I wanted you to know it."

A single tear trickled down her cheek. "No. You were right the first time. I'm in love with you, too." Her words made me feel more like a man than anything we'd just done to each other. And she wasn't even done yet. "I thought you were hot from the first second we met. You only got hotter every second since. I lied to myself that I was fine just being your friend. Because you're right about that, too. We're great friends. Yeah, I wanted more but you were so busy chasing Paisley that I knew I didn't stand a chance."

I didn't correct her that time. I didn't care anymore. I didn't care about anything except Mia. "I was a complete jerk."

"No. You were just... blind."

"Not anymore." My heart stuttered in my chest and my voice sounded like sandpaper as I added, "I can finally see what's right in front of me. And it's more beautiful than I could have ever imagined."

"But how can you..."

I cut her off before she could remind me of what a colossal dope I've been. "I love your smile and your sarcasm and your bravery. I love how you call me out on my shit. I love how you swear in Spanish when you get angry or scared. I love everything about you."

She'd been wearing a small smile that disappeared as she said, "Except my body."

"Your body is beautiful," I said, running my fingers from her shoulder down to her waist before coming to rest on her thigh. "*You're* beautiful. Just the way you are."

CHAPTER THIRTY-EIGHT

I woke up to the steady cadence of Mia's breathing. Last night, I spent way longer than necessary replaying every moment of what we'd done and every word she'd said. And afterward, I fell into the deepest sleep of my life. Without nightmares.

But now, I was wide awake with the woman I loved asleep at my side, trying to sort my thoughts.

Lucas Atticus Mason.

I rolled the name around in my brain, trying it on for size. Even knowing that it was what I'd been called for the first twelve years of my life didn't make it fit.

A sexy, sultry, sleepy voice interrupted my thoughts. "Mmm. Two whole hours of sleep. I'm gonna be sooo productive today."

I sank back down into the bed and threw an arm around her naked middle, pulling her close. "Good morning."

She snuggled against my body and said, "Good morning" against my neck.

I ran my fingertips along her shoulder blade and kissed her hair, causing her to tip her face toward mine, finally opening her eyes.

She peppered soft kisses under my chin, purring, "Mmm. I thought last night was a dream."

"It was." I could feel her smiling against my jaw as I added, "For you, I mean."

She giggled and slapped my chest. "Please. You loved every minute of it."

Unable to stop from grinning, I confirmed, "You're right. I did."

"You're not going to lay any *friend* bullshit on me this time, right?" I laughed as she added, "Not that I'm complaining, but would you care to tell me how the heck this happened? We kinda glossed over the fact that you showed up at my door crying in the middle of the night."

"Too busy fucking to talk, I guess."

Mia snickered, but wasn't going to let me get off that easily. "We can talk now..."

She was right. She deserved to know what was going on. I pulled her in closer—it was easier to have this conversation when I didn't have to look at her—and just spilled my guts.

I told her about my dream and confronting Frederick. How he 'fessed up about finding me after the accident, and how he brought me to the hospital, and stayed there with me for months, all the while lying to me, letting me believe I was really his. How my real parents had died, and how I couldn't even remember them, and the sadness, and the guilt, and the anger that followed because of it....

I talked for what felt like hours. The entire time, Mia simply lay by my side and listened, dancing her fingers across my skin, peppering the occasional consoling kiss against my chest. And when I was finally done talking, finally finished relaying every detail about the stupid, fucking, unbelievable drama that was my life, I realized I hadn't even shed a single tear.

I wasn't sad anymore.

I was *pissed.*

She let out with a huge, cleansing breath. "Wow. This is pretty big."

Understatement of the century. "Yeah."

"So what now? What are you going to do?"

"I really don't know." I exhaled a huge breath and ran a hand through my hair. "I think if I can get some details, this whole thing won't seem like it's happening to someone else. I never regretted losing my memory. Not once. But now, it's all I can think about. I want to remember so bad and it's frustrating that I can't."

"Maybe you should just accept your present reality. Maybe opening up the past will present too many questions that can't be answered."

"You sound like *him,* Mia. I need to know who I was. I had parents. They deserve to be remembered. Maybe finding out more about them will help me to do so."

* * *

Mia went into work late and I headed into Jersey. I needed to see the town I was from, needed to feel it.

I drove through the main drag, smiling at the sentinel of mom-and-pop shops that lined the street: Sweet Norman's Bakery. The Fill-Your-Belly Deli. Barbie's Bodacious Boutique. The town could have been Anyplace, USA, and it was jarring to realize it was where I'd come from. I always thought of myself as a city guy. I wondered if I'd walked these sidewalks in my youth, if I'd ever eaten breakfast at the King Neptune Diner, ever spent my allowance at Give Me Candy.

I started to come to the realization that a small town like this would probably have better information on my parents than any Google search, and turned my car toward the huge clock tower in the center of town.

Pulling into the lot of Norman's municipal complex, I found a spot in front of the courthouse. The focal point of the entire site was a humongous boulder, and it looked as though all the surrounding buildings had been built specifically to accentuate it.

I navigated the winding walkway until I found myself in front of the oversized glass doors of the library, and I wondered if my parents had ever brought me here as a child.

It was strange to be in a town I lived in for years but that didn't look familiar to me at all.

The library's entrance was huge, with an open-air concept and a domed glass ceiling. Two curved staircases framed the large rotunda and led to a second floor lined with bookshelves. One look at the ground level revealed even more rows of books as far as the eye could see, along with numerous, arched doorways that led into separate, smaller rooms. I walked the perimeter of the main entrance, taking note of the carved, wooden signs above each doorway—past the children's section, past the reference area—until I found what I was looking for. The Resource Room was located at the back of the building, and from the looks of the lower ceilings and metal shelving back there, made me think it was very possibly part of the original library. A much smaller and way less modern space than the impressively remodeled entrance.

The woman at the desk smiled as I made my way toward her. "Good morning! You look like you're a man on a mission. How can I help you?"

I matched her smile as I checked her nametag. "Good morning, Roberta. I'm looking for any information you might have on

Janet and Matthew Mason? Specifically their fatal car crash in April of two-thousand."

The woman's face fell. "Oh, I remember. So sad. Did you know them?"

I had to think about that for an extra second before I could answer. "No. Not personally. Did you?"

"I knew *of* them. Small town, you know," she said on a wink. "Well, if we have anything, it would be in our archives."

She waved her hand for me to follow her, so I trailed on her heels as she led me to a far corner of the room. There were rows and rows of metal shelves, filled with thousands of microfiche files that hadn't yet been converted to computer.

"This is every issue of The Norman Gazette published since nineteen-oh-eight." She scanned down the labels until she came to the section she was looking for. "And here we are. Right here is two-thousand. You said April, yes?"

"April twentieth. Yes." I swallowed hard as she pulled a few canisters of the shelf.

She led me over to a low desk with a bulky monitor where she loaded up the first film. She gave me a quick lesson on how to navigate through the pages before offering a pat on my shoulder. "I'm going to head over to my desk and do some sleuthing online while you scan through the microfiche. It's a slow day and you look like you could use the help."

"Thank you."

She left me to my research, and it only took a few minutes before I found the correct paper. It took over the entire front page of *The Norman Gazette*. Guess it was big news for such a small town.

Two Norman residents were killed in a traffic collision with a Freehold Shipping truck at 9:50 PM Wednesday night on Main Avenue at the intersection of Anthony Road. Weather conditions were severe.

The couple's car was determined to be driving at or near the speed limit, authorities say.

Matthew Mason, 45, and Janet Mason, 45, were killed instantly.

Their twelve-year-old son was a passenger in the vehicle. He remains in critical condition at Hackensack University Hospital.

The driver of the truck, Marcus Geist, was treated at Norman General for minor injuries. He was not under the influence of any substances at the time of the accident.

Two separate photos of my parents were embedded within the article, and I stared at the images of their smiling faces. It was hard to make out any detail—the pictures were small, on grainy newspulp, and the microfiche monitor wasn't exactly designed for optimum clarity. There was a third, larger photo at the bottom of the page—a semi-truck turned on its side surrounded by caution tape and the flashing lights of the surrounding emergency vehicles.

But I couldn't see the car that well, thankfully.

I scanned through a few more pages, but didn't find a follow-up story in any future papers. I did, however, find my parents' obituary:

MASON, Janet and Matthew

Mr. Matthew Thomas Mason and his wife, Janet Faith Mason (nee Coffey) of Norman were accepted by the Lord on April 20, 2000.

Matthew (b. 1/31/55), originally from Brooklyn, NY, was a regional sales manager for MetLife in New York City for over twenty years.

Janet (b. 11/11/54), a Norman native, was a beloved teacher in the English department of St. Nicetius Parochial High School. She received the Teacher of the Year award last spring, her third such honor in her twenty-three years as an educator.

Matthew and Janet were married on December 8, 1985.

Both Matthew and Janet were active members of their community. Matthew was co-chair of the Norman Department of Recreation as well as contributor to the Parks Department. Janet served on the board of The Norman Society. She is best known for spearheading the Beautification Project in 1991 which raised the funds necessary to facelift the downtown area.

They are survived by Matthew's mother, Emily, and their son, Lucas, also of Norman.

Services will be held from 4 to 8 PM at Malachi Bros. Funeral Home on April 24, 2000.

Funeral mass will be held at 10 AM at St. Nicetius Chapel on April 25.

They will be laid to rest at Christ Memorial Gardens immediately following the church service.

In lieu of flowers, please consider a donation to The American Stroke Association.

My breath hitched as my throat tightened. *My parents* had been lain out and buried and I wasn't even there. I hoped there were tons of people there to mourn them. I hoped they weren't forgotten.

Roberta came back just then so I was forced to pull myself together. "Oh, you found it!" she said, leaning over to scan her eyes over the document on the monitor. "Would you like me to print it out for you?"

"Yes. Thank you," I said through a scratchy throat. "Could you print this one too, please?" I scrolled back to the accident report as Roberta readily agreed.

"I was able to find a few articles online, if you'd like to see them."

"I would. Thank you."

Roberta sent the microfiche articles to the printer before leading me back to her desk. As the new pages churned out of the printer, she handed me a few sheets she'd already printed out.

The very first one was a picture of my mother and an older man flanking a teenage girl, the happy threesome holding a plaque between them. I checked the caption on the photo:

1990 Creative Writing Award recipient Layla Warren (middle) pictured with her father Kenneth (l) and her instructor, 1990 Teacher of the Year Janet Mason (r).

Wait. Kenneth Warren? The husband Kate left behind to be with my father? Shock reached out a cold dead hand and wrapped around my throat. I couldn't breathe.

I looked into the face of the teenage girl in the picture. She was wearing a smile that didn't reach her eyes. Guilt washed over me, but I had no idea why. It's not like I was the one responsible for her abandonment.

Frederick was.

In any case, this Layla person obviously knew my mother. I found my voice enough to ask Roberta, "Do you happen to know Layla Warren?"

"Of course. She's in here all the time. She's Layla *Wilmington* now, though." She put extra emphasis on the last name, which I guess was supposed to mean something. It didn't.

"Do you know where I can find her?"

"Well, she splits her time between here and California, but if she's in town, it's no secret where she lives. Everyone knows that house."

"I don't."

"Won't be hard to find. Just go straight up North Road and ask for Wilmington at the gate house. If security lets you through, they'll direct you from there."

CHAPTER THIRTY-NINE

After the third degree from the gatekeeper, I finally convinced him to simply call the Wilmingtons' house and tell them a friend of Layla's mother was here for a visit. Her curiosity must have been piqued, because it was only a brief conversation before the gatekeeper was hanging up and waving me in.

The directions he gave sent me up a long, winding street. I could only catch glimpses of the massive homes between the trees, but thankfully, the house numbers were all printed on small metal placards staked at the end of every driveway.

At the top of the hill, I came to a black, iron gate which opened before I could even hit the button on the intercom. Aside from the security fencing, the Wilmingtons must have had security *cameras*, too.

I navigated up the steep, twisting drive until a large, stone house came into view. I parked near the garage and made my way up the front walk.

An attractive, dark-haired woman was standing at the front door. She was smiling pleasantly enough, but her crossed arms showed that she was warily regarding this perfect stranger who had appeared out of the blue.

"Layla Wilmington?" I asked.

"Yes?"

"I'm Lucas Taggart." When she showed no spark of recognition, I clarified, "Frederick Taggart's son. I think you knew him as *Rick*."

Her eyes immediately tightened at the mention of my father's name. "*I* didn't know him at all. My mother did. And I haven't spoken to her in years."

"I know. That's why I'm here."

Her head cocked to the side, eyeing me curiously. There I was on her doorstep, Frederick Taggart's kid, about the right age to be *her mother's* son, too...

Her mouth gaped open as she asked, "Does that mean... Are you... Are you and I...?"

"No, no. Kate wasn't my mother." I couldn't blame her for putting the puzzle pieces together incorrectly. God, I was handling this thing all wrong. "In fact, Frederick's not my father either, I guess. My real parents were killed in a car accident back in two-thousand."

"Oh, I'm so sorry to hear that." She bit her lip as she crossed her arms over her chest again, warding off a chill. "Um, Lucas, was it? I don't mean to be rude, but I guess I don't understand why you're here?"

"It's Luke, actually. And I was hoping you had a few minutes to talk?" She opened her mouth, probably to offer me a polite excuse which would allow her to dismiss me the hell off of her front porch. I spoke up before she could. "I don't really know why I'm here either. I just... I guess I wanted to apologize. And I thought that maybe you'd know someone who knew my parents?"

Her brows furrowed, so I added, "They—*we*—lived in this town right up until the accident. When I was twelve."

"Wouldn't you know more than..."

"I have no memory of the first twelve years of my life." Her mouth dipped open in surprise as I met her eyes and added, "The accident did a number on my brain. Wiped out everything prior to that night."

She blinked a few times, trying to register my words. "Wait. This is too much information. Why don't you come inside. I'll put some coffee on."

She opened the door fully to escort me inside, and I was immediately greeted with an overzealous Golden Retriever, bouncing around at my feet, just itching to leap into my arms.

"Hooza! Don't even think about it!" she admonished.

The dog crouched low to the floor—butt waggling, paws tapping—a bundle of kinetic energy waiting to be unleashed, but he obeyed his orders. His tail thumped in double-time as I bent down to pet him and offer a few encouraging words about what a good boy he was. I ruffled his ears until he calmed down some and Layla was able to send him on his way.

"Sorry about him. He just loves to meet new people," she snickered as she led me to a solarium at the back of the house. "I hope you won't mind if my husband joins us for this conversation?" She directed her next question to a man occupying an easy chair in the corner of the large room. "Babe? You decent? We have a visitor."

I chuckled at that as her husband stood and turned toward me... and holy shit, it was Trip Wiley.

Yeah. *That* Trip Wiley.

What the hell? I was already nervous enough about coming here today. Now I was being greeted by a famous Hollywood movie star?

The situation was entirely surreal, but Layla offered the introductions as if her ridiculously renowned husband was just a normal person. "Luke, this is my husband, Trip. Trip, this is Luke Taggart." Her eyebrows rose as she added, "*Rick's* son."

The name didn't go unnoticed by the man, but he was kind enough not to make a huge deal about it as he held out his palm to me. "Nice to meet you, Luke."

I tried to be cool as I shook his hand, but Jesus. *Trip Wiley.*

His smile put me at ease, though, and made him seem like a regular guy, even moreso as he asked, "Care for a drink?"

"I'm already on it!" Layla called as she started to head out of the room.

Her husband must have been intuitive enough to realize that I was really in their house to speak to his wife, and halted her departure. "Lay, why don't you let me handle the drinks. I'm sure you and Luke have a lot to talk about." He lightly grasped her arm as he passed her by, asking over his shoulder, "Coffee good or is this a conversation for something stronger?"

I chuckled and answered, "Coffee's fine, thank you."

He gave me a thumbs up on his way out of the room.

I am in Trip Wiley's house and he just gave me a thumbs up.

Mia was gonna shit.

Layla directed me over to sit in a side chair. I immediately slumped into it, shaking my head at my feet as I said, "I wasn't expecting that." This entire meeting was bizarre enough without adding a famous person into the mix.

Layla waved off my nerves and took a seat on the sofa next to the chair I was sitting in. "Don't let it get to you." She leaned in conspiratorially to whisper, "The fame thing goes out the window pretty quick when you're tripping over his dirty clothes every morning."

I laughed, unexpectedly finding myself at ease with the whole situation.

"So, Luke," she started in cautiously. "You obviously came here today for a reason."

"Yeah. Yeah. Well," I was unsure how to begin. "I guess I should start with what I know." I took a deep breath and ran down the finer points. "I guess Kate and Frederick—Rick—started dating in nineteen-eighty-four. They broke up in eighty-eight, the same year I was born. I lived twelve years with Matthew and Janet Mason until that car accident in two-thousand, when I lost my memory."

"Wait. Janet Mason? My old English teacher?"

"Yes."

"Oh God. I'm so sorry for your loss. That accident rocked this entire town. Everyone loved her."

"Well, that's the other reason I came to you. You knew my parents. I can't say the same."

"And you want me to tell you about them?"

"If you wouldn't mind."

"Well," she looked toward the kitchen and smiled at her husband's back. "The first time Trip and I met, it was in her classroom, actually."

"Really?" I asked.

Trip must have been eavesdropping, because he snickered as he busted, "Doomed for all eternity from that day forward."

I chuckled as Layla rolled her eyes. "Aside from that, I don't know how much else I have to tell you. She was smart and funny… She never yelled, that much I do remember. She was calm, even in a roomful of dopey teenagers. She never talked down to us. She held us to some pretty high standards. And she was undoubtedly my favorite teacher."

"Mine, too," Trip piped in.

Layla took a deep breath and offered me a sympathetic smile. "I'm sorry, Luke, but I didn't know your mother *that* well. And I only met Mr. Mason a handful of times. I'm sure I could give you a couple names of people to get in touch with, though, if that will help."

"I'd like that. Thanks."

Her head cocked to the side, her eyes squinting in thought. "Why now? Why the sudden interest?"

"Well, I didn't know about their existence until now. All these years, I only knew Frederick as my father. He adopted me right after the accident, and never told me until yesterday that I wasn't his."

Trip returned to the living room carrying a tray of drinks. As we were fixing our mugs of coffee, the sound of singing came from the corner of the room. I looked toward it, and took note of a baby monitor on the side table.

"Welp," Trip said, drying his hands on his jeans. "I guess the baby's up. I'll get her."

"You just had a baby?" I asked Layla. "If you don't mind me saying, you look fantastic."

"Thank you, although my mirror would disagree with you." We both chuckled before she added, "And no, 'the baby' is almost three years old. But she's the youngest of five, so I guess she'll always be the baby."

"Five?" I was stunned at the idea of so many people in one house. "Where are they all hiding?"

"At the school down the street."

I checked my watch and was reminded that it was only two in the afternoon. "Oh. Of course."

Layla took a sip of her coffee, regarding me over the edge of her mug. "Luke?" she asked, getting back to the subject at hand. "While all this is fascinating, and I'm sorry you lost your parents, I guess I don't understand what any of this has to do with me."

We were both aware that she wouldn't know *that* much about my parents. I guessed it was time to fess up to the real reason I came here. "I wanted to apologize for the fact that the man I knew as my father all these years was responsible for *you* losing *your* mother." Despite my resolve, I started to well up. "He never told me the truth until yesterday. He said it's because he wanted me to remember on my own. He's sent me to every doctor in the city. He says he never gave up hope." It was no use. A tear streamed down my cheek. "But I can't forgive him. He lied! He lied to me for sixteen years!"

Layla grabbed a tissue from the box on the side table and handed it over as she rested her other hand on my knee. "Luke, you're being too hard on yourself. And your father, actually."

I swiped my nose with the tissue and tried to get myself under control. Jesus. How humiliating. I was blubbering like a maniac in the house of a perfect stranger. "My father is dead. You're talking about Frederick."

Layla shook her head. "No, Luke. Frederick's been your father for the past sixteen years. And from what I can tell after meeting you, he's done a fine job of raising you."

Trip came back into the room carrying a little girl upside down by her ankles, the dog leaping around at his feet. "Luke... This is Cameron. Say hello, Cam!"

A mop of blonde curls bounced on the top of her head as she waved and said, "Hewooo, Cam!"

Trip threw her over his arm and tickled her until she squirmed to be let down. The dog followed on her heels as she ran into a playroom off the solarium and straight toward a toy box, pulling out everything inside, talking to each toy as she did.

Trip finally realized that the stranger sitting on his couch was red-eyed and using up all his tissues. "Hey. Bad time? You alright?"

"She's cute," I said, trying to deflect the focus off of me.

Thankfully, my diversion tactics worked. Trip let out an exasperated breath as Layla rolled her eyes. "Thank you. She's a terror," she shot back on a laugh.

The comment was enough to jog me out of my sour mood. I gave a last swipe to my eyes and let out a sad chuckle.

"I'd better get in there before she tears apart the entire house. Hey, it was nice meeting you, Luke."

"Thank you. You, too. My girlfriend isn't going to believe me when I tell her where I was today." I didn't even think about it before referring to Mia as my girlfriend. It sounded right, though.

"Well, bring her on by sometime. Now that you know where to find us," he said on a wink. The guy had such a Hollywood grin but somehow, he made it look genuine.

I was speechless as he left the room. I finally turned back to Layla, and saw that she was eyeing me curiously. "I have something to show you," she said as she rose and went out to the hall. She came back a minute later holding a large framed picture toward me for my inspection. Five children. Different skin colors. Obviously not all of them were genetically theirs.

She pointed to three of the children. "This is Katherine, that's Terrence, and you've already met Cam. We made them," she added on a sly grin. Then she pointed to the two younger boys. "And these are our sons, Dayo and Zawadi." She smiled warmly as she looked down at the picture. "We *chose* them. These children are just as much ours as these are." She leaned the portrait against the sofa and sat back down as her words sunk in. As if I hadn't already gotten where she was going, she explained,

"A family isn't defined by bloodlines. I can understand why you feel betrayed that Frederick kept the truth from you, but you can't deny that he's done his best to raise you in a loving home."

"But what about having an affair with a married woman?" I asked. "That he destroyed an entire family? I can't forgive him."

"I assure you, my family isn't destroyed."

Oh man. What a shitty thing for me to have said. "I didn't mean to—I'm sorry, I—"

"I know what you meant. It's okay. But you don't owe me an apology. Even your father isn't entirely to blame. My mother... She had some problems back then. I won't lie and say growing up without her was easy, but I made my peace with it years ago."

Her admission made me smile. "You must have. I couldn't help but notice that you named your daughter after her."

"Well, it was my way of forgiving her. At least in my own heart. I'm... okay now." She gestured toward her husband before placing her hand at my knee again. "*We're* okay. You will be, too. I promise."

CHAPTER FORTY

Layla Wilmington sent me on my way with some names of her other teachers that were friendly with my mother back in the day. I didn't have it in me just then to follow up on any of the people on that list. I'd done enough research for one day.

She also gave me her phone number and asked me to keep in touch. I was grateful but confused. Why would she give her phone number to a random stranger? But then I realized the bizarre connection she and I had. We were almost family in a weird sort of way.

I was so frazzled by the events of the day, the overload of information, that I considered stopping in at a cool little lakeside pub I'd passed on the way home from Norman. But instead, I realized I was simply done with this day altogether. Exhausted, I headed back into the city, back to Mia's apartment.

She was still at work, so I did some shopping and whipped up some dinner, then waited for her to get home. But I fell asleep on the sofa before she could.

* * *

The next morning was Saturday, so Mia and I were able to indulge in a leisurely breakfast. We made love in the shower, and then I got to work frying up some potatoes and bacon at her stove. While cooking, I told her all about my encounter with Layla and Trip Wiley yesterday.

She couldn't quite believe it.

I placed our prepared plates on the island as Mia sat on a stool across from me, gaping in shock. "I knew he was local, but oh my God!"

"Yeah," I snickered. "I actually thought he lived here in the city."

"Was it weird? Did you totally lose your cool? I would have."

"No. Well, I mean, at first, yeah, but they were both really nice. Like regular people. I got over the fame thing within only a couple minutes. He's just a normal guy and his wife is really sweet."

"Hmm." She said, taking a bite of her eggs. "Is he as hot in real life?"

My fork froze midway to my mouth as I raised an eyebrow. "Watch it, Cruz."

After our breakfast, I dropped Mia off for her first therapist appointment. I didn't have anywhere to be afterward, so I ended up just going for a drive. I had more than a few thoughts to sort out. I replayed my conversation with Layla Wilmington yesterday, the things she'd said about my dad. Reluctantly, I had to agree that she was right.

He made it his goal in life to raise me with the best of everything. He took me in, this scrawny little geek, and he gave me a home. A stellar education. Had me trained in every skill imaginable, from martial arts to ballroom dancing.

Jesus Christ, he turned me into Bruce Wayne, for fuck's sake. I used to joke about it, but shit. I really was. Dead parents, endless wealth, the way I liked to think of myself as a superhero...

Without fully realizing I was doing it, I turned my car north and headed home.

* * *

My father was sitting alone in the den when I appeared in the doorway. He had his elbows on his knees and was turning a pocket watch around in his hands.

"Hey," I said warily, trying to gauge his mood, offer an olive branch.

He looked up at my greeting, and I felt guilty when I saw that his eyes were tinged with concern. "Hey."

"I'm sorry I didn't answer any of your calls," I said. "I know you worry." I'd turned my ringer off after the first attempt. It had been easy to ignore the rest after that.

"I figured you were okay. I just like to know it. Even if you're angry with me," he added, lowering a brow. "Thank you for at least texting me last night."

"You're welcome."

"Where have you been staying?"

I could have just as easily told him the truth, but I wasn't exactly feeling chummy with him right at the moment. I didn't want to get into the whole Mia thing right then anyway. "Does it matter?"

"No. No, I guess it doesn't." His eyes dropped to his feet after that. I took a seat on the leather couch next to him and adopted his same pose. "I'm really, really sorry about all this, Luke. In trying to avoid a big mess all these years, I made an even bigger one. I'd understand if you want to stay mad for a little while longer."

"I'm not mad, Pop." I meant it. He'd thrown my entire world into a meat grinder, but I'd already started to forgive him. It was too hard to stay angry at the guy. "I mean, I was, of course, but I'm not now."

"I only wanted the best for you. I'm sorry for assuming I was it."

"Pop, you were. You've been the best father ever." His words surprised me. My resentment was with the situation he'd created by lying to me. Falsehoods aside, our standoff didn't have anything to do with the amazing father he's been. "In fact, I'm glad to have the chance to thank you."

The old man was still beating himself up. "Thank me? For lying to you?"

"For saving my life."

We let the heaviness of my statement hang in the air between us, Pop nodding his head in acceptance. Just because I'd decided to put an end to the anger didn't mean I was ready to bury the subject, however. "I have a lot of questions, you know."

"Yes," he agreed. "Of course you would. I'll try to answer what I can."

"I guess I'm most curious about how... I mean... They just let you take me home?"

"You had no other family to take care of you. You were slated to go to a state facility. They were going to find you a foster home until someone could adopt you. I sort of... I was able to talk them into letting me be your foster father."

"You greased the wheels, you mean."

"Yes. But it's not like I paid them off. I just made a few sizeable donations that expedited the process. I still had to take all the classes, submit to a background check, and file the proper paperwork like any foster parent."

Fact was, I *really* didn't want to know how much he paid for me. I decided not to dwell on the new information, and changed the subject instead. "What's that?" I asked, pointing to the watch he'd been fiddling with.

"This was your father's."

He handed it over, and I immediately ran my fingertips over the engraved surface. From the look of it, it was pretty old. "It was my father's? How did you—"

"I didn't let them include it during the settlement of your parents' estate. It was one of the only things in their safe. Made me think it was something special."

"Shouldn't it have gone to my grandmother?"

"The money from the estate plus a hefty sum from my own pocket was put into an account for her. She's being taken care of."

My mouth gaped. "*Being?* You mean she's still alive?"

"Probably not. To tell you the truth, I really wouldn't know."

I found myself getting agitated all over again. "Well, why should you? Just throw some money at the problem and all is well, right?"

My father dropped his head and spoke to his feet. "That's not how it went down at all. I thought I was doing right by her. Honestly, Luke. I tried to make her as comfortable as possible."

"Alone."

"She'd be alone even if you were sitting right next to her. Apparently, she had one hell of a stroke back in the nineties, and she didn't know who anyone was. The nurses assured me of that. Please believe me, son."

Believe him? After all the lies he's told? He must have been kidding.

"Just tell me where I can find her."

CHAPTER FORTY-ONE

My grandmother's nursing home was out in Jersey. Shermer Heights, to be specific. As in, right down the street from the Shermer Heights Training Facility, the very same place I brought my clients a few times every year.

Yeah. I know.

The Sunshine Center was a fairly large complex which reminded me of a college campus. Small, assisted-living houses were spread out over rolling green lawns along the meandering drive until I came to the main building—a pale-yellow, Victorian-styled mansion with a large, wrap-around porch.

I parked in a spot marked VISITOR and made my way up the porch steps. There was a line of white rocking chairs, and a few residents were outside enjoying the early fall air. I gave them a wave before heading through the doors.

Inside was a small lobby with a reception area. There was a woman sitting at a desk behind a tall counter, partially hidden by a large fern. She stopped writing as I approached and greeted me with a smile. "Can I help you?"

"Yes, I'm looking for Emily Mason?"

She slid her chair over a few inches to get a better look, regarding me with skeptical eyes. "It's been a long time since she had any visitors."

Aaaand cue the guilt. "Yeah. Sorry about that. I'm uh... I'm her grandson, Luke Tag—Mason. Lucas Mason," I corrected.

The woman's eyes went wide. "Lukie? Oh my goodness! I can't believe how much you've grown! Look at you in your fancy suit!"

She came around to my side of the counter to give me a hug, but stopped when I asked, "You know me?"

Her cheery face dropped along with her arms. "It's Gloria. Gloria Kinney. You used to come in every week with your mother and father until they... until the accident. You don't remember me?"

"I'm sorry. I wish I could." When all she did was continue to stare at me, I cleared my throat and explained, "My memory's shot. That accident kinda messed up my brain."

I'd never had the experience of having to explain that I didn't remember someone right to their face before. I didn't enjoy it.

Thankfully, though, Gloria offered me a sympathetic smile. "Oh my gosh, I'm so sorry to hear that." She put a hand to her heart, not knowing what to say. "You know, your grandmother is here because of *her* memory loss, so it would seem the two of you have something in common." She chuckled before adding, "Sorry, that was a bad joke."

I smiled in spite of myself. It was hard not to like this woman. I was glad such a cheerful person was taking care of my grandmother. "I'd like to see her. I'm hoping she can fill in some blanks."

"Of course you can see her. But Lucas, I don't want you to get your hopes up. She can't even fill in her *own* blanks."

"Yeah. Yeah, I figured as much." I was afraid to ask, but there was only one thing I really needed to know. "Do you think she's... Is she happy anyway?"

Gloria sighed heavily. "Oh, sweetheart. There are days when I think she might be. I know she's comfortable, at least. At this point, that's the best anyone can hope for. We give her lots of attention and she gets exemplary care." Gloria pursed her lips for a moment before adding, "Yes. Yes, I think she's happy."

That eased my mind some. If I couldn't be the one to take care of her, at least the good people here had been.

She gave me a pat on my shoulder before escorting me down a long hallway. The walls were painted in a soothing neutral and the lighting was muted in a soft glow. I got the impression that the entire place had been built around the concept of silence. I guess after being alive on this noisy planet for so long, the residents were entitled to a little peace.

That was another thing I liked about this home. It wasn't a depressing weigh-station between life and death. It was a beautiful facility, classy and understated. A fine setting for anyone to live out their final days. I was proud that my parents had chosen it.

We reached my grandmother's room as a knot formed in the pit of my stomach. Would we recognize each other? Would the first sight of my only living relative cause my memory to come rushing back?

Gloria must have sensed my nervousness. A knowing smile broke across her face as she attempted to reassure me. "I think you're going to get along just fine." She gave a knock on the door before opening it, and any illusions I had about an instantaneous brain-repair disappeared. The woman I was looking at was a perfect stranger. Delicate, rosy skin hung on a petite frame, gray hair styled in a simple pageboy. Nothing outstanding about her, save for the mysterious smile playing at her lips.

She was sitting up in her bed, a knitted pink blanket across her lap, a few pillows propped behind her back. The TV was on but she was staring out the window. She almost looked... wistful.

"Emily?" Gloria asked softly. She gave me an encouraging nudge as she added, "Emily, you have a visitor."

At the sound of Gloria's voice, my grandmother looked toward us with a polite smile, and I was met with a familiar pair of brown eyes... I'd seen the same ones in my mirror every morning.

There was no anticipated spark of recognition, though. At least not for me.

I cleared my throat and offered a greeting. "Hi there." I didn't know if I should call her Grandma right off the bat. I wanted to, though.

Before I could tell her my name, her eyes lit up. "Matthew," she said without any hint of doubt.

My surprise at the welcome instantly gave way to regret for having to burst her bubble. "No, Grandma. I'm Luke. Matthew's son." I didn't know if she was a Grandma, a Nana, an Oma, or what, but I decided to just go for it. I'd never had a grandparent before but *Grandma* felt right.

She didn't acknowledge my correction and instead asked, "Cookies?"

I had no idea how to handle that one and looked to Gloria for guidance. Gloria smiled and spoke for me. "Yes, Emily. Luke brought some cookies. He left them at the front desk. I'll go get them." She gave me another pat on my shoulder as she explained, "She's addicted to Nilla Wafers. I'll go grab some."

I was pretty freaked out about being left alone with my grandmother, but what could I do? The woman needed cookies.

Gloria closed the door behind her and the two of us shared a silence. It wasn't awkward. It was just... still. For all my hectic life in the city, stepping back to just *be* was a welcome respite. I could see how my grandmother could be happy here.

I took a cleansing breath, trying to wrap my head around the situation. There was the slightest fruity scent permeating the room, and for one, brief second—and for the first time in my life—something seemed... *familiar*. I couldn't grasp what it was, and the recollection disappeared before it ever fully materialized.

Maybe it was wishful thinking.

Slowly, I made my way over toward my grandmother's bed. There was an upholstered chair nearby, so I took a seat.

Grandma eyed me curiously. "Hello, Matthew."

"It's Luke, Grandma," I reminded her. "Matthew's *son*."

"Yes."

Her certainty was clearly a defense against her embarrassment. On some small level, I think she was aware that her brain was betraying her (I knew *that* feeling all too well), and I felt guilty for pointing it out. Because who cared if she didn't know who I was? I wasn't here for me.

I smiled warmly, an attempt to put her at ease. "It's okay. It's been a long time. I was only twelve the last time I saw you. I can't expect you to remember me."

"Yes."

This was going nowhere fast. I'd already decided to stop correcting her, but I was discouraged at the thought that we wouldn't be getting anywhere by talking in circles.

Just then, Gloria came back with the promised cookies, asking, "So! How's everyone doing in here?"

I leaned back in my seat. "Getting acquainted, Gloria. Thank you." She handed me a plate with six Nilla Wafers arranged in a circle. My grandmother didn't even wait for them to hit the nightstand before scooping one into her mouth.

"Slowly, Emily," Gloria admonished. She shook her head on a smile before announcing, "Okay. I'll leave you two be. *If you need anything*," she stressed meaningfully, "there's a call button right there on the headboard."

Call button was a bit of an understatement. It was a bright red emergency button that would most likely summon every able-bodied human in the entire building within seconds. The adolescent part of me had an irrational desire to push it, just for shits and giggles. "Thanks, Gloria."

She gave me a wink before heading out of the room once more. "No problem. Have fun, you two."

My grandmother must have seen me eyeing up that button, because she raised her eyebrows and said, "I push it sometimes just to scare them."

"What?" I asked, busting out into a laughing fit. Holy shit. My grandmother was feisty as hell!

I waited for her to explain herself, but instead, she scarfed down another Nilla Wafer. "Cookie?" she offered, pointing to the plate.

"I wouldn't dream of it," I snickered back.

She lost interest in the remaining cookies and turned her attention toward the television. It was a rerun of an old *Let's Make a Deal*.

"I'm sorry I haven't come to see you," I said to her profile. She didn't acknowledge my comment, and I started to think she'd forgotten I was even here. Her face lit up as she began clapping excitedly, and I turned to see Monty Hall counting hundreds into a contestant's hand.

Correction: She didn't forget I was here. She had *no idea* I was here.

There were so many things I wanted to say to her. We'd missed out on a bunch of years together and I wanted nothing more than to make up for lost time. But I couldn't even get a proper conversation started.

I mentally chastised myself for my selfishness. As frustrating as her memory loss was for me, it must have been excruciating for her. Or hell. Maybe she didn't have the self-awareness to be bothered about it at all.

I curbed the impulse to sigh, and instead took a moment to glance around her room. "This is a nice place, right? You like it here, right?"

"Oh sure, sure."

Progress. At least she was speaking to me again.

"I noticed the walls are pink. They match your blanket. You like pink, Grandma?"

She finally turned back toward me to answer, "My wedding dress."

My wedding dress was pink? Is that what she was trying to say? I figured she must have misremembered. But I wasn't going to call her out for it. "Oh yeah?"

"Yes," she said, nodding her head. "A pink suit. Like Jackie Kennedy."

I was pretty sure my grandmother had gotten married a few decades before Jackie was ever on the scene. I was trying to think of something else to talk about when she piped in with, "Do you want to see a picture? I have lots of pictures."

She raised an unsteady arm to point a trembling finger toward the low bookshelf behind me. There, among the porcelain knick-knacks and silk flowers... were three photo albums.

My heart sped up as I immediately went over and pulled them off the shelf. I sat back down on the chair and put two of the books at my feet, not quite believing what I was holding. Photo albums! Why didn't I think of that?

With shaking hands, I opened the book on my lap. Sure enough, the first picture I saw was an aged, black-and-white shot of a very young man and woman on the front steps of a brick building. The woman was holding a bouquet of flowers... and was wearing a pale suit. Even in black and white, I could tell it was very probably pink.

I snickered to myself. Grandma knew what she was talking about after all.

I read the date printed along the bottom border of the photo. "April first, Nineteen-fourty-nine."

Grandma craned her neck toward the album, so I put it next to her on the bed. She ran a delicate finger over the man's cheek, but didn't say anything.

"Do you know who that is?" I asked.

She merely smiled in response.

"That's your husband, Grandma." *And my grandfather.*

"Lucas."

"Yes?" I answered, excited that she remembered who I was. But when I looked at her face, her smiling eyes were still trained on the photograph, her fingers still trembling over her groom.

My eyes went wide in tandem with my gaping jaw. "Wait. His name was Lucas?"

She didn't answer, and simply turned the pages. There were shots of my grandparents on their honeymoon (somewhere tropical; I couldn't specify the location), in front of a modest ranch home (somewhere in suburbia), and at numerous parties, surrounded by friends. Grandma would smile at certain shots, but she didn't bother explaining why she found them so endearing. I think she just liked returning the expressions on the faces of the people smiling back at her.

It wasn't until we reached the end of the album that we came across a colorized photo of a newborn baby. "Matthew," she said proudly.

I'd been wondering how if my grandmother had such terrible memory issues, she could possibly remember names and faces. But she'd probably looked through these albums hundreds of times. The names were printed right there under most of the photos anyway.

Because the book had been arranged chronologically, I was confident the next album would bring me up to date. I practically dove for the second book, fully anticipating that I'd find what I was looking for. Sure enough, it was another chronological compilation of photos, lovingly arranged on the pages. I flipped through them, taking in the images of *my father* as he grew throughout the years. Little league games. Playing in the dirt. Swimming. Building a snowman. High school graduation. The older he got in the pictures, the more I could see the resemblance between us. It was eerie, staring into a stranger's face and seeing my own.

The third album was much larger than the other two, and I was pretty sure I knew what I'd find inside. Even still, I was almost afraid to hope. I wanted so badly for the photos inside to be of *me*—of my *father* and me, my *mother* and me—and the fear that they could be of anything else almost had me abandoning ship.

I took a deep breath and opened the book.

A wedding photo. My mother and father. My mother in a poofy, white dress. My father in a simple black tux. Standing in front of a church. Smiling. Happy.

Alive.

My father had to be about the same age I was now, and yeah. We looked like we could be brothers. I'd never seen anyone that looked so much like me before.

There were a few pages of random photos from throughout their early life together, until... I turned the page... and there I was.

A chubby little fart sitting on a red shag rug, chewing on the plastic beak of a stuffed Big Bird.

A laughing baby maniac sitting in a high chair with spaghetti sauce smeared all over my face.

A smiling toddler kissing a German Shepherd.

A toothless pre-schooler laying in a pile of leaves... my mother and father lying at my side.

The sight of that first family photo is what did me in. I mean, seeing any one of those pictures could have affected me just as strongly—it was the biggest compilation of pictures I'd ever seen of myself—but seeing the three of us together? The happiness that I wanted to remember so badly but couldn't?

It broke me.

"Handsome boy."

My grandmother's voice brought me back to the present, and I realized *I* was the one who'd forgotten *she* was there this time. "Yes, Grandma. He sure is."

I swiped a tear from my eye and moved the album closer so we could both have a better view. Page after page, forgotten memory after forgotten memory. I'd never seen so many pictures of myself as a little kid. In one hour, I'd filled in more missing pieces about my life than Frederick ever had in all of the past sixteen years. Although, I guess he'd planned it that way.

Thing was, though, it's not because he was trying to deceive me. I knew that now. The love I saw in that album was the same love Frederick had given to me all these years. The realization helped the last of my annoyance to disappear as I turned the pages, my entire world finally coming together.

The albums were a treasure trove. A revelation. A gift. I wanted to go through each and every picture all over again in all three books, gather up my history and cherish every detail of every captured moment.

I flipped back to the leaf picture and pulled it from the page. "Do you mind if I take this one with me? I'd like to make a copy. I'll get the original back to you."

"Oh, you're leaving?"

"Just for now. But I promise I'll be back."

I stood and retied my scarf before leaning over and giving her a soft kiss on her parchment cheek. I had so many questions that I knew she wouldn't be able to answer. I wanted to ask them anyway.

But my questions could wait. "Thank you for hanging out with me today, Grandma."

"Did you bring cookies?"

I picked up the dish from the nightstand and held it out toward her. "Of course I did." She promptly swiped one off the plate and took a bite as I asked, "Would you mind if I came back again tomorrow?"

Grandma turned her attention back toward the game show on her TV as she answered absently, "Oh sure, sure."

I just smiled and said, "Sounds perfect."

CHAPTER FORTY-TWO

True to my word, I headed back out to Jersey the following day. Only this time, Mia came with me. I was excited for her to meet my grandmother, but I had an important stop to make first.

Christ Memorial Gardens was the cemetery listed in my parents' obituary. I'd already done some research online to find out exactly where on the property they were located, so I navigated my car to the "Holy Spirit" section of the sprawling grounds.

I put the car in park and cut the engine, taking an extra minute to psych myself up for what I was about to do.

"Are you going to be okay?" Mia asked, cutting through the silence.

I turned to look at her, sitting there in her pretty blue dress, and gave her a pale smile. It was cute that she felt the need to get all dolled up to meet my family. "Yeah. I'm ready." I reached over to grab her hand before adding, "You sure you don't want to come with me?"

Mia and I had discussed the situation on the ride over. She was torn between wanting to be right by my side to support me and wanting to let me have a private moment with my parents. Staying in the car was our compromise.

She placed a hand at my scruffy jaw and said, "This is something you should do alone. I'll be right here waiting for you when you get back."

I kissed her hand and smiled into her warm chocolate eyes, grateful for every single thing about her.

I stepped out into the crisp, sunny day, and made my way up a rolling hill toward a huge oak tree, one of only a few dotted across the expansive, park-like landscape.

It took me a few minutes to locate the right spot. But then, a few paces from the tree, I found what I was looking for. My throat tightened at the sight of my parents' names on a shiny, gray stone as a mixture of sadness and remorse sluiced through my chest. I placed the bouquet of flowers on the ground and crammed my hands in my pockets.

I didn't quite know what to say.

Some birds passed overhead, so I looked up, took a breath, felt the sun on my face.

Squatted down, absently pulled some stray weeds away.

Ran my fingers over the carved names, the dates.

Sat down on the cool grass and stretched my legs.

Drew one up and rested an arm over my knee.

Twirled a dandelion at the tips of my fingers.

"Mom."

The word sounded foreign coming out of my mouth; I'd never called anyone Mom before. At least not that I could remember.

"Mom, Dad, I'm sorry it took so long to come see you. I'm sorry I can't even remember you."

I tossed the weed aside and sat up a bit straighter.

"I'm going to try, though. I'm going to keep up with my mind exercises, going to try and bring it all back. I never wanted to, you know. The accident. I never wanted to see it. But I'm not afraid anymore. It was worth it. If seeing it will help me to remember anything about you, then I'll relive it every night if I have to.

"I saw something last night, Dad. You were teaching me to ride a bike. Mom was there, too. It was spring, I think. The bike was green. I could feel you right there with me, cheering me on. I felt safe. And proud. The thrill when you finally let go. The freedom of doing it on my own. The smile on Mom's face.

"I know it wasn't just a dream. I know it was real."

I took a deep breath and ran a hand through my hair, absorbing the quiet, collecting my thoughts.

"Grandma's fine, you should know. She's being taken care of. I'm going back to see her again later this afternoon. Mia's coming with me. Mia's my girlfriend. If you're watching over me, I guess you already know that. And if you have any power up there... Do me a favor and make sure I don't screw this up, okay? She's pretty fantastic. Frederick's taking us out to dinner later so he can meet her. I wish you could meet her, too.

"Frederick's been great. We've got some stuff to sort out, but you should know that he's been an amazing father, gave me the best of everything, took care of me, loved me. I think you'd be happy to know that a guy like that stepped in for you. I think you would have chosen him if you could. Heck, maybe you did.

"It's hard, learning how to forgive him. The hardest thing I've ever had to do. He lied for all these years. He wanted me to forget you, and I did! But he's my father. And I love him. And I know we'll get past this. We have to. I know you would want me to."

There was a stinging behind my eyes, but I held the tears at bay. Despite my resolve, my voice started to shake anyway. I couldn't stop talking, though. I still had too much I needed to say.

"I'm so sorry that I've forgotten you. But it's not like you're completely lost to me. It's not like you're gone. Does that make sense?

"I can feel you. I could always feel your love, all these years, even if I wasn't aware that it was you. You're the voice in my head. If my conscience has a voice, it was always yours, even if I didn't know it. I hope you're watching over me. I hope I make you proud. I'm going to try every day to be a good man."

The tears streamed down my face, so I swiped my eyes with my sleeve, took a deep breath, and pulled myself together.

I placed a palm on the grass and directed my next words toward the earth under my hand. "Thank you for my life."

EPILOGUE
January

The house was packed.

It seemed as if every person Mia had ever met in her life was here to celebrate her promotion. This was hardly the "little get together" she said it was going to be. Aunts, uncles, cousins, neighbors... Mrs. Cruz's little cape was practically busting at the seams.

Mia's mom went a little overboard on the food, but that was nothing new. I couldn't remember a time in the past three months when Mrs. Cruz *didn't* cook enough to feed an army.

Speaking of remembering... I've been keeping up with my mind exercises. Nothing revelatory to report, but every once in a while, a small piece of my past will come back to me. Any new vision was always a gift. And as bad as my grandmother's memory was, sometimes she was able to confirm my stories with a convoluted history of her own.

My grandmother wasn't well enough to make it to the party today, but Mia's mom already put together a takeout container to bring with me to go to The Sunshine Center later.

And of course, she included a shit-ton of cookies.

A week didn't go by when I wouldn't stop in for a visit. Normally, Mia came with me. Even my father came a few times. I was amazed to see how great he was with her. He really had a knack for pulling the best conversations from her. It was how I learned things about my parents like how my father loved his job in the city and how my mother loved old movies.

I guess there's something to be said for genetics.

Swan. Inc. is still going strong. I've recently added group therapy to my program, and so far, my clients have been responding fairly positively. I started going back to therapy myself. Obviously, I had lots to sort out.

Pop and I were able to find some common ground on the whole lying thing. We'd come to an understanding about why he did it, and I wasn't angry about it anymore. It was too hard to stay pissed at him anyway. I mean, look at him. How could I stay mad at a guy who was currently chomping down spare ribs like he was going for a record?

"Have you tried any of this food yet?" he asked, holding up his loaded plate. "Maribel must be a wizard."

I chuckled and said, "Yeah, she's a great cook. Try the *tostones*." I'd been a New Yorker for most of my life—thereby having access to every type of food imaginable—but it was only through Mia's family that I learned to fall in love with Puerto Rican cuisine. Last week, her mom made *asopao*, and it was the greatest thing I'd ever put in my mouth.

Second greatest.

I went over to Mia and put my arms around her, took a huge inhale against her hair, and said, "One helluva 'little get together,' Cruz."

She smiled over her shoulder as she explained, "Puerto Ricans will use any excuse to throw a party."

I'd learned that all too well over the past months. Mia's family was huge, and they insisted on getting together on the regular. I was getting pretty good about remembering all the cousins' names. Jared, however, only seemed interested in remembering *one* cousin's name. He was currently getting a little too cozy with Estella over near the dessert table.

"Well, you deserve it, veep."

Mia had officially gotten the Vice President job two weeks ago, and I couldn't be more proud. She worked really hard for this promotion. She deserved it.

"Oh hey," she said, smiling wickedly at me. "I forgot to tell you. Harry called me today."

"Harry?" I asked, having no idea who she was talking about.

"From that TV station out in Brooklyn."

Oh yeah, right. My brows tightened as I asked, "Why would he call you?"

"To let me know I got the weather girl job."

We both broke into hysterical laughter at the news until I turned her in my arms and pulled her to me in a tight hug, snickering, "Too bad you had to decline. You looked damn cute in that rain hat."

"Who says I declined?" she teased, before planting a kiss on my cheek.

Needless to say, I was kinda crazy about this woman. And hell, she was just as crazy about me. The *real* me, not my fake "stud" act. Fact is, true confidence comes from within. Even through all my bullshit swagger, I'd always actually known I was a one-woman kind of guy. I just hadn't ever found any one woman I'd been willing to commit to.

Until now.

I swiped some hair behind her ear. "I got an interesting phone call today, too."

"Oh you did, did you?"

"Yep." I arched an eyebrow and said, "*Paisley* called this morning. I let it go to voicemail. Apparently, she and Blake are getting married."

"No kidding?"

"Yeah. Next fall."

Mia shot me an impressed smile as she nodded her head. "Good for her. That's great!"

"It really is."

She smoothed a hand up my chest, her face a mask of innocence to ask, "Does it totally mess with your anal-retentiveness that she never finished your course?"

I couldn't help but snicker. "*Attention to detail.* And I'd like to remind you that you never completed *your* final task, either, wiseass."

Her eyelids lowered as she grabbed my butt. "Because we've been too busy fucking all the time."

I laughed in agreement before getting back to the subject at hand. "Well, your present kind of covers it. It isn't happening until tomorrow, though."

She pulled back to look at me. "Wait. My present is a 'happening?' I'm not sure I like the sound of that."

"I'm invoking our trust rule, here."

"Oh *dios mio*, I'm afraid to ask."

My lips twitched as I tried to contain my smile. "We've got an appointment to go indoor rock climbing." Her eyes went wide as I added, "Don't worry. I've got you covered." I pulled a rectangular box off the gift table and handed it over.

Mia eyed me skeptically as she unwrapped her present... a new pair of designer climbing shoes. Her face completely lit up at the sight of them. "I love you!"

I raised an eyebrow at her. "Even when I don't buy you new kicks, right?"

"Of course." Her face scrunched as she slipped a hand around my neck. "But maybe you should keep doing it just to be sure."

What can I say? The woman loved her shoes.

We needed some air. Mia's apartment was nothing more than a maze of boxes at this point, and we were both feeling a bit claustrophobic.

We were gearing up for our move to a much larger place—a row home on 40th Street with a view of the east river. I'd recently rented some office space right down the street from Manhattan Media, so the Murray Hill neighborhood was right near both of our jobs, mere steps to our bases of operations in Times Square. The latest plan was to live in the city during the week but spend the weekends at my father's house out in Greenhaven. The old man still had separation anxiety, after all. But I didn't mind. It was a small price to pay back for all that he'd done for me over the years.

We took a break from our packing and decided to go for a walk through Central Park. We earned it. Besides, it was a beautiful crisp winter afternoon, not the wind-tunnel freeze January usually was in the city. A few other humans were taking advantage of the unseasonably mild day—jogging, riding bikes, feeding the birds—and it was enough to dupe me into believing spring would be here sooner rather than later.

When we reached the big rock at the edge of Strawberry Fields, Mia pulled me to sit down with her so we could do some people-watching.

"Look at this guy," she said almost immediately, nodding her head toward an old man harassing a squirrel.

"Yeah, what a welly beacho."

"We need to work on your accent."

We chuckled as she planted a kiss on me, saying, "I need to show you something."

I waggled my brows and asked, "Is this 'something' presently contained within this green coat?"

I slid my fingers up her thigh but she laughed as she shoved my hand away, chastising, "Yes but not *there*."

She pulled a black notebook from her coat pocket and handed it to me. I recognized it right off; it was the journal I'd given her back in August, at the start of our eight weeks together.

My hands went up in defense. "No way. I can't read this thing. It's your innermost private thoughts."

"I know. That's why you need to read it."

She flipped the book open to the first page and handed it over. I was still opposed, but couldn't help but peek at what she had placed right in front of my eyes. It was kind of unavoidable to notice what she'd written:

Lucas Taggart is the hottest guy I've ever met in my life.

Well, I mean, if she really wanted me to read it, who was I to say no?

The entries in her journal ranged in tone from confused attraction to angry denial to willing capitulation. She'd logged every moment we'd spent together, every good, bad, and ugly thing that had happened between us.

It was the most beautiful thing I'd ever seen.

I was smiling like a total dork by the time I got to the end. As I turned the final page, a folded piece of paper fell out and landed at my feet. Mia picked it up and unfolded it onto my lap, a photocopied monologue from *The Princess Bride* with parts that had been highlighted in fluorescent yellow. I'd just started reading it when Mia shot me a wicked grin and stood up. Before I knew what was happening, she'd climbed onto the rock, cleared her throat, and started reciting the words from memory:

"I love you, and I know this must come as something of a surprise..."

Holy shit. She was really doing this.

"...since all I've ever done is scorn you and degrade you and taunt you, but I have loved you for several hours now, and every second, more."

I stood up to face her. At first, I'd been reading along with her speech, but it only took a few seconds for me to ditch that idea. I stuck the paper in my pocket to concentrate solely on my beautiful, brave girl.

"I thought an hour ago that I loved you more than any woman has ever loved a man, but a half hour after that I knew that what I felt before was nothing compared to what I felt then."

A few people had started to gather near me to watch her speak. Rather than shy away from the attention, Mia proceeded to ham up her performance. Her body flailed dramatically as she recited her lines. "There is no room in my body for anything but you. My arms love you, my ears adore you, my knees shake with blind affection. My mind begs you to ask it something so it can obey. Do you want me to follow you for the rest of your days? I will do that. Do you want me to crawl? I will crawl. Anything there is that I can do for you, I will do for you; anything there is that I cannot do, I will learn to do. For me there is only you."

She really laid it on thick to deliver the final line, clasping her hands to her chest and pleading, "Darling *Lucas*, adored *Lucas*, sweet perfect *Lucas*, whisper that I have a chance to win your love."

She gave an elaborate curtsey as the handful of spectators broke into spontaneous applause.

I, however, was too mesmerized that I couldn't do anything but stare in shock. Finally, I held out my hand to help her down off the rock, and pulled her into my arms. I kissed her, slow and sweet and deep and devoted, reveling in the fact that she was mine. I was such a lucky bastard.

By the time we came up for air, the crowd had dispersed, leaving the two of us to our own private world once again. Mia's face was beaming, so proud and unashamed. "So, how'd I do?"

"Amazing," I answered, awestruck by this incredible woman in my grasp.

"Good enough to earn a dirty water dog with the works?"

The question was unexpected, but then again, there was nothing predictable about Mia Cruz. The girl was amazing in every way, and for some reason, she loved me.

I dipped my head close to hers and ran my nose against her hair, stealing a greedy inhale before I whispered against her ear.

"As you wish."

THE END.

About the Author:

T. Torrest is a fiction writer from the U.S. She has written many books, but prays that only a handful of them will ever see the light of day. Her stories are geared toward readers of any age that know how to enjoy a good laugh and a dreamy romance.

Ms. Torrest was a child of the 80s, but has since traded in her Rubik's cube for a laptop and her Catholic school uniform for a comfy pair of yoga pants. She's a pop-culture junkie, a movie aficionado, and an enthusiast of talking about herself in the third person. A lifelong Jersey girl, she currently resides there with her husband and two sons.

She also really digs it when she hears from readers, and is known to use words like "dig" in a non-sarcastic way. You can find out more about her books at her website: www.ttorrest.com

If you haven't already done so, please come "like" the TTorrest Author Page on FACEBOOK
We have lots of fun discussing books, movies... and the eighties!

You can also follow me on GOODREADS

Or drop by my website to say hi: www.ttorrest.com
and join my mailing list to receive bonus chapters!

I love hearing from readers and am curious about your book club discussions.

If you'd like to drop me a personal message, my email is:
ttorrest@optonline.net
I always do my best to write back!

And lastly, as always, if you enjoyed reading this book, I ask you to tell your friends, loan it out, and please, please leave a review.

TALK ABOUT IT. On Facebook, on Goodreads… any time you're asked about a funny read, a swoony romance, or an awesome book boyfriend.

Word of mouth is *truly* the only way we indie authors survive.

EASTER EGGS

I swear one of these days, I'm going to trip myself up with all these connections.
Someday. Just not today. ;)

Yes, Luke is acquainted with Justice Drake from S.L. Jennings' TAINT. Drake is a crazy-hot, hands-on sex therapist, and you can find his story at all major retailers (Thanks for the loan, Syreeta!)

Luke has some of his clients stay at the *TRU Times Square.* (REMEMBER WHEN Trilogy)

Mia works at *Manhattan Media,* an advertising firm first mentioned in DOWN THE SHORE. So, yes, Victoria and Mia are work colleagues.

Luke arranges a photo shoot at a past client's SoHo loft. That client is Samantha, Livia's artist friend from DOWN THE SHORE.

Wyatt McAllister is now manager of the Shermer Heights Training Facility. In 2003, he was only an assistant manager in BREAKING THE ICE. (P.S. Now I'm dying to write his and Jane's story! LOL)

Luke takes Jared to the driving range at the Shermer Heights Country Club (RW3, A WAY TO GET BY)

Barney's personal shopper, Corinne Cavanaugh, is the sister of Diana (RW2, 3) and Virginia (AWTGB).

Kate Warren and Rick were first mentioned in RW.

When Luke is cruising through Norman, he drives past Give Me Candy (BTI) and the King Neptune Diner (RW).

Luke visits the Norman Municipal Complex—and has to navigate around Norman Rock—to do some research at the library. Afterward, he considers stopping in at The Westlake Pub for a drink. (BTI)

Luke's biological mother, Janet Mason, is Trip and Layla's English teacher in RW. (Sorry I had to kill you. Janet!)

Malachi Bros. Funeral Parlor is a familiar place for any Norman natives. (RW3, AWTGB)

The Backlot is a rag mag first mentioned in RW3.

Acknowledgements:

First up, I've gotta give a big huge sloppy kiss to Moody Haopshy for the inspiration behind this story. He tossed the plot out casually a couple of years ago, and I just fell in love with the idea of a not-quite-superhero version of a modern-day Bruce Wayne. I have people giving me story ideas all the time, but this is the only one I ever felt compelled to run with. Thanks, Mood!

Michelle Mankin, who—while in the middle of readying for her own release, mind you—volunteered to read through this story when it was nothing more than 40,000 jumbled words of mind ramble. Her encouragement and advice gave me the spark to keep going on this book at a time when I thought I'd be shelving it.

Heather M. Orgeron, who is not only a fantastic cheerleader and confidant every day, but gave me the best advice for staying on track while penning a male POV: "Write with your dick, TT!"

Emily Hemmer, Erika Gutermuth and Kari Matthes, all of whom refused to believe this book would be anything less than fabulous, and offered encouragement every step of the way.

My cabal of author and blogger friends who are always there to offer encouragement or lend an ear for bitching purposes.

Ivette W. Portillo for her incomparable help with the English-to-PR translations!

My beta readers! Stevie Kisner, Michelle Mankin, Kari Matthes, Joanne Cowan, Kelly Moorehouse, Anna Roselli, Dawn Nicole Costiera, Roxie Madar, Faith Andrews, Heather Orgeron, Ivette Portillo, Jennifer Mirabelli, Erika Gutermuth.

And of course, wizard-woman Hang Lee for yet another amazing cover.

REAL-LIFE PEOPLE: Huge thanks to my friends and family! They cheer me on from the sidelines, are always interested in what I'm working on, and have provided a support system far beyond the call of duty. I'm grateful that there are too many people in this category for me to name here.

You know who you are.

COMING SOON!

FAREWELL, MY SUMMER LOVE

An 80s romantic comedy that takes place over multiple summers at the Jersey shore.

Turn the page for an excerpt!

FAREWELL, MY SUMMER LOVE
Excerpt from Chapter 3

We spent the first ten minutes of our Big Night Out spying on the party from the dunes. A bunch of people were stationed mid-beach, gathered around a small fire drinking, their laughter drowned out by the classic rock station on the boombox. I didn't recognize a single face and it was definitely intimidating. I wasn't used to going to parties—especially beer parties—where I knew exactly *no one*. Vince wasn't even there yet. Plus, the majority of the fifteen or so people around that fire were guys. Like, full-on, older *guys*.

Katrina was playing the faithful friend, refusing to leave my side. She was either new to this scene herself or was being anti-social for my sake. In any case, I got the impression that she and I could have spent the next twelve hours in that grass before we'd be brave enough to join in.

Kim wasn't having it. "Okay, this is ridiculous. I'm not spending my entire night waiting for you two to grow some balls. C'mon. Just hold your head up and act like you belong."

I bit my lip and asked, "Won't the older kids be mad that we're crashing their party?"

"Nah," she answered, smirking just the slightest bit. "Everyone's the same age down the shore. In the summertime, at least."

I met Katrina's eyes and we both gave a shrug. What did we have to lose?

We followed behind Kimmy, our bare feet digging into the cool sand with each step. "Hey guys!" she greeted casually, plopping down cross-legged in the middle of an unoccupied towel. Katrina followed suit but I, wearing a skirt, however, had to be a little

275

more cautious while lowering myself to the empty space next to them.

The "guys" she greeted were three of the most opposite-looking people I'd ever seen in my life. One had darker skin and shoulder-length brown hair. I couldn't tell if he was black, white, or what, but whatever he was, he was definitely cute. The guy in the chair to his left had shaggy blond hair and was wearing nothing but a pair of swimshorts. There I was, trying to piece together an appropriate party outfit, and Blondie over there was practically naked.

"'Bout time you finally got here. I didn't know if you were gonna make it."

I looked over at the sound of such a deep voice and sized up Bachelor Number Three. He'd been aiming his statement at Kimmy, but he was looking directly at me.

Even from such limited light, I could tell his eyes were a gorgeous, striking blue. Like, full-on, Rob-Lowe *blue*. The movie-star comparison didn't stop there, and I was stunned into silence as I noted even more similarities: Dark brown hair, tan skin, and a gleaming white grin that forced me to look away. I was too disarmed to continue making eye contact, and instead focused on the navy blue *Camden Aquarium* logo blazoned across his gray sweatshirt.

Wow.

Kimmy didn't notice that her friend had just melted me into a puddle, and instead put her hands on her hips to announce, "So who's gonna give me a beer?"

Gray Sweatshirt laughed as he dug around in a Styrofoam cooler and came up with a can of Budweiser, tossing it in her direction. He had these great, thick, expressive eyebrows, one of which was raised as he asked, "Is your sister allowed to have one?"

"Sure," Kimmy granted magnanimously. Then she turned toward Katrina to admonish, "Just one, though."

Kat brushed off the rebuke, trying to look cool as she accepted the can from Gray Sweatshirt's hand. It didn't seem as though drinking was a common occurrence for my new friend, but from the looks of it, this seemed to be standard high school activity. I guessed the both of us would need to get used to it.

"And what about your friend?" he asked, aiming those deadly blue eyes in my direction again. "Does she drink?"

Katrina's mouth gaped as I silently implored Kimmy not to out me as the fourteen-year-old I actually was. When I saw the slight curl of her lip, I knew she'd be playing along.

Before she could answer for me, however, I blurted out a response. "Yes, actually," I said. "She's able to speak, too."

That made Gray Sweatshirt chuckle. "Oh she does, does she?"

"Yep. She can answer questions and everything."

I really couldn't tell you where the balls were coming from. I guess the fact that he thought I was older gave me the confidence to *act* older. And my God! I was totally doing it! I was flirting with this cute high school guy!

He raised an eyebrow and dipped his chin. "Maybe I should've asked her instead of her friend?"

"Mm hmm." I had my lips pressed together in an attempt to avoid the fit of nervous laughter that was threatening to erupt, but I couldn't hold it in for long. Before I knew what was happening, I was grinning like a complete fool. I was about to confess everything right then and there, but he spoke up before I could.

"Well, I apologize, Kim. You're absolutely right. I guess I was just too intimidated by her gorgeous smile to remember my manners."

I choked on my own breath as Blondie piped in to bust his chops. "Dude. She's been here for all of three minutes and you're already hitting on her?"

I almost fainted. Or died of embarrassment. Or jumped his bones.

Gray Sweatshirt elbowed his buddy in the ribs. "I'm not hitting on her. I'm simply making conversation, asshole."

"Yeah right."

The thought that this cute guy was hitting on me was too much to handle. The heat rose in my cheeks, and I was grateful for the dim lighting. I was still reeling from the compliment, trying to reacquire my previous sense of chill, but it was a hopeless cause. It's impossible not to smile when someone compliments your smile. I hoped I didn't look like a conceited snob for continuing to do so.

Thankfully, Gray Sweatshirt launched into a Q and A before I could overanalyze my facial expressions. "Does Kim's friend have a name?"

Screw the confession. I was having too much fun. "Kim's friend's name is Lindsey."

"Well, I'm Jason Delaney. Nice to meet you, Kim's friend Lindsey."

JASON. Rhymes with totally hot. Not really, obviously, but damn. Just... yum.

He cracked open a can of beer before handing it over, asking, "So how come we've never met before?" His devilish grin almost had me bursting out of my skin.

Kim jumped in to save me before I could go *Alien*. "You haven't met her before because this is her first time here."

"Shoe bee?" Long Hair asked.

I had no idea what kind of secret code he was speaking in, but Kim and Katrina both shook their heads in the affirmative.

Kim leaned into me and gestured her finger at Long Hair. "Lindsey, the loud mouth, long-haired hippie over there is Wax, the naked blond next to him is Christian, and the guy *totally hitting on you* may have introduced himself as Jason, but everyone calls him Jase."

Couldn't she have simply murdered me and spared me the mortification?

All three of the guys gave a wave at the introductions as Kim continued pointing to everyone around the rest of the circle, cataloging a list of names I knew I'd never remember. They were all in the middle of their own conversations anyway, so the pressure was off to play social butterfly.

Katrina chugged down the last of her beer and asked, "Hey Lindsey. Wanna walk down to the water?"

"Sure," I said, getting to my feet and dusting the sand from my legs.

I was looking for a place to leave my half-emptied beer can when Jason—*Jase*—hopped off his chair. "Here. I'll put it in the cooler so it'll stay cold for when you get back."

I said "Thanks" among the stifled snickers of his friends, busting his chops for his continued prowling.

I chose to pretend I was clueless about it, and instead simply followed Katrina down to the water. The breeze was just the right temperature that close to the ocean, but I hoped it wouldn't blow my hair into a knotted mess. Or my skirt up to my chin. Kat seemed to be holding up fine though, so maybe I was, too.

"Do *not* tell Jase how old you are," she reprimanded as soon as we were out of earshot.

I choked out a laugh. "Well he's gonna find out eventually. I mean, it's nice and all that he's paying me all this attention, but I don't want to lie to him all summer."

"There's no reason you can't tell him *after*."

"After?"

"Yeah. After you bang him."

If I had any liquid in my mouth at that moment, I would have done a spittake. "Are you crazy?"

"You said you never went past second with a boy."

"Yeah. And I don't plan on rounding third anytime soon!"

She shook her head at her feet. "I don't know. It just sounded to me like you had some regrets about that Brian guy. Wouldn't it be cool to go home super-experienced? Show that goofy old Brian what he's been missing out on?"

As crazy as I thought my new friend's plan was, I had to admit, the idea was quickly starting to grow on me. I mean, I wasn't going to have *sex* with Jase for godsakes, but there was no reason we couldn't hook up a little. Why not gain some experience with someone who was completely disconnected from my real life? Someone gorgeous, and older, and probably knew what the hell he was doing. Maybe learning a few things from Jase Delaney would give me just the edge I needed to make Brian Hollander mine once and for all. Ha! I'd like to see Francine Mentozzi try to compete with *that!*

I started to envision my complete transformation from Virgin Mary to sexy Madonna (the pop star. Not the real one) as the facilitator of my metamorphosis sauntered down toward us.

"Ut-shay up-ay on the ase-Jay," I murmured to Kat as Jase met us at the edge of the water. God. He was so tall!

"Am I interrupting?" he asked.

Kat was already halfway up the beach as she answered back, "No, not at all! I'm gonna grab another beer. Why don't you two go for a walk and find some shells or something?"

Oh my God could she be any more obvious?

But Jase simply raised those thick eyebrows at me to ask, "The girl is a mindreader. That's actually why I came down here. So...?" He gestured his head down the beach, silently asking me to join him.

"Oh yeah. Sure," I answered, trying to keep my cool. Not an easy thing to do because *come on*. The guy was gorgeous, he was charming, and he was way too smooth for his own good.

How could I ever tell him no?

ALSO COMING SOON!

BITCH
(previously titled "Bridesmaid from Hell")

A standalone, dual POV chick-lit starring characters from "Down the Shore."

Turn the page for a preview!

BITCH
Excerpt from Chapter Three

I head to my bedroom via the hallway off the kitchen. The original design of our house intended this area to be the "Maid's Quarters," but years ago, my parents had converted the space into an apartment for my grandmother. When Gram had to move into the nursing home, it became mine.

It's not a bad setup. Lots of square footage and plenty of closet space. I only had to put up a small fight when my younger brother Cooper tried to lay claim to the room. But seeing as he was getting ready to head off to law school at the time, there was hardly an argument.

My dog, Snowball, is on my bed waiting for me as usual. I pick him up and tuck him under my arm as I flop down onto the bed. I pick up the remote and try to watch TV, but my brain is still mulling over the conversation I had with Tommy in the car. He was acting a little weird and I can't make heads or tails of it.

I pick up the phone and call Livia for a second opinion.

"Hello?" she answers.

"Hey Liv!"

She whispers into the phone. "Shana? Are you alright? What time is it?"

Ooops. I quickly check the Piaget clock on my nightstand. One-thirty.

"Shoot, Liv, I didn't realize it was this late. I guess I figured you'd still be up. Can you talk? I'm kinda freaked out right now."

"Yeah, yeah. Hang on a sec, okay?"

I can hear her shuffling around, probably going into the other room so as not to wake Mr. Perfect.

"Shane, jeez, is everything okay?"

"God, Liv, don't be such a worry wart. Were you actually in bed already?"

"Well, yeah. It's one-thirty."

"On a Friday night!"

"Sorry. I didn't realize I was expected to leave my boogie shoes on. In any case, I'm awake now. What's up?"

Man. Ever since Livia got back together with Jack, she's been a wet blanket. In the old days, we wouldn't have thought twice about going *out* at this hour, yet here she is already asleep at one-thirty on a Friday night. I decide to lay off the ballbusting, however. After all, I called because I need to talk and I don't want to aggravate her to the point where she won't. I *did* wake her up out of a sound sleep, for godsakes.

"It's Tommy. He was acting a little weird tonight."

"How do you mean?"

I pause for effect, just so my friend knows how serious this is. I give Snowball a scratch under his chin and say, "Well, we were having a great time at dinner and I suggested that we head over to *Gentleman's* for dessert."

"Wait. *The Gentleman at Leisure*? The strip club? Tell me you didn't!"

"I did. But when I started to give him a lap dance—"

"Shana, shut up!"

I start cracking up. I knew Livia would find a recap of my evening entertaining. "No, *you* shut up and let me finish."

"I can't believe you gave Tommy a lap dance at Gentlemen's. What was it like?"

"The club or the lap dance?"

"Shane!"

"Oh, alright, alright. Lots of red velvet and candles. Very Poconos, very Mount Airy Lodge, only classier."

"Is that even possible?"

"I know, right? Anyway, this big, fat bouncer comes over and tells me I can't do that and threatens to kick us out if I don't stop, so we leave. So, I'm thinking after my little dance number that Tom's probably all worked up and all, but when we get back to my house, he wouldn't even come inside. Isn't that weird?"

"That's what you're so freaked out about?"

"Yes. Don't you think that's a little strange?"

I can hear Livia sighing on the other end of the line. I know this isn't the most pressing matter and it certainly isn't the first time I've asked her to play amateur psychologist with one of my boyfriends, but she seems a little less tolerant whenever we discuss Tommy. I guess she gets a little skittish whenever she thinks there might be a problem between us.

She wasn't crazy about the idea of me dating one of Jack's friends in the first place, probably because if things end badly, it could create a rip in the space/time continuum or something. Maybe she should have thought about that before she practically set us up! The way I see it, she's the *best* person to consult on the matter of Tommy. Who better to offer insight than someone who knows him so well?

"I don't know, Shane. Maybe he was just tired or something. Did he *tell* you why he didn't want to spend the night?"

"He said he had to get up early for work tomorrow." I didn't mention the part about my mother at the window, waiting up for us.

"Well, okay then, Captain Obvious. I may be going out on a limb here, but I'm going to have to go with A: *He has to get up early for work tomorrow.* Final answer."

"Gee, thanks a lot, Liv."

"Ha! Okay, look. I think you're just overthinking this. You *do* this, you know. Just chill out and roll with it, okay? Tom's a good guy, you're a hot, happening babe... Just play it cool, huh? I'm sure he'll call tomorrow and turn back into Prince Charming once he's got a few hours of sleep in him. *Capice?*"

"Yeah, I '*capice*' perfectly." I bite my lip nervously, anticipating the reaction to what I'm about to suggest. "But do you think that *maybe* you could ask your boyfriend to talk to him? Just to find out what his deal is?"

There's a big silence on Liv's end. Crap. I'm thinking I probably went too far with that one. I know she's been trying to keep her distance from the goings-on between Tom and me. So it catches me off guard when I hear her say, "Jack's not my boyfriend anymore."

Shit. Here I've been rambling on about my stupid crap and Livia's been dealing with losing her boyfriend of five years. Some friend I am. "Why didn't you call me?"

"I was planning on it. At a more decent hour tomorrow morning."

"But what happened?"

Liv pauses, unable to find the words. She takes a deep breath and then blurts out, "Well, he *proposed*, that's what happened! So he's not my boyfriend anymore. He's my *fiancé!*"

I can hear her busting a gut laughing over there in Shangri-La, while I'm still trying to digest what she just said. "Holy crap. So you're *engaged?*"

"I am engaged. I am *of the affianced!* We're getting married next year. No date set or anything yet. He just did it tonight and my head is still spinning."

I know the feeling.

All I can say is, "Wow…"

"I know, right? Hey, I'm sorry if I just dumped this on you. *You* called *me*. But I just couldn't wait to tell you. It's okay, right?"

I say, "Yeah, of course. Wow. How's the ring?"

"Gorgeous! I am marrying a man with exquisite taste. Wait 'till you see it. Do you have plans tomorrow night?"

I was kind of hoping to see Tommy tomorrow and make sure everything is still okay between us, but I answer, "No. Not really. Why?"

"Well, I really wanted to do this in person, but obviously, I'd like to ask you if you'd be a bridesmaid. So… will you?"

A bridesmaid. This from the girl who knows she will be Maid of Honor at my wedding someday. Although, I guess it's pretty obvious that her sister will be the one to take the lead role in this wedding.

So, even though I'm miffed, I answer, "Of course I'll be a bridesmaid. I'd be honored."

"Okay, great! Because I'd like to get my *wedding party* together tomorrow for a Girls' Night Out. You in?"

Without thinking, I ask, "Who's going?"

Livia laughs and says, "What are you, brain damaged? The *usual suspects* are going: Vix, Tess, Sam, Isla… and you, hopefully."

Of course. *Those Girls*.

What I try to forget on a daily basis is that Livia has this group of girlfriends that she hangs out with when she's not hanging out with *me*.

The problems go all the way back to high school. Livia and I had met when I was a senior and she and I took the same art and photography classes that year. She was a grade behind me and has been fighting to catch up ever since.

287

The girls in my grade never really formed a "clique," at least not one I was ever part of, but that junior class was as thick as thieves. Her little group consisted of girls who just did not like the idea of Liv befriending someone outside of the five of *them*: (Trumpets, please...) Livia and Victoria Chadwick, Tess Valletti, Samantha Baker, and Isla St. Parque.

Vix is Liv's twin sister who has essentially despised me from Day One. I guess she felt threatened by how close Livia and I had become. But the girl is my best friend's sister, for godsakes, so I've had to put up with her.

Sam and Isla are basically lap dogs. They don't necessarily offend me, yet I've never really found the desire to get to know them extensively for any reason. At least I have the capability to stomach either of those two when I need to.

But Tess...

Tess Valletti has been in a class all her own since the day she came strutting through the doors of our high school her freshman year. What sucks most about her is that she is beyond beautiful. And believe me, I take no joy in admitting that. Back when we were teenagers, she even dated some guy who's now an actual Hollywood movie star. I'd tell you who he was on the off chance you've actually heard of him, but I'm not a name-dropper.

The point is, Tess is the kind of girl that things like that happen to.

Aside from that annoying little fact, she also happens to be an absolute hellraiser. She's never hidden her distaste for me and doesn't know how to keep her mouth shut about it. It's not like I've ever gone out of my way to be friends with her or anything, but at least I have enough class to be civil. That girl can barely contain herself when we're in the same room together, which thankfully, isn't *too* often. Not that she goes out of her way to push my buttons, but I try to steer clear of her whenever I'm in her vicinity, just to avoid giving her any opening for a confrontation.

I can't believe Tess has been married to Ronnie for like four years already. Ron is another friend of Jack's, like my Tommy, so I'm forced to be in her company slightly more lately, ever since he and I started dating. The way I see it though, is if *that* bitch can pull off a happy marriage with one of Jack's friends, then getting Tom to fall in love with *me* should be a cakewalk.

Key words there being: 'should be.' That's always the tricky part when it comes to guys—trying to predict what they're thinking in order to hang onto them.

Attracting them, at least, has never really been a problem for me.

Looking back now, it all seems rather incestual, but Livia and I have always had the same taste in men and we look alike, which naturally put us in the position of dating a lot of the same boys during our school years. Back then, we were so wrapped up in the microcosm of high school that picking the same guys out of that particular dating pool wasn't so taboo.

It was really weird once we grew up and were forced to deal with the rest of the world's time-honored policy: Another girl's boyfriend is off limits for life, even after a breakup.

Which is why I almost choked on my tongue the day her boyfriend Jack walked into *The Studio* for the first time. To borrow a phrase from my mother's dictionary, that boy is a world-class *hunk*. No wonder it took Livia five whole years to wrangle a proposal out of him. If he were with me, I would have closed the deal within a year, two tops. Unfortunately, I'll never get the opportunity to prove that theory.

Jack had broken up with Liv only a few months after they first started dating. Lord, what I wouldn't have given for the chance to sidle on in there. But I was honor-bound to our newly adopted Code of Dating Ethics. And besides, more importantly, Liv was heartbroken at the time. What kind of friend would I be if I made a move on her ex while she was trying to put the pieces of her life back together? Sure enough, those two eventually patched things up anyway.

And now, here I am, listening to my friend impart the news of their engagement. Even worse, however, is the fact that now I have no choice but to spend a night celebrating the event with Those Girls tomorrow.

"Yeah. I'm in," I respond flatly.

I'm sure it will be *tons* of fun.

OTHER BOOKS BY T. TORREST:

The REMEMBER WHEN Trilogy
Head back to the 80s with this decades-long coming-of-age romantic comedy between a Hollywood actor and his high school sweetheart.

DOWN THE SHORE
A contractor-turned-rockstar breaks his own rules when he falls for an infuriating groupie down at the Jersey shore during the summer of '95.

BREAKING THE ICE
A second chance romance between a former-NHL-star-turned-bar-owner and the cold-shouldered event planner who comes barging back into his life.

A WAY TO GET BY
"They started to fight when the money got tight and they just didn't count on the tears..."
Find out what *really* happened to the king and the queen of the prom.

This is a work of fiction. All names, characters and places in this book are the product of the author's imagination and/or are used fictitiously. Any resemblance or similarities to actual persons, living or dead, is entirely coincidental.